Love AT FIRST NOTE

OTHER BOOKS AND AUDIO BOOKS
BY JENNY PROCTOR

The House at Rose Creek

Mountains Between Us

Love AT FIRST NOTE

A NOVEL

JENNY PROCTOR

Covenant Communications, Inc.

Cover image: *Woman with Violin* © FotoMaximum, iStockphtoto.com.

Cover design copyright © 2016 by Covenant Communications, Inc.

Published by Covenant Communications, Inc.
American Fork, Utah

Copyright © 2016 by Jenny Proctor
All rights reserved. No part of this book may be reproduced in any format or in any medium without the written permission of the publisher, Covenant Communications, Inc., P.O. Box 416, American Fork, UT 84003. The views expressed within this work are the sole responsibility of the author and do not necessarily reflect the position of Covenant Communications, Inc., or any other entity.

This is a work of fiction. The characters, names, incidents, places, and dialogue are either products of the author's imagination, and are not to be construed as real, or are used fictitiously.

Printed in the United States of America
First Printing: March 2016

22 21 20 19 18 17 16   10 9 8 7 6 5 4 3 2 1

ISBN 978-1-68047-943-0

For Emily (of course)

Acknowledgments

When I started Emma and Elliott's story, it was meant to be a novella—something easy and quick and fun. It turned out to be all of those things, so much so that it just didn't feel fair to stop with the novella. I'm so glad my editor trusted me enough to listen and agree when I e-mailed and said, "Hey, you know that novella you asked me for? Yeah. You can't have it yet." It was the right call, for sure. Turning this story into a full-length novel was an absolute blast.

Samantha, I'm so glad you're on my team. Your steadiness and loyalty, even through hard times and not-so-great words, mean so much. This journey wouldn't be the same without you. To the rest of my Covenant family, thank you for your support and hard work. To Kathy Gordon, thank you for your graciousness and the time you've taken to counsel and assist and encourage.

Seeing as how I'm not a musician myself, I am most indebted to my musical sister Emily, who answered hundreds of questions about the inner workings of the symphony and the finer points of playing the violin. Any classical piece mentioned in this book is there only because of the numerous times I called Emily and said, "Hey, I need a piece of music that does this and this and sounds like this."

Emily, I'm so grateful for your musical smarts, your talent, your exhaustive research on my behalf, and your enduring patience. To speak so willingly (and so frequently) of fictional characters is the greatest gift you could ever give your baby sister, whose brain somehow depends on these made-up people. That you also happen to be brilliant with words is such an amazing bonus! Thank you, thank you. I loce you forever. (Nope. Not a typo. I really did say loce!)

Special thanks also to Claire Gerhardt, my daughter's violin teacher and my friend who let me spy on her musical life and ask so many questions.

To my critique partners, Braden, Susan, and Michelyn, thank you for the numerous times you so tolerantly accommodated my tight deadlines and selfish requests. That you so graciously read chapters upon chapters instead of the prescribed one or two just to help me finish makes me certain I have the very best critique group ever.

To my beta readers, I am forever in awe of your brilliance. Jolene, Laura, Josi, Caitlyn, Melanie, Kim, and Lindsay, thank you for your time and energy and thoughtful insight. You make me better. The end.

And finally to my enduringly patient family, I couldn't write a single word worth half a grain of salt if it weren't for all of you. Josh, you're my rock. That you read chick lit just because I wrote it is one thing, but that you love it and talk about it and celebrate it means the world. It is no small task loving a writer, but you live as if it is always a joy and never a burden. I am so grateful for that most cherished gift.

Jordan, Sam, Lucy, Henry, Ivy, Jack, you're my people. I love you. Thank you for being the very best kids ever, anywhere, on the whole entire planet and even on Mars.

Chapter 1

MOVING BACK TO NORTH CAROLINA? Social suicide.

No. Not social suicide. More like dating suicide.

See, there were a few things that disqualified me from the general dog-walking, beard-growing, craft-beer-drinking collection of men West Asheville had to offer: I was allergic to dogs, I didn't really like beards, and then the whole religion thing. Mormon girls and Southern boys didn't always mix.

I'd only been in town two months when Lilly, my roommate and childhood best friend, and her boyfriend, Travis, made it their New Year's resolution to try every single native beer brewed in Asheville before Christmas. That might not have been very hard had they started in January, but with only four months left in the year? Asheville hadn't been named Best Craft Beer City three years in a row for nothing. The city grew microbreweries like Kansas grew corn.

It was a fine goal for Lil and Trav—something they enjoyed that they could do together. But had *my* boyfriend wanted to spend every date night touring breweries—

Oh wait. I didn't have a boyfriend.

I tried not to dwell on my looming spinsterhood. I liked Asheville, even if the young single adults group didn't reach double digits. Growing up in a neighboring town, I'd always been a sucker for the city's urban-y, eclectic charm. And it was the perfect place to set up my new violin studio. So it lacked available Mormon bachelors. At least the symphony was great, and I was closer to my family than I'd been in years—compensatory blessings, maybe?

When Lilly asked if I wanted to go in on renting the right side of a little house on Maple Crescent, it felt like a no-brainer. The house was perfect—tall ceilings, original hardwood floors, and bricks from 1924 in the kitchen wall. How do you say no to bricks from 1924? So I didn't. I made West Asheville home. Even with my aversion to dogs, beards, and beer.

I was finally starting to feel settled when, on a late September Sunday just after sacrament meeting, Bishop Bradford called me into his office. "Emma, can I speak to you for a moment?" I glanced at my watch. If my Primary class was left alone too long, I had no doubt they'd stage a revolution. Whatever the bishop had to say, he'd better say it quick.

It occurred to me that maybe he wanted to see me so he could rescind my calling as the Sunbeam teacher. It wasn't that I didn't like three-year-olds, but I was clearly not cut out to teach them. The week before, I'd spent nearly half an hour scrubbing chocolate off the sleeve of my favorite Barbara Bui linen jacket—a New York City splurge I'd never regretted until hanging out with Mistress Chocolate Face and her grimy entourage. We hadn't even eaten chocolate in class—it was like the sticky just oozed from their pores. I was not one to quit on the job, but I also wouldn't have minded a change.

Bishop Bradford sat behind his desk and smiled. "Rose and I enjoyed your performance last night. It was a wonderful concert."

I sat a little taller in my seat. "Thank you. I didn't know you were there."

"A coworker gave us tickets. We'd never been before, but we enjoyed it. Rose wants to go back."

"I hope you do. We've got a great season this year."

"So what does it mean, exactly, when it lists you as concertmaster in the program? Is that because you played the solo?"

I snuck a glance at my watch again, imagining the Primary president pacing the hall outside my classroom. "Um, no, it's not . . . I mean, you do generally play the solos as concertmaster, if there happen to be any, but it's more than that too. I lead the violin section and determine bowing gestures so we all move together as we play; I tune the orchestra before every performance, and if we have to audition new musicians, I help—" His eyebrows drew together, stopping me midexplanation. "Did I lose you?"

He nodded. "Somewhere around bowing gestures. Rose just told me it meant you were the best one. That sounds about right."

A blush crept up my cheeks. There wasn't really a graceful way to say it. *Yes. Yes, I am the best! Thanks for noticing.*

Bishop Bradford's voice softened. "I didn't mean to embarrass you, Emma. We were just proud to see you up there. Was this your first concert in the hot seat?"

I shook my head. "I played for a year as concertmaster in Cleveland before I moved home." I tried not to think about my principal seat in the Cleveland Orchestra—a seat I'd been the youngest musician to occupy in more than forty years—or my former associates, many of them friends I'd known all the way through college. The only time I regretted my decision to move was when I spent too much time dwelling on the life I'd walked away from.

"Well, we sure did enjoy your performance last night."

"Thank you," I said again. Maybe this was all our little meeting was about: *Congratulations on your lovely concert. Also, you're going to teach Sunbeams for the rest of eternity.*

Bishop Bradford smiled and leaned back in his chair. "So, I've got a favor to ask, if you're willing—something I think will be of particular interest to you."

Particular interest to me? *Carry on, Bishop. You have my attention.*

"I got an e-mail last night from a new ward member, someone moving to Asheville from out West. He's set to arrive next week, and I thought you might be able to reach out and help him feel welcome."

"Oh. Okay. Um, why me?"

"He's young—in his twenties—so I thought it would be nice for another young person to welcome him. What's more, he's moving onto Maple Crescent." He squinted at his phone. "Three Forty-Seven Maple Crescent. That's your street, isn't it?"

My brain felt too full of details as I struggled to process. *He . . . young person . . . Maple Crescent.* In other words, a young, potentially hot Mormon guy was moving into my neighborhood. I suddenly felt a little warm.

I lifted my long hair off my neck and slipped it into a ponytail. I'd worked all morning to tame my semiwavy frizz into soft, smooth curls, and the ponytail was bound to ruin it, but it wasn't like the Sunbeams were going to care. Though my first week on the job a little girl did ask why I didn't make my hair blonde like her mommy instead of an "ugly, boring mud color." *Whatever.* I wasn't insecure enough to take fashion insults from a three-year-old seriously. Plus, I'd tried highlights once. They'd looked horrible under the stage lights—a little too much like my neighbor's calico cat. I was happier sticking with my natural dark brown.

Another piece of the bishop's details clicked into place in my brain. "Wait, did you say three forty-seven? I *live* at three forty-seven."

"That's what it says. I guess he could be mistaken."

I shook my head. "No, there are two apartments in the house, and my neighbors moved out last week. I guess it makes sense, but wow. What are the odds?"

He smiled. "I guess saying hello will be easier than I thought."

I never would have listed matchmaking as one of my bishop's responsibilities, but I could tell from the gleam in his eye he'd asked me to welcome the new guy for a reason. I wasn't surprised, really. I already felt like the ward project. Cousins, nephews, grandsons, grand-nephews, old mission companions—nearly everyone in the ward knew someone who was absolutely perfect for me. They all meant well—of course they all meant well. But all that had actually come to fruition were a few e-mails from a guy who had asked if I'd be willing to move to Tuscaloosa (Tusca-where?) and a blind date with Sister Parker's grandson that had ended in Urgent Care after the guy had tripped on the curb and face-planted on the sidewalk. I probably should have been more sympathetic, but his nose bled all over my favorite shoes—Ralph Lauren linen and cork wedges, no less. There was no saving them, and the loss totally wasn't worth it. I mean, the guy had made an actual snoring noise when I'd told him I liked classical music. As in, his head had lolled to the side, his eyes had closed, and he had *snored*.

With the ward's matchmaking efforts going so well, it was hard to feel optimistic. But a glimmer of hope still sparked in my chest. I had never been an excitable, giddy girl. I was always the calm one, the one who read, the one who texted without ever using exclamation points. But a *guy* was moving to the barren wasteland of young single adults. And he was going to be my neighbor. No well-intentioned ward members necessary.

I wasn't the greatest at meeting new people. My nerves were ridiculous, and I was a master at getting tongue-tied. But this was too good an opportunity to pass up.

I smiled at the bishop. "I'd be happy to reach out. He'll be here next week? Do you know when exactly?"

He looked back at his phone and shook his head. "He wasn't specific. I can forward his e-mail address to you if you'd like to ask him yourself, or I guess you can just keep an eye out your window. I'm sure you'll notice the moving truck."

I nodded. "Okay. And his name? With a little social media recon, I might be able to find the guy and know what to expect."

"Elliott. Elliott Hart."

Elliott Hart?

"Wait a minute. Elliott Hart? As in *the* Elliott Hart?" I definitely didn't expect that.

The bishop gave me a funny look. "I didn't know there was a *the* Elliott Hart."

"He's a pianist. Have you ever seen the show *Talent Hunt*?"

He shook his head no.

"It's this television talent search thing. Elliott Hart won the entire competition a few years ago. He's pretty big."

"Famous? Really?"

"I mean, not like bring-bodyguards-with-you-to-church famous, but they did send him somewhere totally remote on his mission so he wouldn't be recognized. He does these crazy videos—pianos in weird places—and his YouTube following is huge. But that doesn't make any sense. Why would Elliott Hart be moving to Asheville? Maybe it's someone different."

"I guess we'll find out when he arrives. But wouldn't that be nice? A musician—you would already have something in common."

I still wasn't going to get my hopes up. It was more likely we were dealing with a computer programmer from northern Idaho. A spelunker from central Wyoming. Or maybe a shoe salesman from Tuscaloosa. Elliott, the famous musician? What were the chances?

"I see what you're thinking, Emma," the bishop said. "I promise I'm not going to scheme and plan you into this young man's life, but I do think you should keep an open mind. If God is trying to open a door, it'd be a shame to kick it closed before you even know what's behind it."

"No door closing. Got it."

He smiled and stood. "You better hurry if you're going to catch those Sunbeams."

Sunbeams. *Yay.*

Chapter 2

I survived Sunbeams with only a little drool on my leather flats. Ha! Black. No ruination there—a small victory considering how distracted I'd been all through class. The kids could have tattooed my arms with markers and I wouldn't have noticed. *For real, Elliott Hart?*

After church, I bypassed dinner at my parents' and opted instead for a quiet afternoon lounging around my apartment, studying my potential neighbor's YouTube channel. Talk about time well spent.

Lilly got home late from her shift at the hospital and flopped onto the couch, her too-long legs extending all the way to where I sat curled up with my laptop.

I nudged her feet onto the floor. "Can you put those things somewhere else?"

"Listen, little short person. You have no idea what it's like to deal with limbs this long." Lilly wiggled her toes, digging them into my leg.

I nudged her away again. "Five foot six does not make me a short person. But those legs *do* make you freakishly tall."

"Maybe, but they also make me look fabulous in a swimsuit."

That was no joke. Lilly's parents were European, her father from Spain and her mother from France, but her dad's genes had definitely won out. She was stunning with her olive skin and shiny black hair. Throw in her supermodel legs? Total knockout. "Fine. You win." I dropped my laptop onto our coffee table/storage trunk and shifted to make more room for her on the couch.

I hadn't seen Lilly in what felt like days. Symphony weeks were like that—so much coming and going and rehearsing that our schedules never really meshed. Her hours were crazy working labor and delivery at the hospital anyway. When mine were crazy too, we'd go days without having a conversation.

"Tell your parents I appreciate them giving me your sister's ticket," Lilly said from her side of the couch. "I'm happy to pay for my seat like the rest of the common folk, but I'll always pick free when free's available."

"Yeah, Mom said she was glad you could use it. Better than it going to waste."

"Why didn't Ava want it? You had a solo. I thought for sure she'd want to be there."

I frowned. My sixteen-year-old sister, Ava, nine years my junior, was a musician as well. But she was also determined to follow her own path, and it wasn't leading her anywhere near her big sister's performances. "I'd hoped she'd want to, but she had something else going on. I don't know what."

Lilly scoffed and tossed her balled-up socks across the room. They bounced toward the kitchen and stopped just shy of the old brick wall I loved so much. The wall didn't do anything—it was only a half wall, separating the kitchen from the living room, and was completely cosmetic, an upcycled element saved from the house's original kitchen—but it was funky and fun and added character, even if it did hurt like total craziness when I stubbed my toe against it. "She's sixteen," Lilly said. "What could she possibly have going on that's more important than your concert?"

"No, you've got it backwards. She's sixteen, which means *everything* is more important than my concerts. Besides, stuff with Ava—it's complicated."

"No, it's not complicated. You gave up a lot to move down here. You stuck out your neck for her, and she's not even giving you the time of day."

"I didn't move down here for Ava. And I would never want her thinking I did." I leaned back into the retro-style Ikea couch I'd moved down from Cleveland—an upgrade from the hand-me-down Lilly had been using before I moved in. "It's fine. Ava's just . . . young."

"Maybe you didn't move just for her, but you're here, and you're trying to help her, and she ought to be taking advantage. Instead she's completely ignoring you. That's not just young; it's rude." Lilly had cemented her right to be defensive for my sake back in elementary school when she'd punched Drew Hamilton in the nose for calling me a crazy Mormon; she'd never failed to be my advocate. But we could talk about Ava all night, and it wouldn't change Ava's practiced indifference.

My mother insisted it wasn't personal; it was just her age, her teenage hormones, the stress of high school, blah, blah, blah. But it *felt* personal. Before leaving Ohio, I'd asked one of my former professors at the Cleveland Institute of Music to review a video of Ava. I'd raved about her skill—total truth-telling there; she really *was* talented—and promised he wouldn't be disappointed if he gave her a shot. He'd agreed—"Only because I have such respect for you, Emma."—and I didn't want to disappoint him.

So much for that. He'd expected the video weeks ago, and Ava couldn't be bothered.

I reached for my laptop and opened it. "Want to talk about something more fun?"

"Doesn't look like you're giving me much of a choice." Lilly scooted closer, looking over my shoulder as I started a video.

"So I learned at church today that this guy might be moving in next door." I tilted the screen so she had a better view. "You remember Elliott Hart? The pianist who won *Talent Hunt* back when we were in high school?"

She scrunched her eyebrows. "Um, yes? I think?" She pointed at the screen. "Is that him?"

I nodded. "He's pretty big still. Lots of fans on YouTube, and he's sold something like a billion albums."

"A billion, huh? That many?"

"Shut up. I don't know exactly how many. But a lot." Out of all of Elliott's various videos I'd watched that afternoon, I'd chosen to show Lilly the one that had quickly become my favorite. Watching him play reminded me of when *I* played. You could tell he felt his music the same way I felt mine.

"Did he film this video here?" Lilly asked. "Those look like our mountains."

I nodded. "Yeah. The comments say it was filmed on the reservation in Cherokee. Apparently he went all out to make sure everything was authentic and approved by the tribe."

"That's decent of him." Lilly leaned in and looked closer. "I *do* remember him. He's cute. And those eyes are amazing. He's maybe a little too pretty for me though."

"Why? Because he doesn't have a beard? Just because you like men to look like lumberjacks doesn't mean the rest of us have to."

"Haha. So is this all in the name of neighbor research, or are you really into this guy now? His stuff doesn't sound like the grandma music you usually listen to."

Grandma music? I chose to ignore her insult mostly because she wasn't completely off base. I had always been pretty old school when it came to my musical tastes. It wasn't that I didn't like contemporary music. I did. But when it came to the classics, I was a purist, and Elliott clearly wasn't. Sure, he played bits and pieces of classical stuff but never without mashing it all up with some boy band's newest top-forty hit. People loved it; and even I couldn't deny that what he did, he did extremely well. But why ruin the brilliance of Vivaldi by throwing in eighteen measures of Bruno Mars? It wasn't even that I didn't like Bruno. I just didn't want him messing with Vivaldi.

"I like his original stuff," I conceded. "Like this one. When he's just playing his own music straight up, it's pretty impressive. And it's not that the mash-ups are bad; it's just . . . I don't know. People train really hard to be worthy of the classics, to be good enough to play them precisely as they deserve to be played. Covering songs people already like, then calling them classical because you throw in four measures of Beethoven, feels like a gimmick."

"Show me one of his mash-ups."

I clicked over and changed the video to some conglomeration of Mozart and a pop song I didn't know. "So this is Mozart right here," I pointed out as we listened to the piece. "But here, it morphs into . . . I don't know what."

"Seriously? You don't know that song? It's "Dance with Me." It's huge right now."

A few measures more and I recognized the melody. "Oh. I guess I do recognize it. But why do that, you know? I just wanna listen to Mozart."

"Yeah, but not everybody wants to listen to Mozart. Maybe it's not hard-core classical, but I'd say getting young people to listen to anything without words is an accomplishment—gimmick or not." Lilly reached over my arm and clicked on Elliott's profile picture, this one a little more rugged. "Okay, I see the appeal in this one. He's definitely nice to look at."

I looked at the picture and tried to imagine what it would be like to see Elliott Hart in person. He had a serious face with a strong jaw, dark hair, and deep-set blue eyes. In most of his online photos, he wasn't smiling. But there was one on a red carpet somewhere that was a little more candid, like someone had caught him in the middle of a great joke. That was the one that made me nauseated, nerves jumping around my stomach like I was a bounce house at a kid party.

"Yo, Emma? You okay?" Lilly waved her hand in front of my face. "You look like you're about to puke."

I shook my head. "I feel like I'm about to puke. I was just thinking about what I'm going to say. I'm supposed to go see him as soon as he moves in . . . to welcome him into the ward."

A flash of understanding flitted across Lilly's face, but she shook it off. "Welcome seems pretty straightforward."

"Maybe for you. But you know how terrible I am at this."

She did know—probably better than anybody. After all, she'd been there beside me when I'd thrown up before every high school debate tournament, unable to handle my nerves any other way. She'd seen me flounder and flush and stumble through awkward sentences whenever I'd been put on the spot. Unless I was holding my violin, which somehow kept all the synapses in my brain firing just as they should, I was wholly unreliable as a communicator.

Lilly rolled her eyes. "Don't psych yourself out. You'll be fine. Besides, it's probably not even him."

"So what if it isn't? It only has to be someone who's mildly attractive for me to act like an idiot." I blew out a frustrated breath. My responsibility to welcome the new guy suddenly felt a little like a death march. Or at least a really bad stomach virus. "Why did I agree to do this?"

"Because you're single and human and he's a guy. This is not rocket science."

"Actually, I think I'm fine being single."

"Because then you don't have to talk to people? Whatever. You'll be amazing no matter who it is. Have you looked to see if you can find any other Mormon Elliott Harts?"

I grumbled at her casual dismissal of my very serious concerns and pulled up one of the minimized tabs on my laptop. "I found three on Facebook that list BYU as their school, but two look already married and old. The other lives in Denmark, so I'm thinking that probably isn't him."

"And your Mormon dating sites?"

"Nothing."

Lilly grinned. "It's gotta be him, Em."

"Or maybe it's just someone who knows better than to catalog his life on public social media platforms. Why would *the* Elliott Hart be renting a tiny duplex in West Asheville?"

"*You're* renting a tiny duplex in West Asheville."

"Whatever. It's not the same thing."

"Maybe not exactly, but don't pretend like you weren't the darling of the classical music scene. You were everyone's favorite soloist—at the pinnacle of your career. And yet, here you are."

I tried not to wince at her use of the past tense. She wasn't trying to be critical, just stating a fact, but it burned anyway. "The difference is that the general public actually knows who Elliott is.

No one cares about classical musicians except other classical musicians. Plus, this guy has made serious money. I'm sure he could afford to live somewhere nicer."

"Lots of people could afford to live somewhere else, but they choose West Asheville because it's hip and fun. Or maybe he's just looking to hide out and keep a low profile. If that's the case, where better to do it than Maple Crescent?"

I didn't want to tell Lilly her suggestion actually made some sort of sense. Mostly because I didn't want to admit how much I really, *really* wanted the Elliott Hart moving in next door to be the Elliott Hart who was finishing the final chords of his Native American–themed original composition on my laptop screen, with just over a million views and 47,000 thumbs up.

"I guess we'll find out this week." I closed my laptop and sank back onto the couch.

Headlights flashed through the front window, and we both turned. Lilly walked over to peek through the blinds, then turned to me, wide-eyed. "Or maybe we'll find out right now."

I scrambled onto my feet and stood beside her, looking through the small gap in the blinds she held open with her fingers. A dark sedan had parked in front of the house. "You're crazy. It's just some random car."

"Look. Someone's getting out."

The two halves of our house shared a front door and an entryway before the apartments split off in separate directions, ours to the right and the other to the left, so we were in the perfect spot to spy.

Still, it was dark, so the man was several paces up the sidewalk, keys jingling in his hand, before we were able to see his face in the yellow glow of our porch light. It was his hands that made my heart stop—the graceful arch of his fingers as he fiddled with the key and fitted it into the old lock of our front door. He had the hands of a pianist.

I had known it was a possibility, but seeing Elliott Hart, a guy I'd watched on YouTube, a guy with artfully disheveled hair and killer blue eyes, two feet from my apartment made my blood pound and my mouth go dry. All I could manage to say was, "Oh my word. It's really him."

Lilly stood up and moved from the window. "Let's go meet him."

She was fast, but I was faster. I slid myself between her and the door, blocking her way. "No! We can't go out there right now. It's ten thirty."

"But he's out there right now, and he's our neighbor." She glanced back through the curtain. "You think he's staying here tonight? He doesn't have any luggage."

"Maybe he left it in the car." Elliott was inside now, but since he'd gone in empty-handed, we waited and watched, anticipating his reappearance out front. "He's probably just checking stuff out."

"Come on. I'm going over to say hello, and you're coming with me."

"No, I'm not."

"Emma, you're a grown-up now. You can't hide just because you had a few bad experiences as a teenager. If it were just some random guy and not Elliott Hart, you'd totally go out there."

"But it *is* Elliott Hart, and I'm still freaking out a little."

She shot me a look that told me just how ridiculous she thought I was. She was right, but I'd expected a few days to compose myself and prepare for the moment we'd meet. To jump right in at ten thirty on a Sunday night, wearing yoga pants and my tenth-grade Summer Strings T-shirt, with no makeup on and my hair in a messy topknot wasn't exactly the scenario I'd had in mind.

"Chicken," Lilly muttered as she snuck out the door. I watched through the window, hiding behind the curtain as she walked down the sidewalk and met Elliott, who must have reemerged during our debate, just as he hauled a suitcase and sleeping bag out of the back of his car. They shook hands, and he smiled, not quite the nerves-in-the-bounce-house smile from the photo, but one broad enough to make my fingers curl into tense, trembling fists. They talked for a few more minutes, then Lilly gestured back to the house. Elliott shook his head, but Lilly motioned again, nodding her head with emphatic certainty. He hesitated a moment more, then glanced at his watch and finally nodded. Something in the tilt of her head, the way she cocked it toward the right side of the house—*our* side of the house—gave it away. She was bringing Elliott inside.

I made it around the couch, across the living room, and into my bedroom just in time. I sank to the floor, leaning against the back of my door as I listened to Lilly and Elliott continue their conversation. The light in my room was off, and I left it that way, hoping Lilly would get the hint.

"Sorry you missed my roommate. She's already gone to bed."

Bless you, Lilly, I thought to myself. I'd make her brownies for not blowing my cover.

"That's okay. It's pretty late." His voice sounded deeper in person. I'd seen online interviews enough to recognize his speaking voice, but hearing it nice and resonant and echoing around my tiny apartment sent shivers up my spine. Oh, this wasn't good. I was not hiding in my room in the dark swooning over the sound of a man's voice—a man I wasn't even brave enough to face.

Or maybe I was. I lowered my head onto my knees and took a deep breath. I was no better than a star-struck fangirl. I had resolved to go out and say hello, introduce myself, and be nice to the guy when Lilly's voice piped up right outside my door.

"This is the bathroom. There are extra towels under the sink, and here's a blanket. I'll grab you a pillow from the closet." Her voice grew farther away as she moved down the hall. Towels, blankets, pillows—it sounded like Elliott was going to stay in my house. *In my house!*

"I really appreciate this. I would have been fine sleeping on the floor for one night, but I admit, your couch does look more comfortable."

"It's not a problem," Lilly said. "Do you have movers helping you unload tomorrow?"

"Yeah. They're supposed to be here with the truck by nine."

As I listened to their conversation, I had to wonder if Elliott knew Lilly was aware of who he was. I was fairly certain Lilly wouldn't have invited a total stranger into our house to sleep on our couch and use our bathroom if she hadn't already known he was a member of my church with a squeaky-clean reputation.

I wondered if Elliott was so much of a celebrity that he simply assumed wherever he went people knew who he was. Had he been shocked when Lilly had invited him to stay, or was he used to people going out of their way just for him? I hoped he wasn't used to it—it might be harder to like him in person if he expected that kind of treatment. Granted, he'd been planning to sleep on the floor in an empty apartment with nothing but a sleeping bag and one piece of luggage. That hardly seemed like entitled behavior.

Regardless of what he did or didn't expect, from my position on the floor, the impromptu sleepover seemed pretty brave on both their parts. And there I was hiding like a total coward. I could hear Lilly's voice in my head. *You sound like your mother, Em. Just live a little.*

"Well, I'll be around tomorrow afternoon after I get off work," Lilly said. "And my roommate should be home then too. I can even get my boyfriend, Trav, to come over. If you need us, just say the word."

"Yeah, that would be great," Elliott said. "Thanks again. It was great to meet you."

I stayed there, sitting on my floor, for several minutes longer. If movers were coming at nine, he would probably be up around . . . what, seven? Eight? With my luck, he was a naturally early riser, awake at five thirty to read his scriptures, do yoga, drink a green smoothie, and see me exiting the bathroom in a towel.

I wasn't completely opposed to running into Elliott but kinda wanted to be at my best when I did. And, you know, also be wearing clothes.

Knowing Elliott was less than fourteen steps away from my bedroom door didn't make it easy to get any sleep. I tossed and turned all night, jumping awake at every little sound. When my alarm finally went off at six thirty, I bolted out of bed so fast I banged my knee against my nightstand and knocked a nearly full glass of water onto my pillow, where it rolled, then crashed onto the hardwood floor. I stood breathless and still, listening to see if the ruckus had woken anyone else up, but the rest of the house remained silent.

It stayed that way too.

Even after I'd showered and dressed and blown my hair dry. Even after I banged around the kitchen making breakfast, then made a big production of retrieving my violin out of the living room. The guy didn't even stir.

I was disappointed. I'd worn my best jean/boot combination and curled my hair, thinking surely he'd wake up before I was gone. But no such luck. When I finally left just before eight, I passed right by the couch to get to the front door. All I saw was the back of his head, his dark hair tousled a little more than usual, and his arm flung up over the side of the couch. I probably stared a little too long at the curve of his shoulder, his bicep visible below the sleeve of his T-shirt.

Totally lame, I know, but even that made my heart pound.

Chapter 3

I TRIPPED OUT OF MY car, wrenching my foot one way and my favorite boot heel the other. Leaning against my door to survey the damage, my stomach sank. Broken. Which felt appropriate considering how my day had gone. Fate had been against me since I'd climbed out of bed, my broken boot just one in a string of unfortunate moments.

I'd hoped to make it home in time to meet Elliott and offer help with his move, but my afternoon lessons had run long, which had made me late to my chamber rehearsal. With the music I knew we had to practice—an original composition sent over by the sister of the bride at next weekend's wedding—there was no way I was getting out of there at a reasonable hour. I jerked off my boots and shoved my feet into a pair of old running shoes I found in the trunk of my Jetta. They were Lilly's, I guessed—a size too big and smelling faintly of beer—but they weren't broken, which made them a decidedly better option. I slammed the trunk closed with a mournful glance at my boots and headed into the church, where my quartet was waiting for me.

I hated being late to chamber rehearsal. It always made the violist cranky, but that night, I was already in such a foul mood, I hardly needed her surliness on top of my own. I pointedly ignored her glare when I finally made it into the practice room. *Whatever.* I was less than ten minutes late. Besides, she was the only one ready to play. No one else was even sitting down. I mumbled a halfhearted hello, then dropped to my knees to pull out my violin.

"Emma?"

I looked up. A tall black man had materialized on the other side of the room. No, not just a man. *Grayson Harper* had materialized on the other side of the room. The chairs set up for our practicing must have obscured my view at first, but there was no hiding him now. He smiled a broad, familiar smile, and my stomach clenched, acting a little like it wanted to crawl out and see everybody. I forced a swallow and took a deep breath, determined not to lose control.

"Grayson?" I finally squeaked.

He nodded as he sat down, pulling his cello into position. "It's good to see you, Emma. I had no idea you'd be here."

"No, I . . ." I shook my head. "Me neither." The longer I sat there, my hands hovering over my violin case like I'd somehow forgotten what I was doing, the more confused I became. Grayson didn't even live in Asheville. How was he suddenly in my quartet? Quartet. As in four people. We already had four people.

Plus, this was not the way things were supposed to happen with Grayson. When I saw him again, I was supposed to be living in one of those beautiful modern-but-old houses with a multimillionaire husband and our genetically perfect children. Not bedraggled after a horrible day, wearing running shoes that smelled distinctly of stale alcohol.

The silence stretched into awkwardness before I finally managed a complete sentence. "So, what . . . How . . . I mean, you're here?" Okay. Almost a complete sentence.

Hannah, the grouchy violist, responded with a typical frown. "Bruno's in Florida. We needed a replacement, and he suggested Grayson. You two know each other?"

Uh, yeah, we knew each other. As in junior-prom, senior-prom, and every-weekend-in-between knew each other.

"We played together growing up." Grayson's eyes stayed on me as he spoke. It was a slight understatement, but for Hannah, there was no reason to say more. I mean, I could tell her I'd made out with Grayson in every corner of the youth symphony hall, but that might make for an awkward rehearsal.

In nine years, his appearance hadn't really changed. He looked a little older, his shoulders broader, and his hair longer, tight curls falling onto his forehead and over the top of his ears. But everything else was the same. His deep, charcoal eyes matched his dark-brown skin, his wide smile bright against the contrast. "Is . . . um." I tried to focus. There was a reason Grayson was here, and it had something to do with Bruno. "Why is Bruno in Florida? He just . . . left?" I pulled out my violin and slid my sheet music out of my bag.

"He had to go stay with his granddaughter. I don't know all the details. Something about his daughter going to China for work and the regular babysitter backing out last minute. He said he tried to call you," Hannah said. "You didn't get his message?"

I shook my head. "I've been teaching." I'd heard a voice mail come in halfway through my last lesson, but I never listened to my voice mails anymore. Most people just hung up and sent me a text anyway. Except *Bruno*. At sixty-three, he still carried a flip phone and probably couldn't send a text if it meant a million dollars.

Bruno. Of course. Suddenly Grayson at group rehearsal made sense. Bruno had been his childhood cello teacher. Funny I hadn't made the connection when I'd joined the group the month before. But, then, I hadn't thought about Grayson—not really—in years. The way his presence now filled the room, it was hard to imagine how he hadn't at least crossed my mind once or twice.

"He says three weeks, but I don't know," Caroline added. "The way Bruno talks about Florida, it won't surprise me if he doesn't come back at all."

I took my seat next to Caroline—the fourth member of our group—and put my music on the stand in front of me. I could feel Grayson's gaze and sense the questions he likely wanted to ask, but there wasn't time to catch up. I had already arrived late, and Hannah and Caroline were ready to get started.

Two hours later—two hours of dismally bad music later— we finally called it a night.

"It shouldn't be allowed," Grayson muttered as he put away his cello. "Music that bad . . ."

Caroline laughed. "Can we really even call it music?"

"No complaining from me," Hannah said. "The bride is paying four hundred extra bucks for us to play her sister's stuff."

"Still." Grayson snapped his cello case closed. "I feel like I just sold my musical integrity at a flea market."

I pulled my phone out of my purse to see if I'd missed anything during rehearsal. There was a text from Lilly. *Elliott's moved in. Sorry you weren't here. :(He's really nice. Bought us all pizza to thank us for helping.*

Well, that was awesome. While I had endured an awkward rehearsal playing bad music with my ex-boyfriend, Lilly had been hobnobbing with our famous musician neighbor.

Fantastic, I thought to myself.

Grayson lingered by the door while I finished packing up. Once my violin was stowed away, he surprised me with a big hug, equal parts awkward and familiar.

"I should have done that when you first walked in," he said. "It really is good to see you."

I only managed an awkward smile. Grayson hadn't just been my teenage boyfriend. He'd basically been my entire high school experience—what little there'd been of it anyway. I'd graduated a couple years early, with special tutors and online schooling making it possible for me to focus more fully on my musical training. Everyone else had treated me like an oddity, calling me crazy for skipping basketball games or parties and dances in favor of rehearsing, but Grayson had never made me feel like my dedication had been anything but normal. Plus, he was a musician too. Maybe his trajectory wasn't quite the same as mine, but he still understood.

Our breakup had been inevitable. When he'd headed off to NC State to study engineering, the age difference between us suddenly seemed larger than ever before. It didn't matter that I was heading to college myself—I was still only sixteen. Our last morning together, we stood in his driveway next to the little Honda Civic he'd bought with money he'd earned teaching guitar lessons to neighborhood kids. The car was weighed down with boxes crammed full of his life, ready to cross county lines and land in Raleigh. I was leaving for Ohio the following weekend.

I wished out loud we could make the distance work, and he shushed me with gentle reassurances. But we both knew we were at the beginning of our end.

A few months later, I was glad we'd lost touch. The challenge of matriculating into a college campus weeks shy of my seventeenth birthday provided more than enough of an emotional challenge. Keeping up with a boyfriend would have been a killer. Still, Grayson was my first love. No matter the logic behind our breakup or the amicability of our parting ways, he was still a boy I'd kissed and loved and trusted with my heart. And the surge of emotion his touch stirred up now? The one that kept me standing still and silent in front of him? I didn't like it. I just wanted to shake it off and head home.

Instead, I stood there, my heartbeat erratic and wholly unreliable. It was dumb. I was a grown woman—who'd had plenty of experiences and boyfriends to demonstrate just how insignificant high school boyfriends really were. And by plenty, I meant two. Or maybe just one and a half since kissing the associate conductor in Cleveland probably didn't qualify as an actual full-scale experience.

"I, um . . . yeah," I finally stammered. "It's good to see you too. Unexpected but good. Are you living in Asheville now?"

Grayson shook his head. "I live in Hendersonville, but I work here in the city. At Deerbourn—it's an engineering firm downtown. Do you know it?"

"No. That's great though. Good for you." I swung my violin over my shoulder and followed Grayson into the parking lot.

"I saw the article in the paper about you moving back home," he said. "Concertmaster of the Asheville Symphony. I guess you've made the big-time now." His words weren't exactly rude, but there was a sharpness to his tone that felt judgmental.

My eyes narrowed. "What's that supposed to mean?"

He held up his hands. "Sorry. I didn't mean to sound critical. I was just surprised. I mean, I kinda understood when you stopped soloing and settled in Cleveland. All that touring couldn't have been easy. But I wasn't expecting this kind of move from you. Asheville's great, but it's a pretty big step down from Cleveland."

I sighed. There might be truth to Grayson's words, but there was also a lot he didn't know. He didn't know my reasons for leaving or my motivations for moving home. And who was he to dog on Asheville Symphony? It was smaller, yes, but it was still a great orchestra.

"Plans change." I didn't even try to smooth the edge out of my voice as I stalked past him toward my car. He'd struck a nerve, and I was happy for him to know it. "I'm happy to be back."

"Emma, is it your mom?"

I spun around to face him, my eyes wide. The question had caught me totally off guard.

He tilted his head to the side and tugged on his ear. It was a gesture I recognized, which made me feel all weird and unsettled.

"How is she?" he asked.

That he'd managed to land on my biggest reason for moving home in less than five minutes of conversation was annoying. But my mother's rapidly progressing MS wasn't allowed to be on my list of reasons for moving to Asheville. At least not the list I talked about. If Mom thought I moved home for her, she'd buy me a ticket back to Cleveland and come over and pack my suitcase herself.

I shrugged. "She has good days and bad. More bad lately, but you know my mom, always wearing a brave face."

He stared at me, hard, his eyes looking deeper than I wanted them to look. "Do you want to go get some coffee somewhere? Wait—" He paused and smiled. "Not coffee. Dinner? Maybe some frozen yogurt?"

I didn't want to have dinner with my ex-boyfriend. I wanted to go home and casually but completely on purpose run into my new neighbor. Plus, I was bugged by Grayson's slight. I could handle my family and friends expressing concern over my career choices, but I hadn't talked to Grayson in nine years. He didn't have the right to question anything. "I don't think that's a good idea."

"Come on. It's just dinner. If we're going to play together for the next three weeks, we might as well catch up. I'd like us to be friends again." A part of me suspected Grayson really just wanted to hear more of why I'd derailed my life plan and landed back in Asheville, but he did have a point. I didn't want every chamber rehearsal till Bruno's return marred by awkwardness. "Okay. I guess dinner's fine."

He laughed. "Don't sound too enthusiastic."

"It's not that. It's just . . . been a long day."

"Come on. Let's go to Rico's Taco Truck. I haven't been there in ages."

"It's not Rico's anymore. It's Rosa's, I think, but word is it's still just as good."

"Then Rosa's Taco Truck. Come on. What do you say?"

I sighed and shrugged my shoulders. "Okay, I guess. It's on my way home, so yeah. Let's go get tacos."

We sat on a bench just down the sidewalk from the taco truck that for two years had served as our favorite post–symphony rehearsal hangout. We held on to steaming to-go boxes filled with Rosa's finest: corn tortillas held together with a thick layer of melted cheese, overflowing with onions and cilantro, grilled chicken, and spicy chorizo. I squeezed lime juice on my first taco and took a bite.

"This"—I nodded my head—"is a taco. Taco Bell does not make tacos."

Grayson hummed his agreement in between bites. "Agreed," he finally said. "I don't know who Rosa is, but I think I like her better than Rico."

A few more bites into our tacos and Grayson put his container down on the bench beside him. "I didn't mean to sound judgmental, Emma." He leaned forward, propping his elbows on his knees. "About leaving Cleveland. I'm sorry if I seemed rude."

"It's not a big deal. You're not the first person to question, but I'm happy here. I'm glad to be back."

"Are you playing anywhere else?"

"Not yet. I plan to, but I'm still trying to figure out how my schedule is going to work. I'm teaching five days a week, and with—" I almost said "with my mom" but stopped short. I spent every Tuesday and Friday morning with Mom, grocery shopping, going to doctor's appointments, and doing housework, but I didn't like to talk about it. It was impossible to mention it without people trying to turn my time with her into some grand magnanimous gesture or near-holy sacrifice. But it wasn't like that. She was my mom, and she needed me. End of discussion. "With other *stuff* that's going on, I'm not sure how much I can commit to. There's an audition for associate concertmaster in Atlanta in a couple of months," I said. "I am thinking about that one."

"Associate? Really?"

I shot him a look. "I'll take what's available. I want to play. I need to stay in Asheville. Maybe it's not the perfect opportunity, but it's enough for me right now. I have other reasons for moving back, so this"—I motioned to the city around me—"has to be enough."

"Enough?" He shook his head. "That sounds a little like you're settling."

"Prioritizing is different from settling."

"It *is* your mom, isn't it?" Grayson asked.

I closed my container and placed it on the sidewalk between my feet. "Can we not talk about this?"

"I'm not trying to pry. But I do care about your mom. I'm sorry if her health is failing."

"Her health isn't failing; she's just had a few setbacks."

"I'm sorry. Would you tell her I said hello?"

Mom had always loved Grayson. She liked that we had music in common and had defended him more than once when our nosy neighbor with her archaic beliefs liked to complain about me dating a black guy. Still, she was happy when we broke up. Grayson wasn't LDS, which precluded him from the perfect little scrapbooks Mom had encouraged me to fill with pictures of temples and butterflies and knights in shiny returned-missionary armor.

"I'll tell her," I said. "So what about you? I wasn't sure you would even play after high school. But you're good. You've kept it up."

"I didn't at first," Grayson said. "But I missed it after a while, so I joined a community orchestra in Raleigh that I stayed with all through college. After I moved back home, I joined the symphony in Hendersonville."

"If Bruno's gone three weeks, he'll probably miss Asheville's next concert. You want to play in his spot? I'll vouch for you with the conductor if you want in."

"That'd be great. I'd love to if they'll let me."

Huh. "So Asheville is good enough for you, just not good enough for me?"

He cocked an eyebrow. "My star was never destined to shine as bright as yours, Em. You know that as well as I do."

I huffed. "And you know I would never put my career over my family."

"That's true," he agreed. "I do know that about you."

It was hard not to feel like Grayson was throwing me a woeful "too bad your star has dimmed" pity party. A part of me wanted to lay it out there and explain all the reasons I'd walked away from my growing career. But I resisted, mostly because I didn't need to justify my choices to Grayson but also because I knew if I started down that road, it would be tough not to throw my own dang pity party. What was done was done. Rehashing the why and how of my departure from Cleveland wouldn't change anything.

Grayson ate in silence for a moment while I picked at my food. I wasn't annoyed, really. I didn't think Grayson was trying to be hurtful, but career discussions always left me feeling unsettled.

When the conversation shifted to high school memories and old friends, the tension in the back of my throat finally started to ease. Talking about the past felt easy, familiar even. We joked; we reminisced. I even managed to eat another taco.

And it was fine. I enjoyed Grayson's company, and we had a nice time. But I couldn't help but wonder: *why* was I eating tacos with my past instead of eating pizza with my potential (in a perfectly reasonable, not overzealous way) future?

Chapter 4

I PUSHED INTO MY APARTMENT on weak legs to see Lilly and Trav at the kitchen table playing a game of Scrabble. I left my bag on the couch, kicked off Lilly's old shoes, and went to the fridge for a bottle of water. I dropped my leftover tacos on the table next to Trav. "You want those? They came from Rosa's."

"You went to Rosa's and had leftovers? How does that even happen?" Trav asked.

"I ate two of the four. That's not too bad."

Trav opened the carton and wolfed down a taco in two bites, bits of cilantro clinging to his beard.

"Seriously?" Lilly said. "Did you even chew it? How are you even hungry after eating all of Elliott's pizza?"

Trav's mouth was already full of his second taco. "It's Rosa's."

Lilly shook her head and tossed him a napkin. "You are a barbarian." She finally looked my way. "What's up with you? How was rehearsal?"

I took a long swig of water. "Bruno's playing super grandpa in Florida, so he sent one of his old students to fill in for him until he's back in town."

Lilly shifted forward. "Okaaayy . . . you just said that like it should mean something to me, and I got nothing."

"The new cellist?" I paused a moment longer, watching Lilly lean so far forward she almost lost her position on her stool. "It's Grayson Harper."

She toppled forward, catching herself before she hit the floor, her eyes wide. "What? Your Grayson Harper?"

I nodded. "Crazy, right? He's living in Hendersonville. I guess he's been back a few years now."

"And he still plays the cello? That's totally hot. Wait, is it? Is he still hot?"

"Maybe hotter," I said. "I mean, he looks older, but yeah. He's barely changed."

Trav leaned forward, propping himself up with his elbows and batting his eyelashes. "So are we talking like hotter-than-Elliott-Hart hot?"

I shook my head. "No one's hotter than Elliott Hart. So what was he like?"

"He was really nice," Lilly said. "You need to go over and introduce yourself."

"I can't just walk over without a reason. That would be weird."

Trav gave a good-natured huff. "No weirder than Lilly inviting him to sleep on your couch fifteen seconds after she met him."

"He was going to sleep on the floor," Lilly said. "And I knew he was a nice guy. He's a Mormon."

"Ah, the Mormons," Trav said. "Forever gleaming with the shine of good character." I turned and tossed a dish towel at his head. He caught it with a smile and lobbed it back in my direction. "Just being Mormon is enough reason to go over there, right? Isn't that all you people need to fall in love?"

"Very funny."

"Besides," Lilly added. "You have a reason. Your bishop said to welcome him to the ward. So go welcome him."

"At nine o'clock at night? I should make him cookies or something. Cookies could be my reason."

"Did Elliott serve one of those mission thingies? With the bikes? Name tags? All of that?" Trav asked.

I nodded. "In French Polynesia."

"Seriously? Tahiti? I bet that was a rough two years," Trav said.

"Ask her something else," Lilly whispered, leaning over the table. "Emma's a fan."

"I'm not a fan. I've seen his videos. He's talented. But it's not like that."

"Where did he grow up?" Lilly asked.

Denver. "I . . . don't know."

"Where'd he go to college?"

He didn't. "No idea."

Lilly rolled her eyes. "How many siblings does he have?"

"Okay, I really don't know that one. Come on. I read the news. I know the basics. Maybe I'm a fan, if that's what you call occasionally enjoying his music, but that doesn't mean I'm a fanatic."

"Then go meet him." Trav spoke with a gleam in his eye.

"Right now?"

"Yeah, right now," Lilly said.

"Without cookies?"

"Emma, you don't need cookies. Just be nice. 'Hey . . . you're a Mormon; I'm a Mormon. I'm your neighbor. Welcome.' I'm sure you can handle that much without saying anything stupid. Just go knock."

Trav stood up. "Come on. I'll go with you. And I promise not to mention how much you like him."

I lunged across the kitchen and pushed Trav back into his seat. "No, no, no. You're not going anywhere."

"So you'll go by yourself?"

I left my water on the counter and walked to the door, pausing briefly to check my appearance in the mirror that hung in the living room. My primping was only fuel to Lilly and Trav's fire, but after the day I'd had, I could look like Medusa, for all I knew. I pulled my dark hair out of its ponytail and shook it out over my shoulders. I didn't look half bad. Two points for running into my ex-boyfriend looking not quite ravishing but still totally acceptable. My blue eyes looked bright against the green of my shirt, and thanks to the lower humidity levels of fall, my hair was actually kind of awesome—no frizz to be seen. I maybe looked a little tired, but there was no helping that, not without reapplying makeup, and there was no way I was giving Lilly that kind of satisfaction.

"You look great, Em," Lilly called. "Go knock him dead."

"I hate you," I called over my shoulder.

"You don't, and you know it," she sing-songed.

I slipped on a pair of navy flats by the door, better than the tennis shoes I'd been wearing all night, and crossed the small entryway to Elliott's door. I could hear the piano, just a few keys here and there, like he was puzzling out a melody. I leaned forward and listened. He repeated the same three notes, added a chord, and then suddenly it was a song. I stood with my fist inches from his door, completely mesmerized. I was a professional musician. I knew my strengths and had worked hard to build a career around them, but I'd never even attempted to compose. My brain wasn't cut out for that kind of creativity—that kind of freedom. Listening to him build something where there had been nothing before was captivating.

The music stopped, and something shifted, then footsteps sounded toward the door. I panicked, not wanting to get caught eavesdropping, and pounded on the door with a little more than friendly force.

The door swung open, and there he was with the hair and the eyes and the long, graceful fingers. He stood barefoot, wearing dark jeans and a T-shirt that clung to him in all the right places. I could see the things about him that made Lilly call him pretty. His features were almost delicate, from the curve of his lashes to the sharp angles of his cheekbones. But standing just a few feet away, seeing the scruff and the T-shirt and the long wiry biceps, he was decidedly masculine. And I was having a hard time getting air through my lungs.

"Hello?" He cocked his head and raised his eyebrows, probably wondering what a girl with wide eyes and a frozen expression was doing on his doorstep.

"Hi. I . . . um . . . from church." *Me caveman. You handsome.* I shook my head. "Sorry. Let's try this again. The bishop told me you were coming, and I just really wanted to see you . . . I mean, not see you like I'm spying on you, just see you to welcome you." All those years of education, and that was the best I could come up with? "And I just wanted to tell you that I really love you . . ." I closed my eyes and felt my cheeks flame red. "No! I don't love you. That would be weird. Sorry. What I mean to say is I'm glad." *What the what?*

"You're . . . glad?"

"Glad." I repeated the word like it was weird he didn't understand my incomplete babbling. "Yeah; I'm glad you're here." I finally finished my sentence. "You know. In the ward." This was a train wreck; a disastrous, cars-ripped-from-the-rails, broken-in-half, consumed-by-fiery-flame train wreck.

Not surprisingly, Elliott was unimpressed by my less-than-graceful greeting. "Uh, thanks."

I silently wished for the cookies I hadn't made him. Having some physical reason to be there would have been way less awkward than just standing there staring.

Make him feel welcome. The bishop's voice echoed in my head. I shifted my weight from one foot to the other. "So, I think you're going to like Asheville." Of course, he probably moved because he already *did* like Asheville, but I was no longer in control of my words. "It's a really great city. And the ward is great too. The singles, I mean, we aren't huge." Me and five other people definitely didn't qualify as huge. "But we do have activities occasionally." I shrugged. "I can maybe let you know when we do . . . um, you know, have them." I paused long enough to wish for an errant black bear to wander through the yard to distract us out of our misery. Okay, fine. A bear might have been pushing it. I would have settled for an angry squirrel. "Oh. I'm Emma. I didn't say that before."

He ran his fingers through his hair and gave me a look—a weird blend of annoyance, pity, and sort of a condescending tolerance. "Right. Emma. Listen, I appreciate you coming by. But I really moved to get away from the singles scene. I'm not planning on attending the singles ward. Really, I'm not looking to be involved in singles anything."

"The singles ward?" Asheville didn't have a singles ward. With so few singles, that would have been a really lonely ward.

"I'm really just here to focus on my music for a little while."

"Your music." I closed my eyes. Why was I repeating everything he said?

"*Not* socializing." He pushed one hand into his pocket and rested the other on the handle of his front door. He didn't seem to mind socializing with Lilly and Trav when they were helping him unpack. Lilly had raved about how nice he'd been. Why was he taking issue with me? You know, aside from the fact that I'd just acted like a bumbling fan who'd said I loved him before introducing myself.

I couldn't stand the thought of him thinking I'd only come over to fall at his feet and swoon. I might have blundered the last minute with my awkward staring and jumbled sentences, but it wasn't too late to change things. Granted, it was going to be tough to undo the love comment, but maybe he'd forget that part of our conversation. So I lied. "You mentioned your music," I said a little smugly. "What do you play?"

He shot me a quizzical look. "Piano."

"Are you any good?"

He had to know I was feigning ignorance, but I didn't back down. It wasn't like I could make things worse. He narrowed his eyes. "Good enough to pay the bills."

Yeah, and then some, I'm sure. There was something in his voice that turned me off. It wasn't pride, really, not blatant pride anyway. But he sounded snobby, and it grated on my nerves. I thought about my own tight budget—the weeks between performances and gigs when my lessons brought in just enough to scrape by. I had made more money when I'd played in Cleveland, even more when I'd been on tour, but in Asheville I joined the ranks of musicians who were constantly juggling, playing in multiple symphonies throughout the region and working day jobs they didn't love because there was no way music alone could pay the bills. It wasn't easy, certainly not as easy as racking up the cash from a million views on YouTube.

"That's all, huh?" In my mind's eye, I watched the shine of Elliott's halo dim. I didn't begrudge him his success, but I did resent him taking his success for granted. Enough to pay his bills? He'd been famous since he was seventeen. He had no idea what it felt like to really truly only have enough to pay the bills. But that was a conversation for another time. I needed to get out of there before I said anything else incriminating and really did make things worse.

"Okay, so . . . thanks for stopping by." He closed the door a couple of inches.

"Oh, sure." I took a step backward. "I guess I'll see you around. Maybe I could hear you play sometime?" I regretted the words the moment I said them. What was I thinking? That he'd invite me in for a private concert?

"Or maybe you could just look up a video on YouTube."

Ouch. "YouTube?"

"I'm sorry. It's been a long day. I'm gonna call it a night."

At least he paused long enough for me to nod a farewell before shutting the door in my face. I turned and slipped into my apartment, where I leaned against the wall and closed my eyes.

"So . . . you don't look like that went well."

I turned my head and looked at Lilly. "It was awful. I don't even know what happened. First I forgot how to talk, and then when I did talk, everything that came out of my mouth was completely stupid. I'm pretty sure I told him I was in love with him, which didn't make any sense since twenty seconds later I pretended like I didn't know who he was and asked him what instrument he played. Then he got all smug and acted like I *should* know who he is 'cause he's just *so* famous, and it just . . . I don't know. It was bad. Worse-than-tenth-grade-debate-team bad."

"Way to hit a home run." Trav spoke without looking up, his eyes glued to his Scrabble tiles.

"Shut up." I went into the kitchen and glanced over his shoulder. "Helix—right there. It'll give you a double-word score."

"Ooh, good word. Thanks." He added the tiles to the board, then counted his points. "Pretty sure that gives me the lead." He looked at Lilly. "Want to bow out now before it really gets ugly?"

"It totally doesn't count. You can't use Emma's word and then rub it in my face like you've beaten me. You never would have come up with *helix* on your own."

I pulled a bowl out of the cabinet and retrieved the ice cream from the freezer. Playful bickering was the cornerstone of Trav and Lilly's relationship. They seemed to thrive on it, but I wasn't in the mood to listen to them squabble. I'd just ruined my one good chance to be friends with the only other single Mormon in all of Asheville. At least the only one who wasn't an eighteen-year-old girl. Or Darren Fishbaum. Add that to my unnerving dinner with Grayson, who made me feel like my life was one giant heap of failed potential, and the only thing I wanted was a bowl of chocolate ice cream and a marathon of *Friends* reruns.

"Oh, hey, Emma," Lilly said. "Your sister called while you were next door."

I turned. "Did she? Did you talk to her?"

"Yeah. I answered your phone since I knew she wouldn't leave you a message. Hope you don't mind."

"No, I'm glad you did. What'd she say?"

"She wants you to call her. Something about an audition piece? I think she wants you to play it for her so she can hear all the dynamics and other blah blah musical terms I don't understand."

As far as I knew, Ava didn't have any auditions coming up, which meant she was probably working on the Barber Concerto for the video I'd offered to send to my professor at CIM. Ava working on the piece was a good thing. Ava asking me for help? That was a miracle. "Okay, thanks. I'll call her back right now." I grabbed my phone and my ice cream and headed for my room.

"Emma," Lilly called before I was out of earshot. "Don't give up on Elliott. Next time will be better, I'm sure."

I waved my spoon in the air before rounding the corner of the kitchen. "Yeah, yeah." *Better like a toothache.*

Chapter 5

I didn't see Elliott for the rest of the week. It wouldn't have been hard to scheme my way into a casual run-in. I heard him in the entryway more than once, and I could have found a reason to go outside at just that moment to check the mail or take out the trash or, I don't know, take pictures of an angry squirrel. But I'd already set myself up as a twitterpated, lovesick fan. The next time he saw me had to feel completely organic. I couldn't make it happen; it had to just . . . happen.

But all my scheming to not seem like I was scheming? It totally backfired. So much so that I actually started avoiding him. Every possible encounter seemed like something I could have set up, and I couldn't stand the thought of him thinking I would do such a thing. It was much better to be guilty of avoiding someone on purpose than it was to be constantly seeking them out. Less weird anyway. Or so I told myself on Thursday afternoon when I sat in my car, my seat all the way reclined so Elliott wouldn't see me as he crossed the street in front of our house and went inside.

I pressed the heels of my hands over my eyes and groaned. I was being ridiculous. I knew I was being ridiculous, but—

A sharp rap sounded on the driver's side window, and I jumped. Ava stood beside my car, her hand propped on her hip and her eyebrows scrunched up in question. She looked annoyed, like she couldn't believe she was related to someone who would do something as outlandish as recline the seat in her car. Never mind the fact that I was actually hiding from my super-hot neighbor. I sat up and looked past her, making sure Elliott was all the way inside, then motioned for Ava to move around the car and get in.

"What are you doing?" The tone of her voice matched her eyebrows—all scrunched up and judgy.

"Nothing. I was just . . . resting."

"It looked like you were hiding."

"I wasn't hiding. I live here. Who would I be hiding from?"

"Right. You live here. Which is why it doesn't make sense that you're resting in your car. Why not just go inside and rest on your couch?"

Suddenly I was thirteen years old, trying to reason a five-year-old Ava out of the sandbox at the park and back onto the sidewalk so I could walk her home. She could dig her heels in better than anyone I knew, stubborn to an I-will-drive-you-crazy fault, and she never backed down. Even when it was something stupid like her big sister sitting in her car a little too long. "What's with the inquisition? It's nice outside."

"Hmmm. I don't buy it. Your windows weren't down. I think you were hiding from your new famous neighbor. He's in the same house, right? Is he home? Is that his car?"

"What? That's ridiculous." I knew I shouldn't have said anything to Mom. "I'm not hiding from anyone."

"It's that black one, right? It looks expensive." It took me a second to figure out she was still talking about Elliott's car. It was an expensive car, more expensive than mine anyway. But this was stupid. Even if I did want to gush about Elliott's car, it wouldn't be with my little sister. I loved her, but she insta-posted everything—from the flavor of her breakfast cereal to the eye color of her current crush. She knew social media better than I knew music theory and wouldn't let something as juicy as her sister living next to a famous pianist go unmentioned. I felt the need to call her off.

I didn't know for sure why Elliott had moved to West Asheville. Despite Lilly's claims that it was cool and hip, which it totally was, it wasn't exactly a popular haunt for the rich and famous. It made more sense that he really was trying to lie low and be off the grid for a while. Which meant Ava blabbing anything to her whatever-hundred followers was not what Elliott would want. Just what I needed to lock in my lovesick fan persona: a little sister revealing his secret location all over the Internet.

"You haven't posted anything online about Elliott, have you?"

"What? No. Why would I?"

"Because he's famous, and . . . I don't know why else. Isn't that enough?"

Ava shrugged. "I guess it's kind of exciting, but it's not like he sings or anything. None of my friends would even know who he is. I mean, he's just some old guy who plays the piano."

"Old guy? He's only a year older than me."

Her eyebrows went up. "Yeah. I know."

I sighed. "So what's up with you? What are you doing here?"

She pulled a loaf of bread out of her bag and handed it over. "Mom's baking again."

"Really? She said she was feeling good on Tuesday but not baking-bread good. I'm surprised." I pulled the loaf to my face and breathed in the familiar yeasty smell. Baking was a good sign, though it made me nervous that Mom had done it without me there. She liked to think she didn't need me around, but it made Dad nervous too when she tried to do too much on her own. Six weeks before I moved home, she fell in the grocery store and broke her wrist. She hadn't slipped or tripped or stumbled in any way. She'd just . . . fallen. Her legs had stopped working and then she'd been on the ground. I would never forget the way Dad sounded on the phone, like it killed him that he couldn't just be there for her all the time. He couldn't, not with his work schedule. But I could.

"Yeah, she's had a good day. She was making cinnamon rolls when I left," Ava said.

"For real? Is she alone? She's been on her feet all day. She shouldn't be doing this if she's by herself—"

"Chill," Ava interrupted. "Dad's home. She isn't alone."

"Oh. Well then, why didn't you wait an hour and bring me a cinnamon roll too?"

"Whatever. You're only getting bread 'cause I have rehearsal and Mom insisted I bring it over on my way. Are you coming over on Sunday to help with my concerto?"

"Yeah, I'm planning on it. I also thought we could look at Juilliard's audition list. Have you looked at it yet?"

She pulled out her phone without responding, her fingers flying over the keys. I waited a beat longer, then huffed out her name. "Ava."

"What? Oh. No, not yet."

For a second, I only stared, feeling the familiar Ava-tinted tension building in my neck and shoulders. "It's not that different from when I auditioned," I finally said. "You'll need a Paganini Caprice. Do you know any Paganini?" She didn't look up from her phone, but at least her fingers stilled. "We'll find you a good one. I like number twenty-two, but seven is good too, or fourteen, maybe. And a Bach sonata. Number three in C Major would be perfect."

Ava still didn't respond. She stared out the passenger-side window, biting at her thumbnail with enough ferocity I was surprised I didn't see any blood.

"Hey. You okay?" I reached over and nudged her shoulder.

"I'm fine."

"I know you've got a year before you audition, but you really do have to start thinking about all this now. I promise I won't be pushy about it. You can totally pick your own Paganini."

"It's not that; it's just . . ." She shook her head. "Never mind. It's fine. I'll do whatever you think is best."

"Ava, what are you not telling me?"

She reached for the door handle. "I gotta get to rehearsal. Feinstein hates it when we're late."

She had a point there. Gerald Feinstein had been conducting the Asheville Youth Symphony for as long as I could remember. He'd been ancient when I'd been in the orchestra; it was hard to believe he was still going strong. It was not hard to believe his distaste for tardiness had done anything but intensify with age.

Ava got out of the car and shut the door without saying good-bye.

I wound down my window and called out to her, stopping her in the middle of the street. She turned around, her hands shoved deep into the pockets of her hoodie. "Are you sure you're okay?"

She shrugged. "I guess."

She turned and climbed into the tiny hatchback she'd inherited after I'd graduated. I could see her violin—another of my hand-me-downs—sitting in the backseat. I tried to wave as she drove past, but she kept her eyes forward, not even glancing in my direction. I didn't need her to glance at me to see the tears though. My heart sank. I remembered all too well the pressure of college auditions, the hours of practicing, and the endurance required by schools like Juilliard and CIM. I could only hope Ava wasn't buckling under the weight of it all.

With her gone and Elliott safely inside, I finally climbed out of my car.

Fifteen minutes later, Lilly found me in the kitchen waiting for my toast to pop, a fried egg sizzling in a pan on the stove.

"Seriously, Emma, do you ever eat anything else?" She sank into a kitchen chair and kicked off her shoes. I glanced over my shoulder, noting how tired she looked.

"Protein, whole grains, butter. Ready in five minutes. It's the perfect meal. You want one?"

"Yes. No. I'm starving, but Trav is coming over in an hour. I think he's bringing sushi from Green Tea." She dropped her head onto the table.

"Mmm, Green Tea. Tell Trav if he brings me a Dragon Roll I'll feed him Scrabble words for the rest of forever."

"Will you even be here to eat it? Fried eggs mean rehearsal. I know the drill."

"Just chamber group, but have him get one anyway. I'll be hungry when I get home."

"Chamber group again? Didn't you just do that on Monday?"

"Yeah, but we have a wedding this weekend, with new music, so we're getting together one more time." I sat in the chair across from her and dug into my food. "What's up with you? Long day?"

"Sooo long," she said. "We had this dad today who was seriously the most obnoxious baby daddy I have ever, ever dealt with."

"Yeah? Do tell."

"There's too much to tell, really. Suffice it to say, he was all about getting naked and getting in the tub with his wife while she was laboring."

"Like, *naked* naked?"

Lilly nodded.

"Please promise you'll stop me if I ever come close to marrying someone who thinks getting naked during labor is a good idea."

She laughed. "You going to add that to your string of first-date questions? What do you do for a living? How many siblings do you have? When your wife is in labor with your first child, would you or would you not feel comfortable taking off your pants?"

"Oh, I'm gonna. I might wait for the second date to ask, but this'll be a deal breaker for me." I finished eating and took my plate to the sink, rinsing it off before sliding it into the dishwasher. "I gotta run. Dragon Roll! Don't forget to text Trav!"

* * *

Vibration still pulsed through my hand as I dropped my bow, exhilarated to have hit that high note just right. Rehearsal was going so much better than last time. It helped that I was no longer shocked over Grayson's presence, but also, we played through the sister of the bride's psycho-awful composition only once before we considered it good and moved on. The rest of the typical wedding stuff we knew well enough not to worry about practicing, which left us time to play around a little. We played one of my favorites—Puccini's Crisantemi—a piece I hoped we would play for our spring concert. It definitely wasn't wedding music. The Crisantemi was composed as an elegy honoring some Italian-born king of Spain from the 1800s, Amadeo something or other. But it was a piece that hit me all the way down to my soul, and I was in a good mood for having gotten to play it.

I placed my bow carefully in my case and took a few extra minutes to wipe the excess rosin from my violin strings, mostly because I kinda wanted to let Grayson get good and gone before I went to my car. I was pretty sure our impromptu taco dinner the week before had been a one-time, nice-to-see-you-again-let's-catch-up kind of deal, but what if he wanted to go out again? What if he wanted it to be a regular thing and I was going to have to endure casual, semijudgy questions about my life choices over and over again? Caroline and I talked over our instrument cases long enough I thought for sure Grayson had left. This made it all the more surprising when I found him leaning against the driver's side door of my car, a fancy white envelope in his hands. He must have already put his cello in his truck because he just stood there, turning the envelope over and over and looking . . . nervous, maybe?

What the heck was he holding?

"Hey." I unlocked my car and put my violin in the back. "What's up?"

"I, um, well, I just wanted to give you this." He held out the envelope. "I don't want you to feel weird, so if you don't want to come, you really don't have to. But I didn't want you to think you weren't invited, and now that you're back in town, you should be invited. So just . . . I guess I'm just saying it's up to you. If you'd like to come, I think it would be nice to have you there."

I pulled a thick piece of cardstock out of the envelope and started to read. "Grayson, are you getting married?" I read a few more lines of the invitation. "I can't believe you didn't mention it on Monday."

"I was going to, but then it just sort of felt awkward bringing it up, and . . . I'm sorry. I should have told you."

"November. That's not very far away."

"Yeah, it's coming up pretty quick."

"Wow. I mean, that's big news. I'm really happy for you."

"Thanks."

I tried to puzzle out the emotions battling inside my brain. Happiness reigned—I knew that much was true. Grayson was a good guy. He deserved a great relationship. I was maybe a little bitter he'd managed to find his happily-ever-after before I had, but I'd never admit as much out loud. I would admit, as soon as I was home and talking to Lilly, that underneath my shock and happiness and stupid old-girlfriend bitterness, there was also a tiny measure of panic. I didn't have anything to wear to a wedding where I wasn't a hired musician, especially not an evening wedding at the Grove Park Inn. More importantly, I didn't have a plus one. And if there was one thing that was absolutely perfectly clear in my jumbled-up brain, it was that I was *not* going to my ex-boyfriend's wedding without a date. Even if that date was Darren Fishbaum.

Okay. Maybe scratch that last part about Darren Fishbaum.

"So tell me about"—I glanced at the invitation—"about Jane."

Grayson's eyes got all bright and happy. "She's great. She's my boss's daughter, actually." He tugged on his ear. "She dropped by one day to bring him lunch, and that sort of started everything."

"Did she grow up in Asheville?"

"Yeah. Then she moved away for school and came back a few years ago after she graduated. She's the hospitality director at Hotel Indigo. Do you know it?"

"I love the Hotel Indigo. We played a gig there last—oh my gosh. I think I met her."

"What? You did?"

"She's teeny tiny, with dark short hair, right? We were playing for this swanky cocktail party, and she and I talked for a few minutes while we were setting up. She was really nice."

"Yeah, that's her. So, are you going to come?" He shoved his hands into his pockets and gave me a hopeful smile.

I looked back at the invitation one more time. "I'll have to check my schedule. Weekends are generally pretty crazy with gigs and symphony concerts, but I'll try. If I'm not busy, I'd love to be there." I answered him with just enough conviction I almost believed it myself.

Chapter 6

LATER THAT NIGHT, I SAT across the table from Lilly, enjoying my Dragon Roll—*I love you, Trav*—while she studied the details of Grayson's invitation.

"Theodore and Agnes Manigault Rockwell. Who even has names like that anymore?" Lilly reached across the table and snuck a piece of my sushi.

"The real question is who includes a pronunciation guide on a wedding invitation?"

"*An-yez*," Lilly said through her nose. "I want to go to the reception and call her plain old Agnes just to see what happens."

"At least they had mercy on their kid. You can't get much simpler than Jane."

"But she isn't just Jane. She's Jane Ravenel Rockwell."

I tried not to laugh. "I'm sure they're all very nice."

"So what are you thinking? Are you gonna go?"

I snatched the invitation out of Lilly's hands and gave it another once-over. "I don't know. I kinda feel like I should, but he didn't send me an invitation until *now*. Which means the only reason I'm invited is because we're in the same chamber group and he probably felt guilty. Do you really think he wants me there? His ex-girlfriend? It's a little weird."

"It's only weird if you're still in love with him. But you're not. You've moved on; he's moved on. You should go. It's free food anyway."

"I'm not going to his wedding for the free food. And I'm also not going without a date, which, you know, probably means I'm not going."

"Why do you need a date? Maybe you'll meet someone there." Lilly tucked her hair, still wet from her shower, behind her ear. I hated her a little for looking so good without makeup, wearing old yoga pants, and sporting an oversized sweatshirt. She pulled off messy casual way better than I did.

"That's true," I said. "I'm sure Grayson is inviting all kinds of eligible Mormon bachelors to his wedding."

Lilly rolled her eyes. "You and your stupid requirements. Anybody could pinch hit as a wedding date though, right? He doesn't really have to be Mormon. Not to take you to a wedding."

"I guess not. As long as it's not my wedding."

"What about Buster?"

"Trav's work friend, Buster?"

"Yeah. He's nice and . . . sort of cute."

For real? How desperate did she think I was? "His name is Buster."

"That's a stupid reason not to like someone."

"Okay. His name is Buster, and he plays Minecraft twenty-three hours a day. And he smells like mushrooms."

"But you like mushrooms."

I pushed up from the table and dropped the sushi to-go box in the trash. "You're not helping."

"Fine, fine." She leaned back in her chair and crossed her arms. "What about Elliott? You've been making out with his YouTube channel all week. Maybe he'd go with you."

"I'm not even going to dignify that comment with a response." It was stupid how quickly my heart picked up speed just because Lilly mentioned Elliott's name. It was almost as stupid as her comment about his YouTube channel. Because I wasn't . . . I didn't . . . Or maybe I did. But I was only listening. Not obsessing.

"Oh, whatever," Lilly said. "You just need to go talk to him again. Give yourself another chance to make a better impression."

"I'm not *ever* going over there to talk to him—not without a personal invitation or a really good, completely plausible, verifiable-with-physical-proof reason. Even if I did have a reason, I would never ask him to go to Grayson's wedding. That would just be . . ."

"Amazing," Lilly interjected. "It would be amazing."

"I was going to say awkward."

"Emma, just think about it. Everybody at that wedding is going to remember you as the Emma who was going somewhere. You said yourself Grayson acted like your star had dimmed. Who knows what kind of things he's been telling people about your fall from Cleveland."

"I didn't *fall* from Cleveland. I left. On purpose."

"I know that, and you know that, but no one else does. What better way to show everyone you've still got it than by showing up to the wedding with Elliott Hart?"

"So, use his celebrity to make myself look . . . what, more important? More accomplished? You know that's not my style."

She frowned. "Okay, no. It's not your style. But . . . I dunno. He'd still be the hottest guy at the wedding. It might be fun for that reason alone."

He would definitely be the hottest guy at the wedding. He was the hottest guy anywhere. But I still couldn't ask him. Because asking required talking, and I wasn't planning on talking to him ever again. It was the only surefire way to guarantee I didn't humiliate myself.

"Have you seen him around at all?" I asked Lilly.

"Who, Elliott?"

I held my hands up and shot her a look.

"Calm down," she replied. "I've just seen him once. He helped me carry my groceries in yesterday. Have *you* seen him around?"

I shook my head. "Only a few times, but I don't think they really count. I saw him, but he didn't see me."

"Yeah, I guess he wouldn't if you're hiding in the bushes." Lilly stood and stretched her arms over her head, then stifled a yawn. "Emma, you live here. You can't hide from him forever."

"I know! But I still feel so stupid. You can't know the extent of our conversation, Lil. It was quite possibly the worst conversation I have ever had with a man. Or maybe with anyone. Ever. There is no way to recover from that." I flipped the light in the kitchen and followed her into the hallway.

"So that's it, then? You'll just never talk to him again?"

No.

Yes.

I have no idea.

"Maybe not forever. But the next time we talk, it has to feel completely natural. I just don't want it to be forced, you know? It has to just happen."

* * *

The irony of my comment was not lost on me when the following Sunday morning, just after sacrament meeting, old Sister Sheehan snaked her way through the crowd and snagged Elliott before he'd made it three steps away from his pew. She gripped his arm and had a gleam in her eye as she looked pointedly in my direction. I was in for a confrontation with Elliott that was anything but the organic encounter I'd been hoping for. With Sister Sheehan at the helm, his second impression of me might actually be worse than the first.

I hid behind the Stevenson kid, grateful for his high-school-linebacker–sized shoulders, and almost made it to the safety of the hallway, now bustling with people. But when my shield stopped to flirt with a girl lingering in the back pew (curse you, high school romances), Sister Sheehan managed to cut me off before I could make my escape.

"Emma dear. I'm so glad you're here today." When she finally released Elliott's arm, he shook his sleeve and shoved his hands in the pockets of his suit pants. He didn't look annoyed, really, just sort of . . . weary.

"When I saw this handsome young man in the back row, I knew he had to be the piano player you told me about last week. This is him, right? I just wanted to make sure you had the opportunity to say hello."

I cringed as I heard my own voice echoing back in my head. *What do you play?* I kept my eyes on Sister Sheehan—dear, sweet, cover-blowing Sister Sheehan—but I could still see the smirk on Elliott's face. "It's nice of you to think of me, and I appreciate you bringing him over, but we've already met."

"Oh, well, that's wonderful." She turned to Elliott. "You know, Emma is a musician too. She plays the fiddle almost as well as my uncle Nesbit."

I tried not to wince. The fiddle? Uncle Nesbit? I couldn't get to my Sunbeam class fast enough.

Sister Sheehan squeezed my arm, her eyebrows dancing as she grinned. "I'll leave you young people to it." She shuffled out of the chapel while Elliott and I stood in awkward silence. I tried to think of something to say that might redeem me from our first encounter, but before I could open my mouth, Elliott gave me a nod and a brief "Nice to see you again," then turned and left.

Awesome.

For the second week in a row, I tried and failed to focus on my lesson. I couldn't think of anything but Elliott's smug expression. The kids were all over the place, ignoring everything I said, and I could hardly blame them. I wasn't making any sense. Finally we ate some animal crackers and colored some pictures, and I mentally vowed that next week we'd learn something useful. I looked at the next lesson. "I Am Thankful for Fish." See? Perfect.

At the end of Primary, I ducked out of church a few minutes early to avoid the crowds. And by crowds, I meant Elliott. I stopped by Maple Crescent long enough to grab my violin, then drove to my parents' house, hoping Ava still wanted to work on her concerto. And also hoping for lunch.

Church in Hendersonville ended an hour earlier than my Asheville ward, so my family was already home and gathered around the kitchen bar, the post-church feeding frenzy in full swing. Dad stood at the counter making himself a peanut butter and jelly sandwich while Ava hovered by the open refrigerator, sniffing her way through containers of leftovers. I left my stuff by the door and plopped onto a barstool.

"Hi."

"Hey! It's Emma!" Dad called. "Karen! Emma's home."

Mom appeared in the kitchen doorway and smiled. She moved around the bar and kissed me on the forehead. "What brings you to our end of the mountains?"

I shrugged. "Ava said she wanted to practice."

"Are you hungry?" Mom nudged Ava out of the way and leaned into the fridge. "Your dad made sweet pork tacos for the missionaries last night. I can warm up some leftovers if you want."

"That's what *I* was looking for," Ava said. She swung her blonde hair over her shoulder. "Is there enough for both of us?"

"There's enough for all of us," Mom said, "though it doesn't look like your father was patient enough for a taco."

Dad grinned through a huge bite of sandwich. "This is only my appetizer."

I took the containers from Mom and pulled a few plates out of the cabinet. "Thanks, Mom."

She moved to the window seat at the back of the kitchen while I made the tacos—a plate for each of us. Ava took hers to the living room, leaving me alone in the kitchen with my parents.

"So." Dad rubbed his hands together. "Have you met the rock star yet?" He sat down next to Mom and pulled a cushion into his lap, then lifted Mom's feet onto the cushion.

"Huh?"

"He's talking about Elliott Hart," Mom said. "Have you talked to him yet?"

"He's in your ward, right?" Dad said.

"He's in her ward, but he's also her neighbor. He lives in the same house, right across the entryway."

Dad's eyebrows danced playfully. "What are the odds of that happening? When's your first date?"

"Go easy on her, Jake." Mom nudged Dad in the chest with her foot.

She was playing all coy, scolding Dad for teasing me, but I didn't buy it. I could almost hear the wheels turning in her brain, fast-forwarding through my potential future with Elliott. I couldn't exactly blame her. I mean, the fantasy had crashed and burned within ten seconds of meeting him, but I'd still done the same thing.

"Tell me about him," Mom said. "What's he like?"

"He's . . ." I had no idea what to say. I couldn't say nice because, well, he hadn't been very nice, not that I'd done much to deserve his niceness. I could say hot; that was totally true, but it was hardly a description that would satisfy Mom. "He's . . . very talented."

She gave me a funny look but didn't press further.

"So guess who's in my chamber group now?"

Mom's eyes sparked with interest. "Someone new?"

I nodded. "New to the group but not to me. He's filling in while Bruno's in Florida with his granddaughter."

"He?" Mom's eyes went wide. "Is it Grayson? Really?"

I nodded. "He's getting married in November."

"Oh! That's so good! And such big news." Ha. She didn't even try to hide her relief.

Dad gave Mom's foot a final squeeze, then got up and retrieved his plate before leaving the kitchen. "I'm going to do some reading. Make sure you come see me before you leave."

I nodded.

"How are you feeling about the wedding?" Mom asked.

"Fine, I guess. Grayson seems really happy."

"Are you invited?"

I nodded again. "Yeah, but only just now. I'm sure he wouldn't have if we weren't in the same quartet."

"Are you going to go?"

"Go where?" Ava reappeared in the kitchen with her empty plate.

"To Grayson Harper's wedding," Mom said. "Emma's been invited."

"Who's Grayson Harper?"

"Seriously? You don't remember Grayson? He was over here all the time."

"Emma's old boyfriend from high school," Mom added.

"What, when I was like seven? No. I don't remember him."

"Ava, his picture is hanging in the music room. It's been there forever."

"The prom picture? Is he the black guy with the curly hair? The one in between you and Lilly? I always wondered who that was."

"For real? You don't remember him coming over? He would play hide-and-seek with you for hours. And you would always ask if you could play his cello."

"Ohhhh! I do remember him! He was really nice." Ava still hadn't changed out of her church clothes. Her fitted green dress had once been mine, but she'd dressed it up with a skinny silver belt and a navy cardigan. She looked grown up—like it would suddenly feel funny to call her my baby sister. I finished the last of my taco, then stood up, leaning over the bar to put my plate in the sink.

"Come on," I said to Ava. "I brought my violin. You ready to practice?"

A shadow passed across her face, and her mouth pulled into a pout, destroying any trace of the grown-up Ava I'd noticed just moments before. She heaved a sigh and turned toward the living room. "I guess."

* * *

Two hours later, I could think of only one good thing about our infuriatingly awful practice session: I was so annoyed with Ava I forgot to be annoyed with Elliott.

Ava wasn't just planning on applying to CIM and Juilliard. She was also thinking about Eastman, and she'd probably apply to BYU. Regardless of where she wound up, if she majored in music, her college application would require a music audition. A month into her junior year, she should have been zeroed in on the process, but her lack of focus was killing me. All she was zeroed in on was her phone. I watched as she snapped a selfie with her violin, then applied a series of filters and sent it off to the digital world, where she spent so much of her time. I rolled my eyes. Apparently Ava had plenty of time to tweet about playing the violin, just not any time to actually *practice* the violin. I'd hoped maybe we'd reached a turning point since she'd called me about the video for CIM, but things were no better.

If she wasn't so good when she did play, I might just throw my hands in the air and walk away. But it felt wrong to give up when she was so close to being ready.

"Ava, please come play this with me." I gave it one final try. "If we play it together, you'll get the feel of it and have an easier time practicing when I'm not here."

She sighed a purposely loud sigh and stood up, slipping her cell phone into her back pocket before retrieving her violin from the back of the piano.

"On my count, all right? One, two, ready, play . . ." We made it through the first eight measures before her phone dinged with an incoming text, and she left me to play Barber's Violin Concerto opus Fourteen on my own.

"Ava, come on! Why did you want me to come over?" There was a reason I wasn't Ava's regular violin teacher. Mom brought it up once, wondering if she could save the money she spent on Ava's tuition. It took about seven seconds for me to shoot that idea down. Even just helping her with her pieces on the weekend was enough to make me crazy.

She shot me a backward glance. "I'm sorry. I know I've been distracted. It's just . . . this is really important. How about you play it for me all the way through and record it so I can listen and practice along with the recording."

It wasn't a bad suggestion. But it would be even better if we could play through the entire thing together. Then I could help her identify any trouble spots she'd need to work on. "I can record it for you, but let's play it through first."

She giggled, her eyes still glued to the phone.

I sighed my own purposely loud sigh. "Seriously? I'm going home."

Mom poked her head around the corner of the kitchen and gave me a pleading look.

"What do you want me to do, Mom? She's worse than the Garrison twins, and their mother pays me to put up with their antics. I can't help her if she won't play more than four measures."

"These are important auditions, Emma." Mom's voice was quiet, soothing.

"I *know* they're important. I went through the same thing when I was her age, and I worked around the clock to be good enough. I had to build an entire portfolio of work, and I took it seriously, without anyone having to browbeat me into practicing."

Ava huffed, finally dropping her phone. "Well, isn't it just too, too bad we can't all be as talented as you. Talented enough to be first chair everything all the time, to get into CIM *and* Juilliard like it was nothing, to be the grand-high-violin-goddess of the Cleveland Orchestra and the Asheville Symphony. Isn't it just so sad we can't all be as perfect as you." She slammed her violin into its case hard enough to make me wince and stormed out of the room.

Mom let out a frustrated breath and shook her head. "I should've bought that girl an oboe."

I sank onto the piano bench. "I shouldn't have rubbed stuff in her face. I just don't understand. She's so talented. Why won't she try?"

"You left her some pretty big shoes to fill," Mom said. "I know you don't expect her to be just like you. Your dad and I don't either, but she puts the pressure on herself."

"But she's better than I was at her age. She shouldn't feel pressure at all—she'd be brilliant if she'd just try."

"She's got a lot of natural talent." Mom kept her voice low. "But I'm afraid you got the lion's share of the one thing she might not have enough of."

I raised my eyebrows and waited for her response.

"Desire. She has to want it, Emma."

I shook my head. "That's ridiculous. We've talked about it. This is what she wants."

Mom looked tired. "I think you're right, but I have to wonder if we aren't pushing her too hard."

"If this *is* what she wants, there's no other way to get her there. She won't make it if she doesn't push hard."

Mom sat down on the piano bench beside me, her movements slow and intentional. "You know better than anyone what she needs to focus on," she said, "but I wonder if it might help if you tried being her sister *without* your violin in your hands."

I scoffed. "What's that supposed to mean?"

"Talk to her. Take her to see a movie. Ask her about school and her friends."

"So just give up on her music?"

"Of course you shouldn't give up. But there's more to life than music, Emma. Your dad and I have been watching her the past few weeks, and we're beginning to wonder if music isn't actually what Ava wants to do."

"Has she told you as much?"

"No. But . . . I don't know. We could be wrong. Just go easy on her, all right? And find a way to be her sister."

"Fine. I'll try. But I can't let her give up on this thing with CIM. If Professor Graham likes her video, she's in, easy as that. It's a huge opportunity." I stretched my neck, hearing the crack as I turned my head to the left, then right. "Here." I handed Mom my cell phone. "Can you record while I play the Barber? I'll send it to both of you. Can you just make sure she listens? It'll help."

"I'll make sure."

I pulled my violin up to my shoulder, bow at the ready, and waited for my mother's nod to start the piece. She hesitated. "Please think about what I said, Em."

I nodded my head and motioned with my bow for her to start. I could think about what she said all night, but that didn't mean it would make any sense. Ava and I had been holding violins since our instruments were only nine inches long and looked like they belonged in a toy store. Music was the only language we'd ever spoken to each other, at least spoken well. Take that away? The thought left me uneasy, to say the least.

I finished recording the concerto and packed up to head home, stopping in Dad's office long enough to wrap my arms around his neck and kiss him on the head.

"You sounded good in there," he said.

"Thanks."

"So how's life in West Asheville?"

I leaned my head against his shoulder, breathing a muffled groan into the still-crisp collar of his Sunday shirt. "Well, my old boyfriend is in my chamber group, my new neighbor thinks I'm crazy, and my entire ward thinks it's their sacred responsibility to marry me off. So, you know, normal stuff. Also, Ava hates me."

Dad chuckled. "It's okay. She hates me right now too." He squeezed my hand. "It'll be all right in the end. It always is."

There was something about my father's unshakable faith in nearly everything that made me smile. Any problem or struggle we'd ever had while I was growing up, his token response was, "Did you pay your tithing? Did you say your prayers? Then it'll be all right in the end."

It might have been annoying if it was all for show, but he really did feel that way. He was always steady, always trusting. The rest of us wavered from time to time, but we never could for long—not with him around.

I gave him another hug. If I squeezed hard enough, maybe I could leech out some of his faith for myself.

Chapter 7

FIVE MINUTES WITH DAD WENT a long way to lift my spirits, but I was still in a foul mood when I made it back to Maple Crescent. Mom wanted me to connect to Ava without music, but how? Besides, I liked it when we played together. While I'd been in school, I'd loved holidays and rare weekends at home when Ava and I had played. We'd holed up in the music room for hours, laughing as much as we'd played, carrying on until well past midnight.

It was hard to believe that was the same Ava I'd just fought with for two hours. I couldn't remember the last time I'd been around her without the crippling tension that seemed to scream, *I hate your everlovin' guts! And your stupid violin too.*

Halfway up the front walk, I ran into Elliott.

"Oh," I stammered. "Hello." We stood there face-to-face for what felt like an interminable pause. He was in the middle of the sidewalk, blocking my path, so I waited, wondering if he was going to step out of the way or, I don't know, say hello back, maybe. Since that was generally the kind of thing neighbors did.

"What are you doing here?" he finally asked.

Wait. What? What was *I* doing there?

He must have mistaken my confusion for embarrassment because he said, "Look—do you want me to sign something? A CD? A photograph, maybe?"

Wait! What?
Sign something?
Words.

I needed words to talk my way out of this one. I spoke slowly, without stuttering, without saying one single um. *Go me!* "I have no idea what you're talking about."

Elliott sighed. "First you show up at my apartment. Then you follow me to the family ward, even though I told you I wasn't interested in singles activities. I've seen you lurking around all week, sitting in your car, watching me. I'm sure you're a really nice person, Emma. It's Emma, right? And I don't mean to take any of this out on you personally, but I moved to get away from this kind of stuff."

Oh my. I couldn't decide if it was more hilarious that Elliott Hart had just accused me of being a stalker or more hilarious that he still thought we had a singles ward. I shook my head. "You've really got the wrong idea."

"Do I?"

He was still blocking the sidewalk, so I cut into the grass and moved to the front of the house. "First of all, I'm here because I live here. It doesn't have anything to do with you."

"You live here? *Here,* here?"

"Right next door to you," I said. "I'm Lilly's roommate."

He closed his eyes and pressed his forehead into his hand—a literal facepalm. Good. Decent of him to at least feel chagrined.

"Second, there's never been a singles ward in Asheville. The young single adults group pretty much consists of four freshman girls from UNCA, Darren Fishbaum, and me. That's it."

He blinked. "Darren, the little tiny guy who spoke today?"

"That's him." I shifted my violin to my other shoulder and reached for the front door. "Honestly, Elliott, I knocked on your door last week because the bishop knew we were going to be neighbors and asked that I welcome you and say hello. I got a little tongue-tied—I guess it was exciting to meet you in person—but really, truly, I'm not going to bother you again. You can play your piano and make your music, and I promise to let Darren know whenever he wants a ride to the stake singles activities he better not call you." I stepped into the entryway and nearly had the door closed behind me when he stopped me with a question.

"Why did you pretend like you didn't know who I was?" He didn't sound defensive, just curious, like he was trying to make new sense of me.

I turned back. "Why did you automatically assume that I did?"

"Maybe I did assume. But I've gotten pretty good at reading people. When people know who I am, they just . . ." He shoved his hands deep into his pockets. "They see celebrity and think that somehow gives them the right to insert themselves into my life. They hang out in front of my house or send hundreds of e-mails to my mother or call up my old girlfriend to see if she'll tell any stories about me. I know that's not what you did, but from the way you were acting, it just seemed like . . ." He shook his head, his words trailing off into nothing.

His answer held more honesty than I'd expected, laced with a hint of what seemed almost like regret. I could only imagine trying to date or have a normal life when so many people were interested in your personal activities. He was probably constantly wondering if people were sincere in their interest to get to know him or just enamored by the glitz of fame. Suddenly I understood why moving to a tiny duplex in West Asheville had such appeal.

Still, he was wrong about me. "So you thought you had me figured out? I was just another fan tracking you down, hiding outside your apartment, waiting for the chance to jump out and get your autograph? Sorry to disappoint you. No Elliott posters on my wall. No love letters hidden under my pillow." I leaned forward now, uncomfortably aware that I might be hissing. My bad mood was making me harsher than necessary. "I don't even really like your music."

I couldn't decide what to make of the look on his face—the tight jaw, confused eyes. But I didn't have it in me to puzzle it out. I shook my head. "I'll see you around." I pushed my way through the front door without waiting for his response.

Inside my apartment, I dropped onto the sofa with a huff, my coat still on, my purse and violin still hanging from my shoulder.

"Hey." Lilly closed her book and looked over at me. "Tough night?"

I frowned. "I went home and tried to practice with Ava, and it was awful. And then I ran into Elliott outside."

"Yeah? Was it better this time around? You didn't ask for his autograph, did you?"

"That would be funnier if it wasn't exactly what he thought I was going to do. He didn't know I lived here. All the times he's seen me getting in my car, or 'lurking' around the apartment, as he liked to call it, he thought I was stalking him."

Lilly laughed, her eyes wide. "Oh my gosh, that's awful. Did you explain? He must have thought you were completely psycho."

"Yes, I explained, but it was just . . . he was so arrogant about the whole thing."

"Emma, he thought you were stalking him. You gotta admit it's kind of hilarious. He has to feel stupid now that he knows you live here."

"I'm sure he does, but honestly, it's just more drama than what I want to deal with. Making new friends shouldn't be so hard."

"Even gorgeous, famous, talented friends?"

I frowned. "Especially those." I stood and shrugged off my purse, then took my violin to its home by the piano. "How did he not hear me practicing? Did he think you were the one playing the violin?"

"Why not?" Lilly shrugged. "He hardly knows me. If he did hear you playing, he'd have no reason to think it wasn't me. And you've hardly practiced at home this week, at least not while I've been around. It's possible he just hasn't heard you yet." She stood from the couch. "Oh, a nice lady stopped by while you were at your parents' house. A somebody Hansen? She wanted to ask you about playing in church next week."

"She stopped by? Like she was actually here in person?" I asked.

"How else does anyone stop by but in person? She was here a few hours ago, said she thought asking you face-to-face would make it harder for you to say no."

"Did she mention what she wanted me to play?"

"Nope. Just said for you to call. I wonder if it'll also have a piano part. Think she'll hit up the new pianist in town?"

I stifled a groan. "She better not, but knowing the way my ward thinks, it wouldn't surprise me if she's considered it."

"You better talk her out of it," Lilly said. "You know if you don't, Elliott's going to think it was your idea."

Chapter 8

SISTER HANSEN ONLY NEEDED A little coaxing when I asked her to accompany me herself instead of asking Elliott, which seemed only fair. The musical number was her idea anyway.

"Elliott is laying low for a while," I told her. "I don't think he's looking to play in public—even church."

She finally relented, which meant I finally agreed to play, which meant I had one more thing to practice in my week that was already full of practicing. I had two quartet gigs to prep for—another wedding, with a very specific set list (fortunately not composed by the sister of the bride), plus an upscale work party that was paying triple our regular fee for booking last minute. I also had new symphony music to look over and needed to polish my audition pieces for the associate concertmaster position in Atlanta.

Still, I was glad for the busy week. It served as a great distraction, making it harder for me to spend any time wondering what Elliott was up to. With Ava and her issues, Grayson and his stupid wedding, and all my practicing, I had more than enough to keep my mind busy.

After chamber rehearsal Thursday night, Grayson followed me to my car and asked again if I was planning to attend the wedding. It was annoying. He'd done his duty by inviting me. I couldn't figure out why he cared so much if I actually decided to attend.

"I'm still not sure if I can make it," I answered. "Is this a dinner menu thing? Like you need my RSVP so you can buy enough steak?"

"Not really. That will matter eventually, but you can just send in the response card. This is more of a favor-to-my-future-mother-in-law type thing."

"How do you mean?"

"She wants to meet you."

Um, what? "Why would she want to meet her son-in-law's ex-girlfriend?"

"She doesn't want to meet you because of me. She wants to meet you because you're Emma Hill." He motioned to my violin. "She knows who you are."

"Really?"

"She's a pretty huge patron of the arts. She makes big donations to the symphony every year and said she'd really like to meet you. She's curious about you."

"Curious why?"

He shrugged and shifted his weight. "Who did you play with in New York? Apparently she heard you play a few times before you came here. You were already on her radar when you moved."

"The better question is who *didn't* I play with in New York?"

Grayson's eyebrows raised in question.

"While I was getting my masters," I explained, "I played everywhere—in every symphony that would take me."

"That's right. I forgot you also went to Juilliard. That explains a lot though. Jane's family is in New York all the time. When Agnes found out you were an old friend . . . what else can I say? It's the price you pay for being a celebrity."

"Ha! I'd like to know where my celebrity paycheck is, then."

"Hmmm." He gave me a pitying look. "Pretty sure you left it back in Cleveland."

My eyes narrowed. "Don't start that again. You can't make me feel bad about leaving."

He held his hands up. "I'm not trying to make you feel bad. You're the one complaining about making less money."

"I was just being funny. Even my full-time salary in Cleveland would be a joke next to an actual celebrity paycheck. Wait—is that why your mother-in-law is so curious? Because she wonders why I'm here? Seriously, if that's how she feels, I won't come. I don't need to be patronized by people who don't support my choices."

Grayson's eyes went wide. "Whoa, whoa, whoa. Take it easy. Nobody's trying to patronize you. I was just teasing. I didn't realize you were so sensitive about it."

I huffed. "I'm not generally. I just . . . something about you makes me defensive."

I knew exactly what it was about Grayson that made me defensive. When I was building dreams and making plans and wishing on stars for my future, Grayson had been my fuel to keep going. He'd believed in me, pushed me, challenged me to be better than I'd thought possible. It wasn't so much that I cared whether he thought I'd made good choices. We'd been apart long enough I was no longer under that particular spell. I just didn't like that he made me doubt my choices myself.

"Don't be defensive. We're cool. I'm glad you're back in town, and I'll be even more glad if you come to the wedding, give my mother-in-law an air kiss, and let her feel important for having met you."

I heaved a sigh. "Okay. I'll come. But no more snarky remarks about Cleveland. Or New York. I'm in Asheville on purpose, and I'm happy about it."

"Deal. So I'll put you down for two, yeah? You'll bring someone with you?"

There was something keenly humiliating about having my old boyfriend question my current relationship status, seeing as how it was very un-boyfriend-ish. Maybe Lilly could count as my date. "Um, sure. I'll bring someone."

"A date?"

Grrgh. Did he really need to push the issue? "A date or a friend, or I don't know. Maybe I'll bring my grandma. Why does it matter? I'll be there, and that's what you want, right?"

"Well, yeah. But I've been pretty honest with Jane about our history, and it makes her a little nervous that you're suddenly back in my life."

"I'm not back in your life. I'm in your chamber group. There's a big difference."

"I know. And it's not a big deal. But if you happened to bring a date . . ." He shrugged and gave me a hopeful smile. "It might be a little easier on Jane."

"So let me get this straight. I'm coming to your wedding to make your mother-in-law happy, but I'm bringing a date so your wife isn't unhappy? Do you realize how ridiculous that sounds?"

"Just think about it, all right? I'm sure there's someone you could bring along. An old friend, a cousin maybe?"

A cousin? Was it that hard to imagine I might actually secure a real date? I tossed my hair over my shoulder and swung open the back door of my car to drop in my violin. I turned back to face him, giving the door a good slam. "Or maybe I'll just bring my boyfriend."

"Oh." He didn't even try to hide his surprise, the jerk. "Well, yeah. That'd be even better."

It was fine. Totally, completely fine. I mean, the wedding was, what . . . six weeks away? Seven? I could get a boyfriend in seven weeks. And if I couldn't, then worst-case scenario, Lilly would probably let me borrow Trav. I wondered if I'd be able to convince him to shave.

* * *

On my drive home, my stomach started to hurt. It was possible I was already internalizing the stress of attending Grayson's wedding with my imaginary boyfriend.

Or maybe I was just hungry.

Thursdays were my longest days: back-to-back lessons from one to five, then chamber rehearsal starting at six. I normally grabbed something quick in between, but my last lesson had run long, and there hadn't been time. I cataloged the contents of my fridge as I pulled onto Maple Crescent, hoping Lilly had cooked something she'd be willing to share. My phone rang just as I pulled into the drive. I pulled it out of my purse and smiled when I saw my grandma's picture lighting up the screen.

"Hi, Grandma."

"Four questions. Do you have time?"

I smiled. Chitchat had never been Gram's thing. "I've got time but only a little. I just got home, and I'm starving."

"Then I'll make it quick. Your mother tells me that old boyfriend of yours is in your quartet. Do I need to worry about that?"

Sheesh. Way to start with the serious stuff. "Did Mom also tell you he's getting married?"

"Well, yes. But you're a talented and beautiful woman, Bug. Men have changed their minds before."

There was something hilarious about my grandmother referring to me as a beautiful woman and also calling me Bug—the nickname she'd been using for me since I was four—in the same sentence. "You don't need to worry," I told her. "It's not like that at all. Number two?"

"The piano player. Do you like him?"

I hesitated. "No. Yes. I don't know."

"Hmmm. I need more. Keep talking."

"Let's say we haven't exactly gotten off to a great start friendship-wise."

"Has he heard you play?" Grandma asked.

"No. Or maybe. I don't know. It's possible he's heard me practicing from next door."

"Not good enough. I don't know why you even try the talking thing. You need to just knock on his door and play something."

"Right. Because that wouldn't be awkward at all."

"So be a little more subtle. What about a serenade outside his window? You know you're at your best when you're holding that instrument. Don't hide your strengths."

"Fine, fine. I'm playing in church this weekend. Does that count?"

"Yes! Splendid."

"Okay. Question three."

"How's your momma?"

"She looks really good. She's up on her feet this week, almost like normal."

"Is she in pain?"

"It's hard to say. She's been masking it for so many years I'm no good at spotting when she's pretending."

Grandma was quiet long enough I wondered if the call had been lost. "Grandma? You still there?"

"I'm here, Bug. Just thinking. How often do you see her?"

"Every Tuesday and Friday until two. We normally do appointments, shopping, and errands and stuff on Tuesdays. Then just hang around while I do housework on Fridays. I'm going over on Sundays now too. For the food."

"And she's letting you help her?"

"I can tell she hates it, but it makes Dad happy. And we have fun together too. It's not bad at all."

"You're a good girl, Emma."

"It's not a big deal."

"No, I think it is. And that leads to my fourth question," Grandma said.

"Yeah? What is it?"

"How are *you*? And don't just give me some random rote answer. You're not allowed to say the word *fine*."

I smiled. "I'm good. I'm happy, I think. I like living with Lilly, and it feels good being closer to home."

"Do you miss Cleveland?"

Now that wasn't a fair question. For starters, she was in Cleveland, and I missed her like crazy. But I knew that wasn't what she wanted to know. "That's question number five. You don't get that many."

"Come on. Throw a bone to an old lady."

I leaned back against my seat, still sitting in my car outside the house. "Of course I miss it, but I'm okay, you know? I feel like this is where I'm supposed to be right now. I just try not to think about where I'm not."

"Tell me three things you love about Asheville."

"You are so going over your question limit. I get extra questions for you next time we talk."

She laughed. "Fine, but only if you give me three things you like."

"I like living with Lilly. I like playing in a smaller symphony and still having time to teach. And I like being closer to Mom. And Dad and Ava too. Maybe not always Ava. But mostly."

"Okay," Grandma said with a satisfied air.

"Okay?"

"Okay. You pass. Go find some food."

"I love you, Gram."

"Love you too, Bug. Wear your red dress when you play on Sunday. Resist the urge to wear black!"

I shook my head and laughed as I hung up the phone. I really did miss a lot of things about Cleveland but nothing more than Gram. My stomach growled, and I climbed out of the car, finally making my way up the front walk and onto the porch.

"Emma."

I almost jumped out of my skin. Elliott was sitting on the porch in the extra-wide rocker in the corner. *In the dark.*

"Geez. You scared me to death. I didn't see you there."

"Sorry. I wasn't trying to scare you."

I pressed my hand against my chest and felt my heart pounding under my palm. I took a deep, calming breath and looked in Elliott's direction. Branches from a large oak tree hung over the left side of the porch where he sat, blocking the light from the street lamps and casting such a heavy shadow I couldn't make out his face at all. He was nothing but a blurry outline against the white of the chair cushion behind him. "Do you want the light on?" I glanced up. "There's a switch just inside the entryway."

"No. Actually I was waiting for you."

Waiting for me? I was kinda surprised he even remembered my name. "In the dark?"

He held up his hand, his phone flashing blue before the screen went black. "I've been reading."

"Oh."

"Do you want to sit?"

Yep. At my kitchen table. With a plate of food in front of me. "Um, sure." I shifted my bags, lowering them and my violin to the porch before moving to the chair opposite his.

"Lilly told me you'd be home soon. Sorry if this is weird. I just didn't want to miss you."

What was weird was hearing him talk to me all normal-like, as though the last conversation we'd had hadn't included him calling me a crazy, psycho stalker. "It's fine," I managed to say. "What's up?"

"Only that I owe you an apology. I made some pretty ridiculous assumptions about you. It wasn't fair, and I'm sorry."

I was impressed. My mother once told me the best way to judge a man's character was to wait for a situation where he owed someone an apology. Elliott was passing Mom's character test like someone had slipped him a cheat sheet. His words were straightforward and clear, no hemming or hawing over what to say next, no elaborate explanation to justify why he'd mistaken me for a nutso fan. Just a straight up "I was wrong, and I'm sorry."

"I can understand how you might have gotten the wrong impression," I admitted.

"Maybe, but that was no reason to be rude."

Elliott seemed genuine and humble and gracious. I shouldn't have been annoyed, but I totally was. I'd convinced myself he was arrogant and condescending, which went a long way to soften the embarrassment of his door-slamming-in-my-face rejection. Now he was messing that up, being all nice and stuff. It just left me feeling embarrassed all over again.

I stood up. "It's really okay," I finally said. "I'm already over it."

"I don't always love what this business does to me." He stood as well, like he wasn't quite ready to let me go. "Sometimes it's hard to stay grounded and remember that everything isn't always about me."

I cocked an eyebrow. Was it really hard to remember that?

"Wait. That didn't sound right," Elliott said. "I'm *not* that guy. I don't want to be that guy. That's what I'm trying to say."

"It's cool," I said calmly. "I get it."

With my eyes finally adjusting to the darkness on the porch, I managed to make out a few details of Elliott's appearance. It was hard not to stare once I really took him in. His dark hair was completely unstyled—long-ish and shaggy, hanging loose on his forehead. He also wore glasses, which I hadn't expected. It was a different look, a little less intentional and a lot less like the polished star image I was used to seeing.

He leaned forward. "So . . . better than Uncle Nesbit, huh?"

I laughed. "I've never actually heard Uncle Nesbit play, but I hope he's good. He's been the benchmark for every single one of my church performances."

"Do you play full-time?"

"Yeah. And teach."

"That's cool."

I shrugged. "Cool enough to pay the bills."

His eyes narrowed at first, then he chuckled. "That was . . . Man, I really seemed like a jerk, didn't I?"

"Yeah. But maybe not more than I seemed like a groupie."

"I don't know." His voice was light and teasing. "I think you'd actually have to like my music to be a groupie."

I cringed. "Right. Sorry about that."

"You shouldn't apologize. You're entitled to like what you like."

I realized with a perfunctory satisfaction that aside from the darkness of the porch, which made things slightly weird, I was having a bona fide conversation with Elliott and wasn't acting like an idiot. I wasn't throwing up. Or even sweating. Maybe it was the anticipation that always made me so sick—all the build-up of wondering how things were going to go. I just needed all our conversations to be a surprise. Or maybe I just needed it to be dark. I still wasn't sure I was ready to forgive him for his earlier arrogance, but at least I wasn't acting like a moron.

"I really like your original stuff, if that's any concession."

"You don't like the mash-ups?"

"I mean, for what they are, you do them really well. It's just . . ." I had no idea how to share my opinion without sounding like I was dogging on his career.

"It's just that you're a purist when it comes to the classics?"

Good word. And spot on. His acknowledgment gave me the freedom to speak a little more plainly. "You can't mess with Vivaldi," I said. "It feels like cheating."

"Cheating? I don't think anyone's ever called me a cheater before."

"Sorry. That sounds harsher than what I mean. I promise it isn't personal."

"Then I promise not to take it personally if you explain."

Explain? Without hurting his feelings? What sort of mess had I gotten myself into? I took a deep breath and sat back down on the seat behind me. "I guess I just feel like every classical piece has this depth, a purpose behind why it was written and what it's supposed to accomplish. There's emotion behind those notes—every single one of them—and the challenge as a musician is to play them in a way that explores that depth. Vivaldi, for example. When you listen to his *Four Seasons*, you capture the threads that tie each movement together. You can literally feel the surge of a summer storm or the fall of leaves in autumn. You feel and hear and relate to the music because of what it represents.

"Or take *Rhapsody in Blue*. Gershwin composed the piece in five weeks in answer to a newspaper article that asked 'What is American music?' He called it a—"

"Musical kaleidoscope of America," Elliott interrupted. He leaned against the porch railing and crossed his arms. "I know."

"Right! And the music is so much more moving when you understand the context, when you think of the sights and sounds and feelings that inspired Gershwin to write it in the first place. To truly do the music justice, a musician has to capture all of it, all that emotion the composer poured into the piece. When you only borrow a few lines here and there? I think a measure of musical integrity is lost." Elliott was silent for so long I started to worry I'd said too much. "Sorry," I said again. "That was probably more of an answer than you bargained for."

"No. I admire your passion. And I get it. I actually think you're right."

There was no way he was agreeing with me right out. "But?"

"But I also think there's something to be said for making classical music a little more accessible. If there's a way to create music that introduces Vivaldi to people who wouldn't hear him otherwise, I don't think that's a bad thing."

"Lilly made the same argument when we had this conversation. But only if it leads to enjoying Vivaldi as he's meant to be enjoyed. It's a valid point, but . . ."

"You'd still rather be listening to straight-up Vivaldi?"

I smiled. "Yeah. I mean, why choose a cheeseburger when I can have steak?"

He frowned.

"Oh gosh. That didn't come out right. I must sound like such a snob."

He raised his eyebrows, one side of his mouth lifting into a half smile. "Knowing what you like doesn't make you a snob."

"No, but implying what I like is best and everyone else is wrong? That's lame." Especially since I'd just been all judgy over his arrogance. What was I trying to prove?

He looked me right in the eye. "That's true. Some people like cheeseburgers best."

I grimaced. I couldn't decide which was worse: Elliott thinking I was stalking him or me comparing his music to a slab of ground meat.

With his eyes locked so unwaveringly on mine, my nerves got all jittery, and I stood up. "I, um, I think maybe I need to stop talking before I say something else ridiculous." I reached down and picked up my bags and my violin. Elliott moved to the front door and held it open for me.

"So I guess I'll see you around," he said.

"Yeah, I'm sure you will."
And suddenly everything with Elliott felt different.

Chapter 9

I PULLED OUT THE PIANO bench in my living room and positioned it in front of my music stand. Four glorious hours with nowhere to be. I'd been tempted to be lazy after I finished my breakfast, to go back to bed and lounge around watching bad television. But I couldn't ignore the pull of a quiet, empty house. I had too much to practice to waste such perfect circumstances.

I thought of Elliott as I pulled out my music, wondering if he was awake, if he was on the other side of the wall close enough that he might hear me play. I'd heard his piano more than once since he'd moved in, and it made me nervous to think that now he might hear me. It was dumb. I didn't get nervous when I played. Except this was Elliott. Of course I was nervous.

I had to wonder if he'd been offended by my less-than-graceful pontifications the night before. He'd probably developed a pretty thick skin after eight years in show business. Even in my tiny niche of the orchestra world, I'd dealt with enough rejection and criticism to learn that one person not liking something couldn't ever be a deal breaker. But still. A *cheeseburger?* It wasn't even an appealing analogy.

I tuned my violin, then reached for Mozart. I played through the first movement, pausing to repeat a few lines, then worked out the bowing of a particularly tricky section. I grabbed my pencil and made a few notes on my music, then raised my violin to play through it again. My fingers were in position, my bow on the string when I froze, straining to hear the music that wasn't coming from my instrument but from the one next door. I relaxed my position and moved closer to the wall. It couldn't be, but . . . it totally was. Elliott was playing Gershwin's *Rhapsody in Blue.*

I leaned against the wall and listened as he powered his way through the piece. That he'd picked that song to play after our conversation the night before was no coincidence. He was sending me a message, and I was hearing it loud and clear.

I'd heard a lot of people play Gershwin, but Elliott's version was perfect, with the same rhythm and energy and insanely fast finger work I'd heard on the original recordings of the piece—*Rhapsody* played by Gershwin himself. I'd known Elliott was talented, but I was ashamed to admit I'd also kinda thought he was a little bit of a gimmick. Famous only because a panel of people on television had decided he should be. But there was nothing gimmicky about the way he was playing *Rhapsody*. The man had skill—more than skill.

I leaned into the wall and wished I could see him play, watch as his long fingers raced up and down the keyboard, reaching high, then low, over and under, then over again. Instead, I only listened, ignoring the itch my fingers felt to join in and play. I'd played the piece enough times I probably could have picked out the melody, but I didn't want to miss a single note of his performance.

When it came to an end, there was a moment of perfect stillness, the echo of his final notes still humming in the air. Those notes were a challenge, a declaration that I'd dang well better not underestimate Elliott Hart.

Okay, so, yeah, I was impressed. But it was just one song, and one song was not enough to make a classical repertoire. I had to wonder what else he could do. I picked up my violin and played the opening movement of Vivaldi's *Four Seasons*: "Spring." He responded almost immediately with a few measures from "Summer." Seconds after he finished, he launched into the opening lines of Joplin's *The Entertainer*. He played the first few measures, then paused and played them again, emphasizing the final two notes.

It was an invitation. I played the next line of the song. That must have been what he was waiting for because he moved on, playing the next line, then waiting for me to pick up the next. A few lines of *The Entertainer*, and he changed it up. When he played the opening lines of Copland's *Appalachian Spring*, it was game on.

Back and forth we went: Beethoven's Fifth, Bach's Brandenburg Concerto no. 3, Debussy, Chopin, Tchaikovsky. He would play an opening line for me to match, then I'd pick one and do the same. I dug through my brain, trying to find those obscure pieces he might not know, knowing the game would be over as soon as one of us was stumped. I started a Shostakovich symphony, and he picked up his part like he'd been ready and waiting for his cue. Then he played the first movement of Rachmaninoff's Third Piano Concerto in all its impressive power, and I wondered if I was out of my depth.

Finally, when my music arsenal started to dwindle, I picked one of Mozart's violin concertos. It was a great piece but lesser known and not something I would expect even a classical pianist accustomed to being accompanied by orchestras to recognize. He was totally stumped, playing back only the lower octaves of the piano, like a rock falling to the ground and landing with a thud. It was the sound of Elliott's defeat.

I was amazed by the extent of his musical knowledge. He knew his classics as well as I did, maybe better. And the way he played them? I mean, listening through a shared apartment wall wasn't quite like watching him on YouTube, but it was still extraordinary. And it was different from everything I'd heard him play before. He wasn't supposed to be a classical pianist. He was contemporary, edgy.

Except he wasn't. He'd known Prokofiev and Rachmaninoff and Tchaikovsky, and he'd known them from memory. Even when he hadn't known the full-blown piano parts, he'd at least known the melodies of every single classical piece I'd played.

On the other side of the wall, Elliott played the last line of the "Hokey Pokey" with ridiculous flourish. *That's what it's all about!*

I started to laugh. That *was* what it was all about for me. Moments like that—when music became a living, breathing, incredible thing—trumped just about everything else.

I put my violin away and reached for my iPhone, pulling up the web browser. I keyed in Elliott's name and opened the Wikipedia page that detailed his musical training. I'd watched a lot of his videos on YouTube and read all the news articles *Deseret News* and *LDS Living* had done about his rise to fame and how he'd transitioned into missionary service, but I'd never thought to look up the finer points of his musical education.

He had started young, when his parents realized he had a natural affinity for the piano. He blazed his way through teachers until he was studying at university level by age eleven, spent two years with private tutors in Europe, then attended a performing arts high school for all but the summer months, which he spent at Juilliard's Summer Institute Program. That definitely counted as classical training, even if he didn't continue on to college. I couldn't help but wonder how, with all his ability, he wound up with a career playing mash-ups and covers of top-forty radio.

I tossed my phone onto the couch with a resigned sigh, realizing with growing certainty and frustration that not thinking about Elliott wasn't even an option.

Chapter 10

I WAS KEENLY AWARE OF Elliott's presence in the congregation on Sunday when I stood up—wearing red, of course—to play with Sister Hansen. I didn't have anything to prove, especially not to him, but I'd looked stupid in front of him enough, and I was ready to look good.

We played a beautiful rendition of "Come Thou Fount of Every Blessing." I wasn't good at bearing my testimony, but playing that song felt more personal and more revealing than anything I could ever say over the pulpit. Every single note felt like a little piece of my heart. By the time we finished, Sister Hansen and I were both in tears.

After the meeting, I left the stand, violin slung over my shoulder, and walked toward the back of the chapel. I smiled my thanks as a few members of the ward stopped me to compliment my performance. I noticed Elliott watching me from the doorway as I moved through the room. He wore a light-gray suit and a deep-blue tie that matched his eyes so perfectly I had to wonder if he'd had it custom made. I mean, celebrities did that kind of thing, right? The closer I got, the more his eyes pulled me in. I tried not to stare, but it was hard. He just looked so *good*.

When I finally reached the door, Elliott joined me as I walked into the foyer. "That was really beautiful," he said. "You're very good."

"Thanks." Things were definitely different between us. Mostly because he wasn't avoiding me and I wasn't hiding behind the ficus tree in the corner. But there was also a new kind of spark in his eyes, something that made my heart get all flip-floppy. We walked together to the end of the hallway. "I've got to get to Primary," I said.

As if on cue, the Primary president rounded the corner. "Emma, I'm glad I found you. Can you also take the next class up today? We're missing a teacher."

Three-year-olds and four-year-olds? That sounded fun.

"It'll be kind of a big group, eleven kids total." She looked at Elliott with raised eyebrows. "I don't know, maybe you could ask someone to help out?"

I glanced at Elliott. "That's okay. I think I can handle it."

"How about you, Brother Hart? Are you up for helping Emma today?"

Seriously? She wasn't even being subtle.

"Sure. I'd be happy to."

I didn't want to be excited about spending an hour with Elliott and eleven preschoolers. I didn't want to worry about whether my breath was bad or my hair looked all right. I didn't want to care. But I totally did, which was just annoying.

Elliott excused himself, claiming he'd meet me in the classroom. Except he didn't even know where my classroom was. I didn't want to think he was making an easy escape. It was sunbeams, after all. Could I really blame him? I tried to move away, but the Primary president grabbed my arm. "So did you hear about the e-mail?"

"The e-mail?" I had no idea what she was talking about.

"There's been so much chatter about Elliott being here that the stake presidency sent an e-mail to each unit, reminding everyone that he's here as a member of the Church, not as a famous musician, and we are all to respect his privacy. I heard about it in ward council."

"Huh. I guess that makes sense."

"It also says he's not looking to do performances of any sort, so we are to refrain from asking."

I knew Elliott wanted to lie low and had figured what I'd told Sister Hansen about his disinclination to play was at least close to the truth. But I was still surprised to hear it officially. No performances at all? His music was his livelihood. How long was he planning on keeping that up?

Turns out Elliott really was happy to help with my class. He showed up right before we started. Fifteen minutes later, I decided Sunbeams was maybe my new favorite place to be. Elliott was right at home interacting with the kids. It was fun to watch such a different side of him. When the kids settled around the table to draw pictures of their fish, Elliott and I managed to steal a few minutes of normal conversation.

"Do you come from a big family?" I asked.

He nodded. "I'm the youngest of five."

"So that means lots of nieces and nephews."

I saw it coming, the lift starting around his eyes, but it still took all my willpower not to fall out of my chair when he smiled. The man was so good-looking it literally made my breath catch. As in, I had to remind myself to start breathing again.

"There's sixteen of them. I guess the oldest is, let's see . . . almost fourteen? I can hardly remember a time before I was Uncle Elliott. What about you?"

"Just one sister, Ava. She's sixteen." I reached down and pulled one of the Sunbeams off the floor and set her back on her seat. "You have to keep your bum in your chair, Chloe, and here, let's put your shoes back on. Can you leave them on for me?"

"I wanna take dem off," she grumbled.

"I know, sweetie, but if you take yours off, then everyone will want to take their shoes off, and then we'll have twenty-two shoes all over the room, and yours might get lost."

"Also the room might get really stinky," Elliott said. "I hear Jasper over there has really smelly feet."

"I do not," Jasper said with a giggle.

I was completely charmed by Uncle Elliott's interactions with the kids. It was also eye-opening to see him out of the context of his stardom. In my mind, and in our few brief encounters up to that point, he'd always been the critically acclaimed Elliott Hart, famous and he knew it, which was pretty dang intimidating. But in the Sunbeam classroom, he was just a guy—a really hot guy—hanging out with some preschoolers, talking about how God wants us to be nice to animals.

It could have been a perfect beginning to our second-chance friendship.

Then one of the little miscreants puked on Elliott's shoes.

Elliott had every reason to lose his cool, what with vomit dripping into his socks, but he didn't. He was still standing in the middle of the vomit puddle when he crouched down and looked Jasper right in the eye. Jasper had tears streaming down his cheeks, his face a sickly green. "Hey, you okay?" Elliott asked.

Jasper shook his head. "I want my mommy."

"Let's go find her, okay?" He picked Jasper up—Jasper, who had *vomit* on his shirt—and held him against his chest. Elliott looked down at his shoes, then looked to me for help. "I'm not sure I thought this through."

"Here, I guess . . . Can you step out of your shoes?"

He slid them off one at a time, stepping wide to avoid getting any messier than he already was.

"There's a little on your pants, but it doesn't look like it'll drip."

"This might be the most disgusting conversation I've ever had," he said.

I couldn't help but laugh. I was amazed that he was being such a good sport.

"So I'm going to go clean him up a little bit. Do you want to find his mom?"

I looked at the ten other kids cowering in the corner behind me, their hands pressed over their noses.

"Jasper is really stinky," Chloe said.

"No, you stay here," Elliott said. "I'll walk past the Primary room and let them know what happened." Jasper had laid his head on Elliott's shoulder, and Elliott rubbed his back. "Just sit tight," he told me. "I'll get you some help." He stepped into the hallway in his socks and glanced one more time into the classroom before giving me a sympathetic grin. "Don't breathe too deep."

Says the guy who's covered in kid vomit. I mean, it wasn't even his kid and he was still patient and gentle and helpful.

I wasn't the only one charmed by his gallantry. Later, as he walked to the parking lot, suit pants rolled up, socks and shoes in hand, the Primary president leaned over to where I still stood in the hallway and said, "Emma, if you don't marry that man, I'm gonna."

"You're already married," I replied. "Nice guy? Doctor? Father of your three children?"

"Oh. Right. Well, I guess that means you should. Really, really, Emma. You really should."

I wasn't ready to propose, but I did follow Elliott out to his car. "Elliott," I called.

He dropped his shoes into the backseat and turned to wait for me.

"I just wanted to say I'm sorry about your shoes. And your pants." I looked at his shirt. "And your shirt. Can I get them cleaned for you?"

"Don't worry about it. The suit was probably due to be cleaned anyway." He loosened his tie and unbuttoned the top button of his shirt.

It made me blush, which was totally stupid. "I, um . . ." I swallowed. "Thanks again for helping. I think the kids really liked you."

"It was no problem. I was happy to do it." He reached for the door handle of his car, then paused, turning to face me one more time. "I really did enjoy your playing today. I know I already told you that, but I appreciate how connected you were to the music." He shoved his hands into his pockets. "I guess I didn't realize how much I missed that connection."

I was speechless. His compliment-turned-confessional was not what I'd expected to hear. It was a pretty personal revelation to make, and it surprised me. He was a professional performer. To think he felt like something was missing from his music? I never would have guessed. "Thank you," I finally stammered. "That means a lot."

He turned and leaned against the side of his car, which was encouraging because it seemed like he wasn't anxious to leave my company but worrisome because he also looked a little sad. I took a few steps closer and leaned against the car too, not too close but close enough to let him know I was listening if he had something else he wanted to say.

He remained silent, his eyes locked on the pavement beneath his feet. I thought of my first week at the Cleveland Institute of Music when my hopes and dreams had been huge and my ego sized to match. I'd been completely overwhelmed by all the talent that filled the school. I'd never had to work very hard to be the best in my high school and youth symphonies, but in Cleveland . . . I'd been playing in a different league. At the end of my first week of symphony rehearsals, my conductor, who would later turn out to be one of my biggest advocates, had taken my bow out of my hand and, with great flourish, said, "No more! You're playing like a robot. Like all we need to hear from you is the notes. Where is your heart, Emma? Where is your music?"

So I guess I understood just how possible it was to play, to even play with technical perfection, but to still be missing the most vital part of any performance: the heart. My career wasn't even a shadow of the success Elliott had found, but those early weeks in college, I'd been so caught up in the business of being a professional musician the magic of playing was lost. It wasn't hard to imagine a brutal career in show business sucking the life right out of a performer.

"I've felt it before too—that disconnect from my music," I said. "When I'm working too hard and focusing too much, that's when it happens for me. And sometimes when I'm scared of what I have ahead of me and I'm not sure I can do what's expected."

Elliott shifted, and I saw his jaw clench.

"It's safer to be disconnected, you know?" I continued. "Because when I'm all in, it almost feels like I'm playing naked. Like the music is me—all of me—and I'm just throwing it out there for everyone to see. It feels risky because what are people going to make of it? What are they going to make of me when I've just emptied my entire soul into each note?"

"That's what makes you so good." He spoke without looking up. "That you're willing to be that transparent."

"Thank you." It was more than a little unnerving to be having such an intensely personal conversation with someone I'd only just begun to know. But, then, we weren't really speaking as Emma and Elliott. It felt more like we were speaking musician to musician, the commonality of our experiences pulling us closer than our regular acquaintance allowed.

"I used to feel that way," Elliott said. "Every performance, every composition was my whole soul."

"But you don't feel that way now?"

He was quiet a moment longer before he pushed himself off the car. "I'm sorry," he said. "I didn't mean for this to turn into . . ." He shook his head and opened the driver's side door of his sedan.

"No, it's okay. I think I get it."

"Yeah." His eyes held mine for a beat longer than necessary. "I think you probably do."

He was halfway into his car, but I wasn't ready for him to leave yet. This was the best conversation I'd had in years. "You play a mean Gershwin."

He grinned. "He's one of my favorites."

"I should have known when you quoted him the other night."

"Was that symphony music you were playing? Before I crashed your practice? It was Mozart, right?"

I wanted to ask him how he knew I was in the symphony, if he'd Googled me after our music battle as quickly as I'd Googled him. Instead, I nodded. "Yeah. For next week's concert. It was also Mozart that finally stumped you."

"*Whaaat?* You stumped me with Mozart? I would have sworn there isn't a note of Mozart I don't recognize."

"It was one of his violin concertos."

"Well, that's totally fair since he wrote, what, forty? Fifty of them?"

I smiled. "I was getting desperate. You know your classics."

"I like cheeseburgers," he said with a sheepish grin. "But I can grill a pretty decent steak if I want to."

Ha. To say the least. The man was a $200 filet at a five-star restaurant. *Decent* was a massive understatement.

It was no small thing to realize Elliott cared about my opinion enough to show me he could play the kind of music I valued. He was trying to impress me, for whatever that was worth.

In my not fan-girly, totally reasonable and leveled-headed opinion, that was a pretty big deal.

Chapter 11

MOM LOOKED UP AND SMILED as I entered the kitchen. "You look like you're in a good mood," she said. "What's up?"

Of course I was in a good mood. Elliott had proven over the past couple of days he was way more than an arrogant, pretty face. From his apology to helping in Sunbeams and then our conversation after church, I had more than enough to be smiling about. I didn't, however, feel like it was quite enough to initiate a Mom confessional. At least, not yet.

"Nothing much," I told her. "It's just a nice day. Where's Dad?"

"He's in the living room. Can you help me get this cake out of the oven?"

I nudged Mom out of the way and lifted Dad's birthday cake onto the stovetop. "Go sit. I can finish this."

She nodded and patted my hand. "Maybe just for a bit."

I turned off the oven and finished making the frosting Mom had started, the ingredients gathered on the counter, then wiped down the counter and swept the floor. When I finally joined everybody in the living room, I noticed Mom's wheelchair sitting next to the couch. I rolled it out of the way so I could sit next to her. I hadn't seen it out in weeks. "Mom, are you using your chair again?"

She lifted her shoulder in a halfhearted shrug. "Just a little. Something's off with my meds, I think. The pain has been flaring up in the afternoons."

"Since when? Since Friday? Why haven't you told me? I was here all morning, and you didn't say anything."

She leaned back into the sofa and closed her eyes. "That's because it happens in the afternoons. I'm fine when you're here."

"But if I'd known, I could have been doing things to make your afternoons easier."

"Like what?"

"I don't know. Making dinner. Making sure you're comfortable."

"Emma. Relax. I see the doctor on Tuesday morning. We'll figure it out."

"Good. What time on Tuesday?"

She gave me a dismissive wave. "It's too early for you to bother coming. I'm fine in the mornings. I can handle getting to this one on my own."

She wasn't fine. I could tell just by looking at her she wasn't fine.

I looked up at Dad. "Back me up here. Tell her she has to let me take her on Tuesday."

She opened her eyes and shot me a look. "Now you're not playing fair."

"I'll make you a deal. You let me come with you, and I'll let you buy me lunch after."

"How is that a deal?" Dad asked. "She *gets* to buy you lunch?"

"No, no, it is a deal," Mom said. "She never lets me buy her anything, even food. Something about the violation of her adulthood and independence."

That definitely had something to do with it, but also, I could buy Mom lunch for the rest of forever and it wouldn't come close to what my parents had spent on my education. I had to draw the line somewhere.

"Be here by nine," Mom said, turning back to me. "Lunch will be on me, but that means I get to pick the place."

I nodded. "Okay."

"So what are you going to do about Grayson's wedding?"

I repositioned the pillow behind me. "I told him I'd be there, so I'll go. His wife will just have to get over it if I show up by myself."

"I ran into Grayson's aunt at the grocery store the other day," Mom said.

"Which one? Aunt Pam?"

"Yeah. She asked about you."

"Huh. That was nice of her, I guess."

Mom shrugged. "She told me a little about the fiancée's family. She called them Southern gentry, whatever that means. Something about old family money and country clubs and Sunday bridge parties. They live over in Biltmore Forest, which I guess says enough right there."

"Says enough about what? That sounds like a really judgy thing to say."

"I'm not trying to sound judgmental, but I think they're probably the kind of people who care a great deal about appearances. I'm sure they want everything at this wedding to be proper."

"Which is why you really think I should find a date?"

"Not necessarily. Your happiness is always my biggest priority. But if it'll keep the peace at the wedding, surely there's no harm in taking someone along."

"Fine. I'll borrow Lilly's boyfriend."

"What about Michael Jefferson? He just got home from Peru. He's a nice-looking boy."

"Mom. He's, what, twelve?"

She tried not to laugh. "He may look twelve, but he's completely legal. He's a returned missionary. Doesn't that count for something?"

"Maybe if we wanted him to stand in as Ava's prom date, but I'm twenty-five years old. I'm not asking out someone who was still a seventh grader when I graduated from high school."

"What about Elliott Hart? Have you found out if he's single?"

"He's single, but I don't know him well enough for something like this. He can't just come to the wedding as my date. He has to come and pretend to be my boyfriend."

"Or you could just tell Grayson the truth."

"Yeah. That's not happening."

Mom shrugged. "You still have six weeks. Maybe you'll know him well enough by the time the wedding rolls around."

"Maybe."

"If not, you can always run an ad in the paper like that movie—*The Wedding Date*." She was trying hard to keep a straight face, but she couldn't manage long. She started to laugh, her arms wrapped around her sides like she was trying to hold it in.

I huffed. "I'm glad my life is so entertaining. Between you and Lilly, I've been laughed at this week way more than I deserve."

She reached across the couch and brushed the hair out of my face, tucking it behind my ear. "I'm sure you'll figure it out. You know I have faith in you."

"Thanks. But honestly it's not a big deal. I'll go. Maybe I'll have a date; maybe I won't. But I'm not going to lose sleep over it."

"That sounds more like my girl," Dad said as he passed behind the couch and left the room. I'd almost forgotten he'd been listening to our conversation.

"Why don't you come with me, Dad?" I called after him. "Want to be my date?"

He poked his head back in the room. "I have a feeling you'll find someone else," he said. "And, obviously, I can't pretend to be your boyfriend. But if it means not going alone, I'd be honored to be your back-up."

I looked back at Mom. "See? Problem solved."

* * *

An hour later, I unlocked my front door to hear Elliott's music filling the entryway. I leaned against the wall and listened, my eyes closed as the melody seeped through his apartment door. It was something I'd heard before—one of his original compositions from his first album, or maybe his second. It sounded like a sunrise, like that moment of stillness when the world is not quite awake but almost. It sounded like hope. How that man ever thought he was disconnected from his music was beyond me.

I'd hardly realized the music had stopped when Elliott's door flew open, startling me so badly I dropped my keys on the floor, where they landed with a noisy clatter.

"Oh, hey." He paused. "Are you okay?"

I smiled and wiped the tears off my cheeks, then reached down for my keys. "I'm fine. I was just . . . listening."

"Ohhh, sorry. I can go play something happier if you want me to."

"No, it wasn't sad. It was beautiful." I sniffed one last time. "This is just what music does to me."

"Must get annoying considering your line of work."

"Ha, yeah. That's the truth."

"That one always makes my mom cry too. It's her favorite."

I smiled. "I'll consider myself in good company, then."

"Are you just getting home?" Elliott asked.

"Yeah. I spent the afternoon at my parents' house. Are you heading out?" It was a dumb question. He didn't look like he was heading out. He wasn't even wearing shoes.

"No, I'm just grabbing my shoes from outside. I left them there to air out earlier this afternoon."

"Ah, the vomit shoes." I stepped out of his way while he moved onto the porch and grabbed his shoes.

He held them up for inspection once he was back inside. "Not too bad, right?" He lifted them to his nose. "They don't . . . Okay, no, wait. They do still smell." He wrinkled his nose. "I might have to declare them casualties of war and just get a new pair."

"A new pair of Ferragamos? Seriously?"

He looked confused. "Is that a big deal?"

"Um, I guess not if you're used to buying $700 shoes."

"Are you for real?"

I raised my eyebrows. "You didn't know you were wearing $700 shoes?"

"No! I mean, they just brought them into the dressing room before a performance a few months ago and told me to wear them."

"So you just wear whatever they put in front of you?"

He shrugged. "I care about the important stuff, like whether or not I'm going to have a decent piano for performances. But I learned early on it was a lot easier to let someone else worry about my wardrobe."

"It must be tough now that you're living in the sticks and actually have to dress yourself."

"Don't judge. You're the one who recognized they were Ferra-whatevers."

"Fair point, but only because of my college roommate. Any knowledge I claim is only what rubbed off from her."

Maybe it was something in the way he looked at me—his smile cocked just slightly to the side—that had me asking the question before I had the good sense to just go inside already and let our neighborly conversation end on a good note. "Hey, can I ask you a question?"

Elliott set his shoes on the floor beside his apartment door and pushed his hands into his pockets. "Sure."

"I have this wedding thing."

His eyebrows went up. "A wedding?"

My nerves were scrambling, and I started to feel sick. This was stupid. We'd had, what, two normal conversations? But the look in his eyes. He looked into me, like he *wanted* to know more. "It's my ex-boyfriend's wedding. He and I are in the same chamber group, only temporarily because our cellist, Bruno, is out of town and Grayson is filling in. He plays the cello too, naturally, or else he wouldn't be filling in . . . So he's invited me to his wedding, and I kinda promised him I would be there. But I don't really love the idea of going alone." I realized, as the words tumbled out, that even a simplified, less drama-filled version of the truth was probably still too much information for Elliott. I could have made the invitation so much simpler. *So I'm going to this wedding. It's a free steak. Want to come along?* Did he really need to know about Bruno's travel plans?

"So you're asking me to go with you?" Elliott leaned against his door.

"Yeah. Is that weird? It's totally fine if that's weird."

He smiled. "It's maybe a little weird. I mean, your ex-boyfriend's wedding. Not exactly classic first-date material."

Just the fact that he mentioned me in dating terms had me all kinds of flustered. "No, you're right. But it wouldn't necessarily be a first date. It's not for another six weeks." I cringed. I'd just implied I wanted to date him. That we would spend the next six weeks having multiple dates. "Wait, that's not what I mean. I'm not saying I want to date you. I mean, I'm not saying I *don't* want to date you. I'm just saying . . ." I shook my head, wishing I could erase the blush blazing on my cheeks. "Oh boy. I'm gonna stop before this gets worse."

He smiled just enough for me to know he was about to let me down easy. "Don't worry about it. Honestly I'm flattered you would even consider asking me. And if my circumstances were different . . ." He ran a hand through his hair. "Emma, I think you're really great."

I backed up a few steps and reached for the handle of my apartment door. "It's okay. You don't need to explain."

"But I want to explain. Things with my career are sort of complicated right now. I've got this album I'm supposed to be working on, and it really deserves my full attention. My agent was angry enough when I moved across the country. He made me promise I'd stay out of the social scene and just work. So that's what I'm trying to do."

I tried not to sound disappointed. "That's an excuse I can totally understand." I did understand. The ability to ignore the world and bury yourself in music was often the difference between someone who made it as a musician and someone who didn't. Considering the unease he'd expressed in our conversation just after church, he probably had extra reason to focus on his music.

But the rejection still stung. I wasn't so much disappointed because he'd said no as I was embarrassed that I'd asked him in the first place. It wasn't like me to be so impulsive. I'd finally managed to start behaving like a normal person, and then I had to go and ruin it. *I'm not saying I* don't *want to date you* . . . Sheesh. What was my deal?

Elliott reached down and picked up his shoes. "For real though, thank you for asking. I wish I could give you a different answer."

"Don't even worry about it," I told him. "I'm sure I'll work something out."

We said good night, and I let myself into my apartment. Once the embarrassment of our conversation faded, one line kept repeating in my head. *Emma, I think you're great.* He was probably just saying it to be nice, but there had been a certain sincerity in his eyes that made me wonder if it was more than that. And with the way we'd connected after church . . . I needed Lilly. She'd know what everything meant.

Chapter 12

Lilly wasn't at home, which was weird for a Sunday night and annoying, considering how much I needed her to be around.

I tried to kill time reading a book but was distracted when Elliott started playing his piano. I moved to the wall and leaned against it, listening as he played. He was working on something new, that much was clear, with starts and stops and repeated lines . . . multiple starts and stops and repeated lines. It sounded a lot less like music and a lot more like he was trying to pound the piano into submission. I wasn't an expert in composition, but in three hours of listening, it didn't sound like he'd made much progress.

The piano was finally quiet just minutes before Lilly came through the door. The idea of hashing out anything Elliott-related was gone the second I saw her tear-streaked face.

"Lil, what happened? Are you okay?"

She sniffed and wiped her sleeve across her nose, a very un-Lilly-like thing to do, and collapsed onto the couch. "Trav and I had a fight."

She reeked of cigarette smoke and beer—also un-Lilly-like—and I had to wonder where their argument had taken place. I went into the kitchen to get her a glass of water before sitting on the couch beside her.

"Here. Drink this, then talk."

She took the water gratefully and gulped it down. "I'm a mess."

"You are," I said gently. "Completely. And you smell awful." I reached over and pushed back the hair hanging in her eyes. "Tell me what happened."

She sighed. "We were at the brewery over in Mills River. They were having this festival thing, and it was crazy. So many people."

"On a Sunday night? Where do all these people work that Monday morning is an acceptable time for a hangover?"

"You sound like a Mormon, Emma."

"I'm not judging. I'm legitimately curious."

"Not everyone that goes to a beer festival gets hung over. Some people just go and drink a beer and then go home."

"What, like ten, fifteen people?"

She smiled—that was good—and shot me a look. "Maybe twenty-five on Sundays."

"Okay. So you're at a not-everyone-is-drunk beer festival in Mills River with Trav, and . . ." I gave her an expectant look.

Her shoulders fell. "I didn't want to be there. I told Trav I didn't want to go. I have to work early tomorrow, and he was supposed to meet a whole bunch of his friends, and I knew what that was going to mean. I don't love the combination of Trav and his friends and unlimited servings of alcohol. He gets so stupid. I just didn't feel like babysitting tonight."

I was looking at a different Lilly. She'd always been cool with Trav's partying. *Babysitting* was more of an Emma word. "So what happened?"

"He begged me to go, and I finally caved, but then he just acted like a jerk all night. He kept saying I don't like to have any fun and I ought to just live a little and I'm holding him back from the kind of life he really wants to lead. Which doesn't make any sense. What kind of life does he want that he doesn't already have?"

"Are you sure it wasn't just the alcohol talking?"

"He was drinking, way more than normal. But you know Trav. He's sometimes obnoxious, but he generally has good judgment, and he's never rude—especially not to me. I just . . . I can't figure it out."

I thought for a moment. "I do know Trav," I finally said. "And nothing he did tonight sounds like him. What's going on at work? Anything stressful? Is stuff okay with his family?"

Lilly blinked. "I don't know. He hasn't said anything in particular. No, he did talk about work yesterday at dinner. Things are good at work. He just landed a new client that he's crazy excited about. He's building them an entire website from the ground up, and he says the payout's gonna be huge. He was so pumped about it."

"So work is good."

Lilly rubbed her temples with her thumbs. "Please just tell me what you're getting at. I'm so tired, and this is making my head hurt."

"I'm just saying that for Trav to act so completely out of character and treat you so badly, there must be something going on that's stressing him out. Those words he said to you tonight—that's not really him. You know he doesn't really feel that way, so what's eating at him? My hunch is it's something he's not sure he can talk to you about, which means what he needs is for you to ignore all the crap he's dishing out and be there for him anyway."

"Just ignore the fact that he walked all over my feelings tonight?"

"Okay, don't ignore that. He acted like a jerk and owes you an apology. But maybe also let him know whatever stuff he has going on, you're willing to support him through it."

She leaned her head against the couch cushion and closed her eyes. "You're probably right. But . . . I'm kind of afraid to say this out loud: I think maybe I'm just tired of the entire scene, you know? I mean, I'm going to work every day, seeing these moms and dads that are starting this incredible chapter of their lives. And I want that. I think I'm ready to move on to the next part of my life, and I've got this boyfriend who thinks the only reason we have weekends is so he has an excuse to get hammered."

I'd never had to hide how I felt about mindless drinking around Lilly—we'd known each other too long for that—but it wasn't exactly the time to be preachy either. I reached over and rubbed her shoulder. "That's a hard truth to realize."

She sniffed. "Yeah."

"Just sleep on it. Everything makes more sense after a good night's rest. And then maybe you write those words down, the ones about moving into the next phase of your life, and when the time is right, talk to Trav about it. Maybe that's what had him acting off. He's feeling the same thing, and he's terrified to admit it."

"So tonight was all about denial?"

I stood up and retrieved her water glass from the floor. "Maybe. I have no idea how Trav feels, but I do know I've never seen him be anything but good to you. I'd give him the chance to explain himself. I'm sure he'll want to."

"He would kiss you if he knew how much you're taking his side."

I smiled. "Do you think he'd shave for me? I might need to borrow him for Grayson's wedding."

"You want to *borrow* my boyfriend?"

"Why not? I'll bring him back in one piece."

Lilly heaved herself off of the couch. "You're completely hopeless. You still have weeks to get a date. You'll find someone."

"You're right. I am hopeless. Which is precisely why I won't find a date. Where did you leave Trav? Is he somewhere safe? Do I need to go pick him up?"

She pulled out her cell phone and swiped through a few screens. "He's with Buster, and Buster isn't supposed to be drinking, but . . . I don't know. I'm not sure I trust him not to."

I stood up and steered her to the bathroom. "Okay, you go take a shower. I'll see if I can get ahold of Buster and find out if they need some help."

She sniffed. "You're a good friend."

"Yeah, yeah." I held out my hand for her phone. "Is Buster's number in there?"

"Yeah." She handed it over. "Thanks, Em." She paused halfway to the bathroom and turned around. "Wait, what about you? How was church? Did you talk to Elliott?"

I tried to hide my smile, but she saw it, and her face brightened. "You did talk to him! What happened? Why are you smiling?"

"We had a really good conversation today. He helped me teach my Primary class, and then we talked about music, and I behaved like a normal, rational person. I think there was a little bit of a connection."

"You mean, like, sparks-fly-at-his-touch kind of connection? Or just a we're-both-musicians-so-there's-lots-we-could-talk-about connection?"

"Both, maybe? No physical contact yet, so I don't know if sparks will fly, but how could they not? You've seen him. He's—"

"The hottest guy you've ever met. I know. You've mentioned it a few times. But remember you also said he was the most arrogant, condescending man you've ever met less than a week ago. Being hot doesn't negate being a jerk."

"True. But he's not a jerk. I think I was wrong about him before." I scrolled through her contacts and found Buster's number, then shooed her away. "Go. Bathe. We can talk about Elliott tomorrow."

It took three tries to get Buster on the phone, but only three seconds to decide there was no way he was driving anybody home. "Just stay there, all right? And don't let Trav leave," I told him. "I'm coming to pick you up."

I pulled my jacket out of the closet and slipped on my boots.

"Emma, no. I can't let you drive all the way over there to pick up my stupid, drunk boyfriend. That's not fair." Lilly stood in the hallway, wrapped in a towel.

"Yes, you can. My homeschool group cancelled our session tomorrow, which means I can sleep in, something you can't afford to do. I promise I don't mind." I scooped my keys off the table by the doorway. "Go to bed. I'll get Trav home safe, and then I'll come straight home. It'll be fine."

She finally nodded. "I really do love you."

"I know. Be back soon."

I made it all the way down the front walk before I stopped dead in my tracks, an overwhelming sense of hesitation slamming into me like a wall of bricks. I was alone. And I was headed into the middle of a beer festival after midnight. It hadn't occurred to me to feel nervous when I'd told Lilly I would do it, but now I was second-guessing. I'd never even been to the Mills River Brewery.

I backtracked onto the porch and pulled out my phone, scrolling through my contacts. There had to be someone who could come along to help. The most obvious answer was Dad. He loved Lilly and wouldn't judge her idiot boyfriend. But this late, there was no way he wasn't already asleep. I hated to pull him out of bed. My finger hovered over his picture in my favorites list, indecision winning the moment, when the front door opened and Elliott stepped out carrying a bag of trash.

"Oh, hey. What are you doing out here?" he asked.

"I'm trying to decide if I should wake up my dad."

"Everything okay?"

"No. Trav and Lilly had a fight, and he's stupid drunk and can't drive. I just had a conversation with the friend who was supposed to be the designated driver, and he's totally wasted."

"So you're going to pick him up?"

"Yeah. And I'm thinking I shouldn't go alone. He's at this beer festival, and . . . I don't know. He's kind of a big guy. What if he isn't cooperative?"

Elliott moved past me and dropped his trash into the can at the corner of the house, then turned around, sliding his hands into the back pockets of his jeans. "I could go with you."

I looked up from my phone. "For real? I hate to ask that of you."

"You shouldn't go by yourself, and I don't mind. Just give me a second to grab my coat."

He emerged from the house moments later wearing a dark hoodie and a baseball cap pulled low on his head. He followed me to my car and climbed into the passenger seat.

"Thank you for this." I looked over my shoulder and backed my car out of the driveway.

"No worries. I was awake anyway. Might as well be doing something useful."

"Do you always practice at midnight?"

He grimaced. "Oh man. Sorry about that. I normally switch over to the keyboard so I can use my headphones."

"It doesn't bother me, and Lilly's been complaining about my practicing since I moved in. What's one more instrument for her to contend with?"

"Do you know how to get where we're going?" Elliott asked.

"Mostly. Want to pull up your GPS just to make sure?"

Elliott pulled up the brewery's address and started navigation, then set his cell phone on the center console between us.

"So tell me about Tahiti." It was fun to see his face brighten when I asked him about his mission.

"Ahh, Tahiti. It was paradise."

"I've seen pictures. It looks beautiful. You spoke French, right?"

"Yeah. And a little bit of Tahitian."

"Tahitian? Is that similar to French at all?" I pulled the car onto the highway, which was almost completely deserted at this hour, and headed toward Mills River.

"Not even a little bit. It's an old island language. It sounds completely different."

"Okay, say something in Tahitian. I want to hear it."

"I'm probably pretty rusty. It's been a while. Let's see. To say hello, you say *la ora na*."

"*La ora na*." I repeated the phrase back to him.

"You got it. If you'd like to say good morning or good evening, you change the last word. *La ora na oe* is good morning, and *la ora oe i teie po* means good evening."

"That's a lot of vowels."

"Yeah, and you pronounce every single one. What about you? Do you speak any languages?"

I shook my head. "Just English. And music. I get to count that one, right?"

"I totally do," Elliott said. "If you could learn any language, what would it be?"

"I don't know. I took a few years of Spanish in high school, but I think I'd learn French. I know people say Italian is the most beautiful, but I like French better. Or maybe I just like France better and that's affecting my opinion about the language."

"You've been to France?"

I nodded. "Lilly and I spent three weeks there the summer after Lilly graduated. Her mother is French, so she has tons of family over there. We stayed with her great-aunt a few hours north of Paris."

"Does Lilly speak French?"

"Probably not as well as you do, but she does all right. She knew enough to get us around Paris and communicate with her aunt, who doesn't speak a word of English."

"I've never been there."

"No?" That surprised me.

"I've been to Russia, Germany, Japan, Scotland, Denmark, Austria . . . but never France. I changed planes in Paris once. That's it."

I paused long enough to listen to the robotic voice of the GPS tell me we were approaching our exit. "You speak languages for all those other countries too?"

He laughed. "A little bit of German. Definitely not enough to claim fluency. And Russian. I spent six months studying in St. Petersburg when I was sixteen and picked it up then."

I shook my head and smiled. "You just picked it up? No big deal, right? Like picking up a gallon of milk or a loaf of bread or a language that uses an entirely different alphabet."

Elliott looked down. "Sorry. I wasn't trying to brag. Languages are kind of a hobby."

"No! You weren't bragging. I didn't take it that way at all. I've read that musicians are supposed to be better at languages, so collectively it's good you speak five. It helps balance out that I only speak one."

"I could help you learn French if you want. I bet you'd pick it up quick."

I stopped at the end of the exit ramp and glanced at Elliott's phone. "Did I miss which way I'm supposed to turn?"

"Right," Elliott said. "Then you'll take the first left just up ahead."

I followed his instructions, slowing down in front of the large sign that marked the brewery's entrance. I turned onto the wide, newly paved road that led past the brewery and to a large field where the festival was taking place.

Things were winding down, but I was still surprised by how many people were hanging around. Finding Trav suddenly felt a lot harder. I parked in an empty spot next to a long row of porta-johns and pulled out my phone. I tried to call Trav and then Buster, but neither of them answered.

"Now what?" I said to myself as much as to Elliott.

"I guess we go find him," Elliott said.

I walked close beside Elliott. I wasn't scared, really, but I felt a little out of my element. When we passed through a particularly raucous group of partiers, I took hold of his elbow, pulling myself even closer.

He reached over with his other hand, covering my fingers with his, and gave me a reassuring squeeze. "You okay?"

I felt the heat of his touch all the way down to my toes. Lilly had asked about sparks? Yeah. There were definitely sparks. "I'm good. Just glad you came with me."

"We'll be fine. Just try not to make eye contact with anyone," he said.

We circled the festival grounds twice before we found Trav slumped over the end of a picnic table, his head resting on his arm, a beer in his other hand.

"Emma!" Trav sat up, beer sloshing over the side of his cup, and smiled. "You came! You want a beer? I'm gonna get you a beer."

"Where's Buster?"

Trav's face fell. "He's gone, man. He left with some chick. Can you believe that? He just up and left me, just like Lilly did. But not you, Emma. You're my one true friend in this world."

Elliott put a hand on Trav's shoulder. "Come on. Time to go home."

"Elliott? You're here too? Aw, man, ya'll are awesome. You want a beer? I'm gonna get you a beer."

"I don't want a beer, Trav. We're gonna leave now, all right?"

"Come on. I'll buy. A beer for my friend Elliott Hart." Trav raised his voice. "Yeah, you heard me. The famous Elliott Hart. He's here with me."

Elliott's jaw tightened. "Trav. Shut up. It's time to go." He positioned himself on one side of Trav, looping his arm over his shoulders, and motioned for me to do the same. Trav grumbled a little but didn't hesitate as we started walking back to the car, an ungainly trio.

"Lilly's real mad, isn't she, Em?"

"Yeah, she's mad. You weren't very nice to her."

"She's gonna forgive me though, right? She won't stay mad. Lilly loves Trav."

Elliott rolled his eyes. "You start taking that for granted, and you may be begging her to keep you around."

"Beg? Naw, man. I won't beg for nothin'!"

We were within sight of the car when I took a wrong step and stumbled, falling to my knees. I scrambled back up and found myself face-to-face with a very large, very foul-smelling man wearing a sleeveless T-shirt that bore a single word: *STUD*.

"Hey, sweetheart. You looking for me?"

"Sorry. I just need to catch my friends." I moved to the left to get around him, but he lunged sideways, blocking my way. I turned the other direction, and he did the same thing. "What's the matter?" he said, his tone mocking. "Can't get past?" He snaked his arm around my waist and pulled me against him. "I think that means you ought to stay right here with me." The heat of his body seeped through my clothes and pressed into my skin. I leaned away, trying to find a pocket of air that wasn't soured by the sticky, sweet smell of alcohol on his breath. It was enough to turn my stomach.

I pushed against his chest. "Let me go."

He only held me tighter, laughing and trying to sway to the music.

A cry of help froze in my throat when I saw Elliott approaching, fury in his eyes. He grabbed the guy by the shoulders and yanked him backward, spinning him around so they stood facing each other. Elliott was a good three inches shorter and wasn't nearly as broad through the chest, but he had the element of surprise on his side. Also, he was sober.

He swung a punch, his fist colliding with the guy's jaw, and knocked him back several steps, where the guy tripped over a chair and landed on the ground with a graceless thud.

Elliott grabbed my hand. "Time to run."

We covered the short distance to the car at lightning speed. "Your keys, Emma." He moved around to the driver's side door.

"What?"

"Your keys. We need to get out of here."

"Oh." I pulled them out of my bag and tossed them to him.

It was good he was taking charge. I was still so stunned by my encounter with the massive, sweaty drunk man I hardly knew what end was up. "Trav, get in the car," Elliott said.

Despite his inebriation, at Elliott's command, Trav managed to get himself into the backseat with relative ease and speed. As soon as we were all in, Elliott took off, tearing through the parking lot so fast spinning gravel sprayed up from either side of the car. I'd never been so happy to be reckless.

I was still in shock. Had that guy really just grabbed me? What would have happened had Elliott not been there?

Trav hummed in the backseat, his fingers absently tapping against the window as he stared at the trees flying past.

"Are you okay?" Elliott finally asked, his voice gentle.

"Yeah." At least I thought so. Everything had happened so fast. I was relieved and grateful Elliott had intervened, but it was hard to get rid of the fear that still sat in my belly, an immovable dead weight pressing into me, through me, reaching every nerve ending in my body. I'd had very little control over a situation I'd been in just ten minutes before. When I looked down at my hands, they shook. I balled them into fists, not wanting Elliott to see.

"I think you gave that guy a fat lip," Trav slurred from the back. "He was a big dude too."

"He deserved it," Elliott said under his breath. He looked my way one more time. "Are you sure you're okay?"

I nodded. "Thank you for helping." My voice was a squeaky whisper. Elliott's brows scrunched together, and he frowned but said nothing more.

When we finally pulled into the driveway on Maple Crescent, Trav snored loudly in the backseat.

"Are we going to take him home?" I asked.

Elliott shook his head. "He can sleep it off at my place."

"I'll help you get him inside."

It took fifteen minutes of juggling limp arms and legs and a lolling head, but we finally managed to get Trav onto Elliott's couch. I pulled his shoes off and shoved a pillow under his head, then draped a blanket across his shoulders.

Elliott stared at the near-stranger sleeping in his living room. "That's more than he deserves."

"Yeah, but it's what Lilly would do."

Elliott leaned against the wall opposite the couch and yawned. "You think they'll work it out?"

"I don't know. This isn't typical Trav behavior. I've never seen him this drunk. But . . . Lilly's pretty tired of the whole scene. If he's not willing to give up beer festivals for a woman like Lilly, she should probably get out now."

Elliott flexed the fingers on his right hand and winced.

"Elliott—" I moved to where he stood and reached for his hand, holding it gently. His knuckles were slightly swollen, one of them split and bleeding. "Oh my word. You can't punch people with these hands!"

"What would you have had me do? Leave you there with that guy?"

"No, but your hands are so much more important than everyone else's! Wait here. I'll be right back."

"Emma, it's fine. Nothing's broken. I'll be okay in a couple of days."

"Please—just let me do this." I turned and hurried across the hallway, retrieving a washcloth and a first-aid kit out of my apartment.

Back at Elliott's, I pulled him into his kitchen, where I washed and treated his split knuckles. I worked in silence, trying to hide my shaking. Stupid hands. It had to be nerves from being so close to Elliott. The drunk man was gone. I was home. Or almost home. But the replay of what might have happened ran through my head like a never-ending movie reel. Strong hands. Rank breath. How I pushed and gained nothing. I took a deep, steadying breath.

"Are you okay?" Elliott asked. "You're trembling."

I looked at my hands and tried to smile. "I'm probably going to have 'what could have happened' nightmares for weeks. But I think I'm okay. It'll pass."

Something flashed through his eyes, a glint of steel reminiscent of the fury I'd noticed seconds before he'd strong-armed the guy off me and punched him to the ground. "I'm sorry, Emma. Some guys are stupid. And when the stupid ones get drunk, it's worse."

"I'll be okay," I said again, rubbing my hands together. "I'm just glad you were there to help."

He pulled me into an embrace, resting his chin on the top of my head. I wrapped my arms around his waist and pressed my cheek against his chest.

He held me a moment longer before his grip loosened and I pushed back, afraid he might see how much I enjoyed feeling the weight of his arms around me or the tickle of his breath through my hair.

"I should get some sleep," I said softly. "We both should."

He nodded. "No nightmares tonight, all right?"

I smiled. "I'll do my best."

Chapter 13

"It doesn't matter what his motives were. He hugged you. He pulled you against his body and wrapped his arms around you. Guys don't do that if there isn't some flicker of interest." Lilly lay on the worn braided rug that covered our living room floor, her legs propped up on the couch. "Are you going to let me eat any of that popcorn, or should I assume you only popped it for yourself?"

I passed her the bowl. It was Monday night, a rare free night in for us both, and we'd decided unanimously that navel oranges, popcorn, cheese, and crackers made a perfectly acceptable dinner menu. "But big brothers hug their little sisters all the time. What if he was just feeling protective and angry and somehow obligated to make up for the stupidity of his gender?"

"It wasn't a half-shoulder squeeze. It was a 'Hey, baby, wrap your arms around me' *hug*. Just own it. The guy's into you."

"Okay, true-confession time."

"After all these years, you really feel like you have to qualify the conversation?"

"Shut up. I'm just saying now I'm getting ready to say something serious so you need to listen and not make fun of me." I tossed another piece of popcorn into my mouth and grabbed a slice of orange off the plate.

"No making fun. Got it."

"How do I decide if I like Elliott because he's someone I would like no matter what or if I like him because he's famous and talented and gorgeous?" I picked at the orange peel.

"Emma. You're too smart to fall for someone's celebrity status. If you guys do wind up together, it won't take you long to decide whether or not he's a guy worth your attention, YouTube views notwithstanding." She grabbed a cracker, smeared it with Boursin cheese, and handed it my way.

"But I'd be lying if I said I wasn't enthralled with his music career," I said, taking the cracker. "I mean, I was a total idiot when I first met him because I couldn't believe it was actually him. I *was* starstruck, no matter how foolish it makes me feel to admit it."

"But is it his fame, really, that you're enthralled with? Or his talent?" She made another cracker for herself. "Do you care about the media attention or the online presence or the record label? That's exactly why you stopped touring yourself, right? Because you didn't like all the hype?"

Fair point. After Juilliard, invitations to be a guest soloist poured in from symphonies all over the country. For six months, I traveled, returning to New York in between performances. It's what I'd always wanted, and yet it wasn't at all what I'd expected. There was so much about it that didn't have anything to do with the music: parties and photos and socializing and schmoozing; it sucked me dry. Returning to Ohio for a full-time position in the Cleveland Orchestra had been a welcome relief from all that pressure. At least there I was among friends.

But Elliott's fame was a totally different animal. I'd only dealt with hype that existed inside the small and somewhat exclusive symphony world. *Everyone* knew who Elliott was. "I'm just worried I'm using all the hype and excitement of who he is to propel my feelings forward faster than I would if the circumstances were different."

Lilly tossed a piece of popcorn at me, hitting me squarely in the middle of my forehead.

"Hey! What was that for?"

"'Cause you're being stupid. Trust me, Em. You're not that kind of girl."

"What makes you so sure?"

"If Elliott was a struggling musician, teaching lessons out of his living room and playing the piano at a local jazz club, would you still be interested?"

"Absolutely, yes."

"What if he wasn't a musician at all?"

That one took me longer to answer. I loved that music was so important to him, and, yeah, I loved that he was so talented. But I also loved the way he entertained a classroom full of three-year-olds and spoke five languages and saved me from STUD guy without a single hesitation. Those things didn't have anything to do with his musical abilities. "I *love* that he's a musician because it's something we have in common. But yes, even if he weren't, I think I'd still like him. I'd still be interested."

"Are you physically attracted to him?"

"Is the sky blue?"

Lilly pushed herself into a sitting position. "Okay, you pass. I declare you officially not shallow and give you permission to pursue Elliott simply because you want his body."

"I don't want his body."

Lilly cocked her eyebrow, reaching over to steal the last slice of orange.

"Okay, fine. But it's not the only reason I like him." I grabbed the popcorn bowl, sliding it out of her reach before she swiped the last handful. "For real? You're terrible at sharing," I told her.

She rolled her eyes. "It might not be the only reason you like him, but it is the most fun. Don't stress over it. You like him; he likes you. It doesn't have anything to do with his career or his fame."

I wanted to believe Lil was right, but an hour later when she came bursting into my room seconds before I fell asleep, I wasn't so sure. "Emma, are you asleep?" She crawled onto my bed.

"Yes, completely. Please go away."

"You need to see this." She handed me her phone.

In my almost-asleep fogginess, it took me a second to figure out what I was looking at. It was a picture on an online photo-sharing app. I had to read the caption three times before I actually processed what was in the photo. "Elliott Hart fist fighting at a beer festival? If this dude isn't him, he should get a job as his look-alike. Cast your vote below: Is this Elliott Hart?" I read out loud. The photo was blurry and only caught the side of his face; even that was in shadow from the hat he'd put on before we'd left. It looked like him, for sure, but had I not been at the festival myself, I wouldn't have been able to vote with any certainty.

"How many people have seen this?" I asked Lilly.

"Eleven thousand have voted so far. That's not too many, right? Not in Elliott-land."

"I don't know. It's probably only a matter of time before it gets more attention." Elliott had a lot of fans who weren't Mormon, but he was pretty public about his faith and his standards. "If any of the gossip websites come across this picture, they'll have a field day with the speculation."

"You should comment and explain what he was doing there," Lilly said. "I think his fans should know he wasn't actually drinking and fighting. Defending your honor is a way better story."

She was right. Someone should speak up and defend Elliott's character. But it felt too meddlesome for me to do it without talking to him first. "I don't know."

"What do you mean you don't know? Just comment on the picture. Tell his side of the story."

"Not until I talk to him," I said. "For all I know, he's seen the picture and his press people are working on a statement. I can't pretend like I know how to handle this stuff."

"It just really stinks," Lilly said. "You should read some of these comments. People are obnoxious, talking about the white knight finally falling in the mud. It's lame."

"I don't want to read them. It'll just make me mad."

I lay there after Lilly left my room, tossing and turning, unable to get to sleep. It was hard not to feel guilty. Elliott had been at the festival only because he'd been helping me. Plus, how crazy was it that all those people cared enough about the minutia of Elliott's life to study a picture and vote on his supposed identity? *Thousands* of people. If they were that interested in one stupid night at one stupid festival, how interested would they be if Elliott started dating someone? Casting myself in that role, imagining that level of scrutiny turned on me? It was enough to make me queasy. But there was no way around it. There was no way I could even dream of a relationship with Elliott that wouldn't include the unwelcome third wheel of his stardom.

* * *

I spent the next morning with my mom, returning to Asheville with an hour to spare before the start of my afternoon lessons. I left my purse in my apartment, then crossed the entryway to knock on Elliott's door.

He smiled wide when he saw me, and my heart did a little flip-floppy thing.

"Hi," I said. "You got a minute?"

"Sure, come on in." He moved aside, then followed me into his living room. "What's up?"

"Have you seen this?" I handed him my phone.

He studied the photograph for a moment before dropping onto his couch with a sigh. He slid the phone across the coffee table in my direction. "How many people have seen it?"

"It's gone from ten thousand to twenty-seven thousand votes since last night. I did a quick search, though, if that matters. So far the traffic is limited to this one photo-sharing site."

He shook his head and echoed my words from the night before. "It's only a matter of time. Thirty, maybe forty thousand hits and it'll generate enough buzz for some gossip rag to pick it up."

"What are you going to do?" I sat on the couch beside him.

"Nothing. There's nothing that can be done. It'll run its course, people will talk about it for a few days like it matters, then they'll move on."

"But do you worry about people thinking you were at a beer festival? Won't it bug your fans to think you were fighting? And drinking? Elliott, I'm willing to comment and explain what really happened. If it would help, I'll totally do it."

"I appreciate you offering, but you can't play their game. If you comment, you'll confirm I was actually there. Right now 42 percent don't even think it's me in that photo. Explaining will only bring more questions. Who's the girl he's defending? What caused the altercation? Are they dating? How long have they known each other? What's he doing in North Carolina? It's like feeding seagulls on the beach. You give in once, and they never leave you alone."

"It just feels wrong for people not to know the truth."

"People don't care about the truth, at least not the people who are posting that picture. They care about what sells, what sounds the most scandalous, what generates the most traffic."

"But truth is still truth. Don't you have to care, even if they don't?"

"I care about the people who matter—my family, my close friends—what they think is important. But I can't care about what everyone else thinks. I'd be eaten alive if I did."

"I guess that's what it means to have thick skin."

"Yeah. It still stinks. This'll tick off my agent more than anything—hanging out at beer festivals isn't exactly on his list of approved album-generating activities—but you do learn to filter out the nonsense. You have to treat it like background noise."

I propped my elbow up on the back of the couch, resting my head on my hand. "Is it worth it? All that background noise?"

He was quiet a beat too long, leaving an uncomfortable silence hanging in the air between us. "It's worth it," he finally said. "Playing is the only thing I've ever been good at. And I love the energy of performing. If I have to deal with some unwanted attention to get the kind that feeds my career, then that's life, you know? You take the good with the bad."

"I get that," I said. "It's the same thing in the symphony world. There are parts of it I hate, but I could never give it up."

"But you did give some of it up, didn't you?" Elliott asked.

"What do you mean?"

"I Googled you, Emma. You're not some small-town violinist. New York, Cleveland—you're kind of a big-shot, aren't you?" He nudged my knee.

I dropped my eyes and shook my head, ignoring the thrill that came from knowing he'd searched for me online. "I don't miss New York, but Cleveland . . ." I shrugged. "Sometimes I still wonder if I did the right thing."

"Yeah? Would you ever consider going back?"

"I don't know. My mom has MS—she's had it for years—but it's gotten worse lately. She's in pain most of the time and can't always get around on her own. She'd die if she knew she was the reason I left, but I can't say it wasn't a big part of my decision. I feel like I need to be close enough to help."

"I really admire that," Elliott said. "Why does she think you moved?"

I winced. "I might have maybe told her a little white lie."

Elliott gasped in mock surprise. "You lied to your mother? I'm shocked!"

"It wasn't really a lie. I just . . . exaggerated a little."

"I sense a story coming on."

I groaned and pulled a throw pillow up to hide my face. "It's not a good story."

"Oh, I think it *is* a good story."

I pushed out a resigned sigh. "Fine. There was this conductor in Cleveland: an associate conductor who took an interest in my career and was nice and attentive and charming, and then one night he came onto me, I lost my head for fourteen seconds, kissed him, then decided it was all a mistake and backpedaled as fast as I possibly could."

Understanding flashed across Elliott's face. "So your Mom thinks Asheville is your escape from the arms of a jilted lover?"

"It's not entirely untrue. The timing was convenient."

"But not a big enough reason to make you move."

I shook my head. "I moved for Mom. I just can't tell her as much."

Elliott's cell phone rang from across the room, and he stood to retrieve it. "Don't go anywhere. I'll just be a minute."

When he glanced at the screen of his phone, his face darkened, and he retreated into his bedroom, closing the door softly behind him. His conversation was mostly muffled, but I still caught a few words here and there, enough to guess he was having an angry conversation with his agent. I pulled out my phone and opened a web browser, running a search for Elliott's name. Sure enough, in the short period of time we'd been talking, the photo had been discovered, and a few online tabloids had picked it up, fueling the fire of speculation about his supposed presence at the festival. One annoying headline read *Mormon Gone Wild?*

Poor Elliott.

He emerged from his bedroom moments later, his jaw tight, his brow creased. "Sorry about that," he said.

"No worries." I glanced at my watch and stood, wishing I didn't have a reason to leave. "I gotta get to my afternoon lessons. Is everything okay?"

He nodded his head sadly. "Yeah, it's just stupid public relations stuff."

"Mormon gone wild?"

"You saw that one, huh? It didn't take them long."

"I'm sorry, Elliott."

"Don't worry about it. His voice hardly sounded encouraging. "It's nothing I haven't been through before."

Yeah, but before it hadn't been my fault.

Chapter 14

"Lilly!" I pushed into the apartment and dumped my stuff on the couch. "Are you home?"

"In the kitchen," she called back. "Trav's here too."

"Hey, Em," Trav called.

Huh. It was good he was around. It'd been almost a week since Elliott and I had rescued him from his drunkenness, and he'd been pretty scarce since then. He was embarrassed, probably, and likely trying to figure out a way to apologize to Lilly. By the looks of how wrapped up in each other they were—literally limbs wrapped up everywhere, arms, legs all tangled from one kitchen chair to the other—he must have figured it out.

"Um, should I come back later?"

"No, come sit down," Lilly said, though she made no move to take her head off Trav's shoulder. "We're just talking."

I pulled out a chair and sat across from them. "It's nice to see you, Trav." His eyes met mine, and he shifted, disentangling himself from his girlfriend. Once on his feet, he reached for my hand and pulled me up into an enormous hug. When he released me, he kept his hands on my shoulders and, with a glance back at Lilly, who was clearly enjoying his performance, cleared his throat. "Thank you, Emma, for helping Lilly see that maybe I wasn't such a bad guy and shouldn't be judged on one bad decision. Thank you for risking your safety by venturing into a festival full of drunken idiots to bring me home. And thank you for bringing Elliott with you. That dude's the real deal."

"Why is he the real deal?"

"One, because he saved you, and if anything had happened to you, I'm pretty sure Lilly would never have spoken to me again. But also, he had some good stuff to say to me that night. Good stuff, man."

"What kind of stuff?" I looked to Lilly, but she only shrugged, her eyes bright against the pale blue of her scrubs.

"Naw, man. I can't break the bro-code, but he's legit. You really oughtta keep him around."

I sank back into my chair. "I wish I had a reason to keep him around."

"Are you serious? He's into you, Em," Trav said. "You don't have anything to worry about."

Lilly brushed a crumb off the sleeve of Trav's plaid shirt. "How do you know this, and why haven't you told me before now?"

"Yes, please," I added. "More details."

He shrugged. "I don't have details. I can just tell. Plus, he talked about you Sunday night."

My nerves jumped at the thought, but only for a moment. "You mean the Sunday night when you were totally wasted? Forgive me for not considering you a credible witness."

"Specifics, Trav," Lilly said. "We need more than drunk-man intuition."

He looked annoyed. "I already told you I'm not breaking the bro-code. But trust me. He likes you."

I wanted to believe Trav was right. I'd felt something when Elliott had given me that hug, but he'd made it very clear he couldn't even be a fake date to a wedding, much less a real one.

I turned my attention to Lilly. "So tell me what I'm supposed to do about this." I pulled out my phone and scrolled to my voice mail. I hit the speaker button, then put the phone in the middle of the table so Trav and Lil could both hear.

"Hey, Emma. This is Blake Johnson. I hope you don't mind me calling. I'm going to be in Asheville in a few weeks, staying with my aunt, Sharon Jensen, from church? Anyway, she suggested I give you a call. I know. Totally lame way to introduce myself, but she's convinced we'd have a good time, and . . . why not, right? So yeah. Give me a call. I'd love to take you to dinner, your choice, obviously, since I don't know anything about Asheville. Okaayy, so I'm rambling. Call me. Only if you want to though. Right. Okay. Bye."

"Oh, he sounds cute!" Lilly said.

I grabbed my phone and pulled up the last page in my web history, turning it around for Lilly to see.

"Oh my word, is that him? He *is* cute."

"I know, right? What should I do?"

"What do you mean what should you do? You should totally go," Lilly said.

"But what about Elliott?" Trav asked.

Yeah. What about Elliott?

"Elliott is a nonissue," Lilly said. "It's not like *he's* asked you to dinner. But this guy has—a guy who's cute and Mormon and clearly interested in taking you out. Go have some fun. You're long overdue. If nothing else, maybe it'll make Elliott jealous."

I didn't necessarily want to make Elliott jealous, but I was due for some fun. I'd been working like crazy lately, between symphony rehearsals and quartet gigs and teaching lessons. Not to mention all the time I was spending with my mom. I hadn't had an actual for-real date since I'd moved. What could it hurt, really? "Okay, I'm gonna do it."

"Good girl!" Lilly said.

I grabbed my phone off the table and a water bottle from the fridge before heading to my room. "Thanks for the apology, Trav," I said from the door. "I hope you meant it."

"I'm a changed man, Em. I promise."

Chapter 15

I dropped another dress onto my growing stack of not-even-possibles. I'd hoped I'd find something at least slightly wedding-ish in Lilly's closet, but most of her dresses were hardly bigger than a piece of sheet music. There wasn't anything I could wear for Grayson's wedding. Which meant I could wear the green dress already hanging in my closet. Or there was shopping in my future. *Dress* shopping. The thought made me queasy. *Stupid wedding*. It wasn't that I didn't like to shop. I was all about finding those classic pieces I could look great in for years. But I might wear a dress for a wedding like Grayson's *once*. Unless maybe I went with something black . . .

A knock sounded on my front door. I glanced at my watch. Two hours until lessons started, which meant I probably needed to practice and wasn't in the mood for a surprise drop-in from a few well-intentioned visiting teachers. I swung the door open anyway—I'm nice like that—and was surprised to find my old Young Women leader, Laney Frampton, standing there.

"Emma! You're home!" She sounded relieved. "I was sure you wouldn't be here."

I hadn't seen Laney in years, since before college, even. We'd been really close when she'd served as my youth advisor because she'd been only a few years older than I was, but then she'd had a baby and I'd gone to college and our lives had veered off in different directions. It was hard to stay in touch after that.

"I have a couple hours before lessons start. Do you want to come in?"

She looked off to the left, then back to me, then back to the left one more time. "Well," she finally said, "I have Oscar with me." She reached out her hand, motioning for someone to come closer. A little boy, maybe five or six years old, moved into the doorway and reached for Laney's hand. She looked back at me. "This is my son, Oscar. Oscar, this is my friend Emma. Can you say hello?"

"Hello," Oscar whispered. He moved behind Laney so all I could see was his little arm wrapped around his mother's leg, gripping her hand so hard his fingers were nearly purple.

"Come on in," I told Laney.

"Actually I was sort of hoping . . ." She paused, then her words started tumbling out so fast I almost struggled to keep up. "So I have this job interview at the Wells Fargo right around the corner. Obviously people don't usually take their children to job interviews, but a water pipe burst in the cafeteria of his elementary school, and I had to go straight there to pick him up if I wanted to have any chance of making the interview on time, and there wasn't time at all to think about trying to find a sitter, so I was going to try and just endure having him along with me." She took a deep breath. "But then your mother called to check in—she's my visiting teacher—and when I told her where I was, she told me how close you live to the bank. So it was her idea, really. She thought if you were home, Oscar could stay with you while I go to my interview. I know it's last minute, but he gets so restless, and I just . . ." She looked at me, her eyes pleading. "I really need to get this job."

"Wow. Um, sure." I glanced at my watch. "I have to leave for my afternoon lessons at two forty-five. Do you think that's enough time?"

"It should be. I can't imagine the interview taking longer than an hour. Are you sure, Emma? I appreciate you helping me out like this."

"It's fine. I'm happy to help."

Laney pulled a backpack off her shoulder and handed it over.

"Is there anything I need to know about Oscar?" I asked. "Allergies? Aversions? Fears?"

She shook her head no. "I don't think so. He's shy and has some anxiety about new situations, so it might take him a little while to warm up to you. But that's it. No allergies. Well wait, he doesn't love dogs, but if you don't have one, he should be good to go."

"Sounds easy enough."

"And there's coloring books and a Nintendo DS in his backpack. That should keep him entertained for a little while."

"Got it."

"Are you sure?"

I tried to give her a reassuring smile. "We'll be fine. Go be great at your interview."

When Oscar realized his mother was leaving him behind, he wrapped both arms around her legs and started to cry.

"Mommy will be really quick," Laney told him. "I promise. And Emma will take good care of you. Can you be strong for me? Like we practice at home?"

He slowly nodded his head. Laney pried Oscar's little fingers off her hand one last time. "Thank you," she said. "I'll hurry."

Oscar watched her leave, then turned to me, his bottom lip still quivering.

"So." I filled my voice with enthusiasm. "What would you like to do?"

He leaned onto the corner of the living room sofa and shrugged.

"Do you want to color?"

He shook his head.

"Do you want to show me a game on your DS? I bet you're better than I am."

Another shrug.

"Do you want to play a game? I think I have Uno cards somewhere."

Through all of my questioning, he kept his eyes down, his eyebrows drawn close together.

When Elliott started to play next door, Oscar finally looked up. "What's that?" he asked.

"That's a piano." His eyes were suddenly bright, interested. I pointed to my piano in the corner. "That's my piano over there in the corner. My neighbor Elliott has one too. Have you ever heard one before?"

He nodded. "At church. But it doesn't sound like that."

"That's because Elliott is very good. Playing the piano is his job."

"Like his everyday job? People pay him to do it?"

I smiled. "Pretty cool, huh?"

Oscar moved to the wall where the sound of Elliott's playing was loudest, pressed his ear against it, and closed his eyes. His entire body leaned into the music, feeling it on a level I recognized as a musician but that I'd rarely seen in someone as tiny as Oscar. I had a couple of students who felt music down to their core, who experienced it instead of just heard it, and I never grew tired of seeing the magic of learning a language that was spoken on such a personal, soul-deep level. Watching Oscar was particularly poignant because I was pretty sure he was experiencing that soul connection for the first time.

I crouched down beside him. "Oscar, do you want to go next door and watch Elliott play? We can go right now if you want."

"Will he let us watch?"

I hesitated. I hadn't seen Elliott outside of church in over a week. He'd said he needed to focus, and he was staying true to his word. But I had to believe this was a reason good enough to break the rules. "I'm sure he will."

"Do you think he'll show me how?" Oscar sniffed and used one finger to push the glasses that were sliding down his nose back onto his face.

"How to play?"

He nodded, his eyes wide, his voice soft with reverence. "I want to be able to do that."

I remembered the moment I'd heard a violin for the first time. I had been six years old at a folk music festival with my parents when an old man dressed as a civil war soldier had played "Ashokan Farewell." It was part of a dramatic reading; a woman stood beside the violinist, reading an old love letter from a Civil War soldier to his wife, the last she would ever receive before he was killed in battle. At first my mother thought my tears were from the letter, but I was too little to understand the soldier's flowery sentiments. It was the music that I understood. I couldn't sleep that night until my mother promised she would find me a violin.

As I walked Oscar across the hallway, pausing outside Elliott's door to knock, it felt like I was about to be a part of something big, like maybe this was going to be a moment Oscar would remember.

I knocked, and the playing stopped, and Elliott came to the door. "Hey." Album-focusing or not, he still looked pleased to see me.

"So this is my friend Oscar," I said, my hands resting on the boy's shoulders. "He's hanging out with me for an hour and was literally pressed against the wall, trying to hear you play. Mind if we come in and listen for a while?"

Elliott crouched down in front of Oscar. "You like the piano?"

Oscar nodded, his face solemn. "Can you teach me?" His voice was so earnest there was no way his words didn't punch Elliott in the gut just like they had me. The kid was every music teacher's dream.

Elliott stood and reached out his hand. He looked up long enough to meet my gaze and smile. "Come on in," he said to Oscar. "I'll pull a chair right up to the piano so you can sit beside me."

I settled on the couch in Elliott's living room and watched as he played for Oscar. He was animated and engaging and funny and such an incredible teacher. By the end of half an hour, Oscar could play a simplified version of "Twinkle, Twinkle, Little Star" while Elliott played an accompaniment, making the song sound impressive even to my ears. By the look on Oscar's face, he was completely blown away. As soon as they finished, he looked up at Elliott, all smiles, and said, "Again!"

Elliott laughed. "You practice through once without me, okay?" He slid off the piano bench and crossed to where I sat on the couch. He sat beside me and leaned forward on his elbows. "Does Oscar have a piano at home?"

"I don't know. I'm guessing probably not. This all seemed pretty new to him today."

"He's a talented kid. He's got a great ear, and . . . he needs a piano. You don't see kids like that every day."

"Really? A little miniature Elliott, huh?"

"Don't sell him short. I think this kid has serious talent."

"Right. 'Cause you're completely average, Elliott."

He smiled and shook his head. "Okay, he's a lot like I was as a kid."

"So teach him."

"What? No. I'm not a teacher."

"Yes, you are. I've been watching you the entire time. You're incredible with him. You are a teacher."

"Well . . . but . . . I have this album I have to finish . . ."

I wanted to ask him how it was going, but I bit back the words. Living next door, I'd heard enough of his efforts to recognize the only emotion shining through was frustration. "Are you sure holing up in your apartment is providing the inspiration you need? I mean, what could be more inspiring than helping Oscar discover his love for music?" *Aside from me*, I thought to myself. I could be more inspiring. I could be *very* inspiring.

He leaned back on the couch. "I don't know. If you knew the stuff the record label is saying to my agent—I'm on thin ice as it is."

"I can't tell you what to do here," I said with a shrug. "I'm sure Laney will be able to find him a teacher regardless, but maybe it's supposed to be you."

"Elliott, listen," Oscar called from across the room. "I did it without making any mistakes."

"Good job, Oscar. Can you do it one more time? I'll come play it with you again in a second." He turned back to me. "What's his situation like at home? Will they be able to afford lessons? A piano?"

I shook my head. "I don't know. His mom went through a divorce a couple years ago. She's interviewing for a job right now, but from the way she talked when she dropped him off, I'm guessing it's pretty tough."

Elliott nodded his understanding, then stood and moved back to the piano. "Okay, Oscar. You ready? Let's do it again."

As they played their song one last time, I couldn't stop thinking about Elliott teaching Oscar. If he wasn't feeling connected to his music or composing with any success, he needed to get outside of his own head. What better way to do that than by serving other people? Especially if *people* meant a musically inclined little whiz kid.

* * *

Three days later, I checked my phone after my afternoon lessons and had a voice mail from Laney.

"Emma, please call me," her message said. "You'll never believe what just happened."

She answered her phone after one ring. In the background, I heard the distinct sound of little fingers working through the melody of "Twinkle, Twinkle, Little Star."

"First of all," Laney said. "You did not tell me Elliott Hart was your neighbor."

"Oh, yeah. You know his music?"

"Not his recent stuff, but I remember watching him on *Talent Hunt*. I voted for him. You can imagine how surprised I was when my doorbell rang and it was *him* standing on my front porch."

I smiled. "He's a nice guy, right?"

"Emma, he brought us a piano. A keyboard, really, but it's full size, and it's beautiful, and it's so much more than I ever expected. He's agreed to teach Oscar for free."

I really wanted to listen to the rest of Laney's explanation, but it was hard not to race home and find Elliott right that moment. He *gave* them a piano. I closed my eyes. Could the man be any more perfect? "Oh, Laney, I'm so glad. I've never seen a kid like Oscar—the way he just lit up from the music. He's special."

"I knew he was special, but he's just always been so shy. I was afraid no one would ever see him for who he really is. But this—he's a different kid when he's sitting at the piano. I can't get him to leave it alone."

"Music can do amazing things for kids. I'm sure this will be a good thing for him."

"Please tell Elliott I said thank you, again. I was pretty much a weepy mess after he showed up this afternoon, then he and Oscar played for me, and I was just so emotional I didn't really thank him properly. Can you imagine? This world-class pianist teaching my little boy. I can't even wrap my head around it."

I resisted the urge to knock on Elliott's door the second I arrived home. I wanted to say thank you, but I kind of wanted to do a little something more too. What he was doing for Oscar was big. Giving him a keyboard that was probably worth close to two thousand dollars was pretty spectacular, but I was more impressed that he was willing to invest in a relationship with a kid he barely knew for nothing but the love of music.

Chapter 16

I RUMMAGED THROUGH MY KITCHEN pantry trying to decide if I had what I needed to make brownies. Elliott deserved a thank-you dessert, and no dessert turned out better than my mother's homemade brownie recipe.

Lilly wandered out of her room an hour later, lured, no doubt, by the smell of chocolate filling the entire apartment. "Ohh, are those your mom's brownies?"

I motioned to the empty batter bowl still sitting on the counter. "I saved it for you."

She squealed and hopped onto the counter after fishing a spoon out of the drawer.

I hated squealing, but for brownie batter, I could almost relate.

"So what's the occasion?" She slid her spoon across the bottom of the bowl, then licked off the batter with a sigh.

"They're for Elliott."

"What? All of them? You mean I have to smell them but not eat them? What kind of a roommate are you?"

"You'll get some. Don't worry. I'm making him a brownie sundae."

She raised her eyebrows and gave me a pointed look. "Does he know you're making him a sundae? Is he expecting this little overture? Perhaps bringing the ice cream and the caramel sauce so you can snuggle up side by side and make your sundaes together?"

"Shut up. Don't turn this into something stupid. He just did a really nice thing today, and I want to say thank you. So, a thank-you dessert."

"What did he do?"

"He gave a piano to a kid. And he offered him free piano lessons."

"An entire piano? Geez. Way to be generous. A kid you know?"

I nodded. "A friend from church."

"Know what I think?" She dropped her spoon into the sink and picked up the bowl. "I think you're falling for this guy." She peered down. "Would you think I was gross if I just put my whole head inside this bowl?"

I took the bowl from her hands. "Yes. That would be gross. And I'm not falling for him. It's not a big deal."

"Yes, you totally are. I worried the whole beer-brawl punch-out thing was going to throw you, but I'm impressed. You're sticking with it."

"What do you mean? Why would it throw me?"

"Here's all I'm saying. I know you were all worried that you liked Elliott just because of his fame, but that was before you'd really experienced what it actually meant. And what it might mean for you if you guys got together. Now that you have seen it, I kinda thought you might bail." She slid off the counter and wandered to the fridge. "I mean, you gotta admit it's not a very Emma-esque lifestyle."

I grabbed a dish towel off the counter and started wiping down the stovetop, channeling my sudden discomfort into full-throttle stain removal. "So what are you saying? You don't think I should be interested in Elliott?" I dropped the towel and faced Lilly.

"No! You should absolutely be interested. He's totally hot. And he's clearly interested in you. You should go for it. I'm just surprised thoughts of being a celebrity girlfriend haven't scared you off. Super proud of you. Don't back down. But, surprised."

I huffed. "I'm *not* a celebrity girlfriend. You're turning this into something it's not."

"Not yet, you're not. But your eyes are all dreamy and hopeful, and I can see exactly where this is going. You've crossed over from 'I like this guy, and maybe I'll have some fun' to 'I'm seriously falling for this guy.' It's only a matter of time."

"I'm just making brownies. Brownies I don't intend to eat with him, I might add. I'm taking a sundae to his door, then I'm leaving." I pulled the finished brownies out of the oven and set them on the stove. "Besides, I'm having dinner with Blake next weekend. Blake, who happens to be a *lawyer* and is interviewing for a job while he's in town. Did I tell you that part?"

"Hmmm, look at you playing the field." Lilly smirked and gave me a nudge.

"I'm not playing anything. It's just dinner and just brownies."

"What if Elliott invites you in?"

I'll do a happy dance and say yes. "He won't ask. He already turned me down when I asked him to the wedding. He's focusing on his music. Not his neighbor."

"He will too ask."

"Then I'll say no."

"Ha! You will not."

I finished washing my hands and flung a few drops of water in her direction. "Brownies," I repeated. "Not a wedding cake."

"Fine, fine," Lilly said. "How long till you cut them?"

"Ten minutes."

"So plenty of time for you to go change."

I looked down at my clothes. "Why do I need to change?"

"Because you have flour on your butt. And chocolate on your shirt."

"Uggh, fine." I headed down the hallway, wondering what I could put on that wouldn't look like I'd intentionally dressed up to carry a brownie sundae across the hallway.

"Wear something green," Lilly called from the kitchen. "You look good in green."

Something green . . . I grabbed a flowy silk tank top out of my closet. "Have you seen my black cardigan?" I yelled to Lilly.

"You say that like you don't have forty-seven black cardigans hanging in your closet."

"Me and everyone else in the symphony. I need the one with three-quarter-length sleeves. With the ribbon trim? And the little pearl buttons?"

I was digging through my clothes hamper when Lilly tossed the sweater at my head. "You left it in the bathroom."

"Oh, that's right. I did. Thank you."

I changed my clothes and threw my hair into a messy bun before hurrying back into the kitchen. "What do you think? Good? Not too dressy?"

"You look perfect. Here." She handed me three empty bowls.

"Three?"

"You're not just making him a sundae, are you? All that effort, and we don't get to enjoy too?"

I smiled and lined the bowls up on the counter while Lilly pulled the ice cream out of the freezer.

"So how's Ava?" Lilly asked. "You haven't mentioned her in a while. Elliott's gone and stolen all our conversations."

"More stubborn than ever," I replied. "I haven't seen her in a couple weeks. She's supposed to be working on her concerto for the Cleveland video, but she hasn't asked me for any more help, I'm sure since things went so badly last time. Mom thinks I need to try to find a way to just be her sister. So far, I got nothing."

"That's tough. Why not take her to the mall or something? Let her help you pick out a dress for the wedding."

"That's actually a really good idea." I topped off each sundae with some whipped cream, a drizzle of caramel sauce, and a cherry. "There. Finished."

Two minutes later, I knocked on Elliott's door, holding the most fabulous brownie sundae ever made in the history of all brownie sundaes.

"Hi," I said when he opened the door.

"Hi—holy ice cream sundae; that thing is huge."

"It's not just ice cream. There's a brownie on the bottom too, and it's the best brownie you'll ever taste. Says my mom, who I tend to agree with when it comes to things like brownies. Here." I held it out to him. "This one's for you."

He looked surprised, which was dumb because who knocks on your door to show you the sundae they're getting ready to eat without offering you one? "What is this for?"

"Consider it a thank-you dessert. Like a card but better 'cause you get to eat it."

"I am in full support of thank-you desserts." He reached out and took the sundae. "Thank you for this. It looks great."

"What's great is what you're doing for Oscar. I talked to Laney tonight, and she was so overwhelmed she couldn't even get out a complete sentence. This is so big for them. Thank you."

"Actually, I'm really excited. I've been thinking about what you said, and I think you're right. I think it'll be good for me."

"Good. I'm glad." I took a step back toward my own door. "Well, enjoy."

He started to close his door, then paused. "Emma, wait . . . Do you want to come in?"

I motioned to my apartment. "I left my sundae on the counter."

"Oh. Well, your counter's, what, like twelve steps away? You want to grab it, and we'll eat together?"

So I didn't actually do a happy dance for real, but I totally felt like it. "Okay."

Back in my kitchen, Lilly watched me retrieve my ice cream, then turn back toward the door. "Ha! See? I knew you'd say yes!"

"Shut up," I whispered. "He's still standing in the hallway."

Lilly laughed. "Go get 'em, tiger."

Chapter 17

I loved Elliott's living room mostly because aside from the small sitting area by the window, the rest of the room was basically a studio. A grand piano occupied the entire far corner, and a long table, covered in recording equipment, sat against the wall. Half-filled sheets of staff paper covered the back of the piano, music notes in tiny, even print scrawled across each page. I couldn't keep myself from walking over to take a closer look.

"I didn't think people composed like this anymore. Isn't there digital software that does all of this for you?"

"Yeah, there is. And I use it most of the time. But sometimes picking up a pencil helps. I know—I'm old school. It's just part of my process."

Conspicuously absent from Elliott's living room was the digital piano that used to sit opposite the couch.

"Wait a minute," I said, sitting across from him. "You gave Oscar *your* piano?"

He lowered his gaze, looking a little sheepish. "It was sort of an impulse decision. I wanted to tell him in person that I'd like to give him lessons, but it didn't feel right to go empty-handed."

"So you just grabbed your piano on the way out the door."

He shrugged. "I'll replace it. If for no other reason than to spare Lilly's ears late at night."

I took a bite of my sundae. "What about that one?" I motioned to the grand piano in the corner. "I can't even imagine how you got that thing inside."

"It wasn't easy. We took the legs off and managed to get it through the front door, but Lilly had to open your apartment door so we could angle it the right way to get it through here."

"Had to go with the grand, huh? An upright wouldn't have sufficed for your stay in Asheville?" I smiled, hoping he realized I was trying to be funny.

"Listen, it was hard enough not to bring my piano all the way from Denver. I'm just renting this one while I'm here. It's a great instrument, but it's still not the same."

"I feel you. I'd never be able to handle a substitute violin, at least not long term."

"Yeah, but you can take your violin as a carry-on bag."

"That's true. So what's so special about your piano in Denver?"

"It belonged to my grandfather. He played, and before he died, I would go over and sit with him, play all his favorite hymns. Sitting at that piano is where I've written all my best work."

Of course he played piano for his dying grandpa. Because that was exactly what I needed to hear to not hyperventilate and fall in love with him right there on the spot.

After a few more bites of sundae, he looked up. "For real, this is the best brownie I have ever had."

"Mom spent years perfecting the recipe. She even does this thing where halfway through the baking you pull the pan out and shake it against the counter. It's supposed to make them chewier."

He smiled and shook his head. "That sounds completely ridiculous."

"Sure it does, but these brownies—I'm not willing to risk messing them up. I will bang pans against the counter every single time if that's what it takes."

We talked about our families for a while, siblings, parents, experiences growing up. It took only a few minutes to determine that we both hailed from families that paid little attention to sports, loved to read books, and could sing entire Broadway musicals from beginning to end. The coincidences made us laugh more than once.

But without our really trying, whatever topic we landed on always seemed to lead us back to music. Like mine, his family had always been musical. His older sisters played the piano, his brothers were singers, and both brothers played the guitar. It made sense with so much music in the background the youngest would be musically inclined as well. But his family never expected Elliott, at four years old, to sit down with a little toy keyboard and pick out the melody to "Twinkle, Twinkle, Little Star." His mom sat next to him and started naming songs, and every single one, he picked out after just a few experimental notes. The music was in him. All they had to do was give him the tools to get it out.

"Did you always love it? Through all the practicing?" I asked.

"Not always. I quit once, when I was thirteen. Told my parents I wasn't ever going to play again."

"How long did that last?"

"About twenty minutes." He smiled. "I couldn't do it. Mostly because there was always music in my head; I needed to play so it had some place to go."

"So you've always been composing." I put my empty ice cream bowl on the floor beside the couch.

"Always. I heard music in my head even before I was skilled enough to play its complexity. That was actually frustrating: to hear it but not know how to make it all work."

"That's amazing." *He* was amazing. Hearing him talk about his music, it was hard to put into words how it made me feel. Because I knew without a single doubt that he understood how I felt about my music. I'd long since grown weary of trying to explain how it wasn't just a hobby or a thing I liked to do because I was good at it. It was more like breathing. I *had* to play. I had to feel the music in me and around me. If I couldn't do that, I would only be a shadow of myself—always lacking.

"So let's talk about your music," he said. "I really liked playing with you through the wall. Have I told you that yet?"

"Even if you did, I don't mind you telling me again."

"I've been studying up on my violin concertos. I think I'm ready for a rematch."

"Have you? Now you've got me worried."

"Oh, you should be worried. You're going down."

Flirty, funny, competitive Elliott? He was really adorable. "So the symphony's playing Beethoven's Fifth?" he asked.

"Oh yeah, next week. You've heard me practicing?"

"Yeah. Great music."

"The whole season is great. After the first of the year, Antoneli Baronovsky is coming to play Prokofiev."

"For real? Baronovsky?"

"Do you know him?"

"He's the reason I was in Russia. I was studying in his studio. He's incredible."

"You'll have to come to the concert. I'm sure he'd love to see you."

"Which Prokofiev? Is it the Third? That one's my favorite."

"In C Major. Op. 26."

"Ahhh, great piece. Hard as all get out though."

"I keep forgetting you can hear me every time I practice. Somehow that makes me nervous."

His eyebrows went up, and he gave me a mischievous grin. "I hear your practicing about as well as I hear your conversations."

I froze, suddenly trying to replay every conversation I'd had with Lilly in the past . . . three weeks? Luckily, we weren't home much. We worked, I rehearsed; it wasn't like there were hours of time to sit around with our feet up talking about boys. But . . . I could feel the blush creeping up my cheeks . . . *Yeah*. We'd definitely had our fair share of conversations about Elliott.

I couldn't decide which was worse: the idea of him hearing my earlier ill-conceived rants about his arrogance and idiocy or hearing my ardent declarations that he was most beautiful man I'd ever seen. "So we're going to just rewind our conversation about thirty seconds and pretend like I never heard you say that," I said.

"I promise I'm not spending hours camped out by the wall eavesdropping, if that makes you feel better. I've only heard bits and pieces here and there."

I held my hands up and shook my head. "No! You've heard nothing! It never ever happened!"

He laughed. "Fine. It never happened." He leaned forward and placed his bowl beside mine, then settled back on the couch.

"Why did you move to Asheville anyway?" I asked. "Of all the places you could go, why here?"

His eyes darkened, and he fiddled with a loose thread on the ripped knee of his jeans. "I just needed to not be in L.A.," he finally said. "My focus has been off for a while now, and I was hoping the change of scenery would do me some good."

"But West Asheville? How did you even find Maple Crescent, not to mention this house?"

"Oh. My mom's cousin owns the house."

"What? Julio is your mom's cousin?" I had a hard time drawing a family tree line from Elliott to my short, stocky Hispanic landlord.

"Not-quite cousin but almost? Let me see if I can get this right. My mother's cousin's sister-in-law is married to Julio."

"So basically you're not related at all."

He smiled. "I always see him at family reunions. I stayed with him when I filmed a video over in Cherokee, and he knew how much I loved the area. When he heard I was looking to come east, he called and asked if I wanted the apartment."

"And here you are."

"Here I am."

"Has the change of scenery helped?"

Elliott frowned. "Not really."

"What's tripping you up?"

"The biggest problem is the album my label wants me to make isn't the album I want to make. I want to do all originals, and they want top-forty covers. I'm hoping we find a middle ground, but so far, it's not looking good." He spoke with a detached calmness that hinted at a history of disagreements with his label.

"Your original stuff is brilliant. I can't believe they wouldn't want it."

"They only want what they think is going to sell. They branded me as a crossover contemporary pianist, and that's where they want to keep me. They get to say what I play, where I play, and when I play it."

"Is that why the stake sent that letter about you not performing in church? Because of your label?"

He sighed. "I really didn't love that letter. And performing in church isn't actually the issue. They don't care about stuff like that. But the invitations from Church members are usually for other stuff. Birthday parties, graduation parties. The church gives them an in, and they just ask without really considering the implications."

"And your label doesn't want you to play just anywhere, right? You've got to maintain that feeling of exclusivity."

"It's lame."

"It's lame that you don't have more control over your career. You're so much more than where they're trying to keep you."

"Nope. I'm not allowed to be more than that. Granted, my contract is worse than most. *Talent Hunt* negotiated the entire thing and pretty much sold my soul."

I shifted on the couch, pulling my legs up under me. "So why not just walk?"

He shot me a weary look. "It's not that easy."

"Why not? If you don't like the music they want you to play, why play it? It ought to be about the music, and if the music isn't working for you, you're the only one who can change it."

Elliott's entire posture changed, and I immediately wished I could take back my words. Who was I to tell him what he needed to do for his career?

"Sorry. That was an overstep on my part. I can't pretend to know all the complexities of your contract and . . . everything." *Lame. Lame, Emma!*

"No, you're fine," Elliott said with a shrug. "But yeah, it is complicated."

"It's not always all it's cracked up to be, is it?"

"What? Fame?"

"No, not just that. I mean, all I wanted was to perform all over the country, to be good enough that people called *me*. When I actually made it, I was on this high for months, like I couldn't believe I was actually living my dream. But then . . . I don't know. The novelty wore off, and I realized how lonely I was. I'd made my life about nothing but music, and recognizing the things I hadn't made room for was hard."

"That's when you went back to Cleveland?"

I felt a little tug at my heart. I nodded. "And it helped. I was closer to my grandma, and my schedule was a little less demanding. But even still, there were things I didn't like. Sometimes I would go weeks without making it to church because my weekends were full of performances. And my social life was almost nonexistent."

"Your grandma's still in Cleveland?"

"Yeah. Twenty minutes outside the city. I might miss her most of all."

"How different is it playing here in Asheville?"

"It still feels good to perform, but I went from more than a hundred performances a year to less than fifteen. The plan was to play with other symphonies—Hendersonville, Knoxville, maybe. And there are auditions in Atlanta next month. But I'm not sure it's going to work. I can't be as busy as I was in Cleveland if I'm also going to be around to help my mom."

"Not many people would have the courage to walk away like you did. That you were willing to sacrifice so much for your family says a lot about your character."

"Thanks. Sometimes I worry I made the wrong decision, but I don't know. Things are good here too. I like being in Asheville."

Elliott shifted so he was sitting sideways on the couch, facing me. His movement only made our knees touch, but in my hyper-aware state, even that felt like a big deal. He smiled. "I think I like you being in Asheville too."

There was an energy sparking between us—something slightly nervous and slightly exciting and completely new that made my insides get all twisted. It was ridiculous how good it felt, how much it had me wanting to rub my fingers across the stubble on his jaw line or feel the softness of his lips against mine. I could tell by the look in his eyes he was feeling something similar. He leaned in, his gaze dropping to my lips, but then pulled back like he'd suddenly thought better of getting that close. He jumped off the couch, sweeping the ice cream bowls off the floor with such dizzying speed I hardly knew what had happened before he was halfway into the kitchen.

"So how long have you been playing with the symphony?" He spoke over his shoulder as he disappeared around the corner.

I tried not to sound too deflated. "Um. I guess it's been three, almost four months now."

He reappeared in the living room. "That's it? I didn't realize you'd been here such a short time."

I shrugged. "That's it. I moved in June."

Elliott moved to the piano and sat down. When he didn't look up from the keyboard, his fingers jumping silently from one key to the next, I wondered if maybe I'd outstayed my welcome. I got up. "I think I'm going to head home."

He stood from the piano bench. "No, don't. I didn't mean for you to go." He pulled a kitchen chair around the corner and sat it a few feet away from the piano, facing him. "Here. Sit here." He looked at me with such boyish enthusiasm I couldn't help but grin.

"Okay," I said slowly. "Why?"

"Because it's been a good night and I'm feeling a little . . . inspired." His right hand danced over the keys, forming the shadow of a melody—soft and sweet. He paused and looked up. "I think maybe there's music in here somewhere. If you leave, you might take it with you."

I moved to the chair and sat. "Just how long are you expecting me to sit here?"

He only smiled.

And then he started to play.

An hour later, I'd moved to the bench beside him, watching the melody pour from his fingers. His face was flushed, his eyes focused, and his attention wholly on the music he was working out minute by minute. At one point, after a ten-minute stretch of nothing but music, I nudged him and asked if he wanted me to go. It wasn't meant to be a selfish question. I could just tell he was in the zone. I didn't want to distract him. He looked up and smiled. "Please don't. I like you here."

So I stayed and watched and listened as the song took shape.

"So this part here," Elliott said. He played a few measures high on the keyboard. "This will be violin." He turned. "You want to try it? I'd love to hear how it will sound."

"I do want to try it, but . . ." I glanced at my watch and gave him an apologetic look. "It's after midnight."

He looked surprised. "Oh man. I'm sorry. I didn't realize it had gotten so late."

"Please don't apologize. This has been amazing. To see your brain work through the music like that . . . I'm glad I stayed."

He shifted a hair closer, and my heart started pounding. I was close enough to feel his warmth, see his pulse pounding in the hollow of his throat. "I'm glad you stayed too." It felt like an echo of our earlier conversation right before he'd bolted off the couch, but this time he wasn't moving away. His words were soft and slow and almost sultry, and I felt completely incapable of getting myself back to my own apartment. Walking shouldn't be hard—left foot, right foot, and all that—but I couldn't move, my hands gripping tightly to the sides of the piano bench where I still sat. I was keenly aware of his gaze moving from my eyes downward and lingering on my lips.

He leaned in, and I closed my eyes, waiting for his lips to meet mine. His kiss was feather light at first, a soft brush against my cheek that moved closer and closer to my lips, one tiny kiss at a time. The anticipation was enough to drive me mad; when our lips finally touched, I leaned forward, one hand moving to his cheek, the other grabbing a fistful of his T-shirt while I deepened the kiss. Heat flared between us, a crackling, delicious tension that I felt all the way down to my bones. He moaned a low, guttural moan, then tensed and pulled away. "Emma, wait."

"Sorry. Was that . . . too much?"

"No. Don't apologize for that. *That* was amazing." He heaved a sigh and dropped his head, his eyes staring into the floor. "But I don't know that I can do this."

I'm sure we can. And we should. Again. Right now. "What do you mean? What changed in the past thirty seconds?"

He pushed his hands through his hair and shook his head. "Nothing changed." He reached up and aimlessly brushed his fingers across the piano keys, forming silent chords one after another. He finally played an arpeggio that climbed two octaves, then shifted into a few measures of the melody he'd been working on just minutes before. He let his hands fall from the keyboard and turned his attention back to me. "The thing is, I've been trying so hard to stay focused. But when you show up, I don't want to focus on anything but you. I can't think straight when you're around."

"I'm not sure thinking straight is really all that important."

He gave me a small smile and shook his head.

"Are you saying you want me to go?"

"No." He answered quickly. "Of course I don't, but you saw how my agent reacted when that photo surfaced from the festival. I know I told you a little about my album struggles, but it's worse than I let on. My career is in a really rough place right now, my label literally watching my every move. They are waiting for me to screw up and will jump on any reason they can find to drop me."

"Why would *they* drop *you*? I thought they wanted another album."

"They wanted it months ago. The fact that I haven't delivered makes me a liability. The second they think I'm not prioritizing to give them what they want, I'm done."

"But you could walk away, right? They don't own you."

"They do. Every ounce of my success is tied to that label."

"Still, they aren't the only record label out there. Surely you could find someone who would let you play what you want." I was starting to feel like a nine-year-old arguing about the stock exchange—completely out of my depth. Plus, I had to sound a little desperate. He was telling me he didn't want our super-amazing, hot-and-steamy kiss to happen again, and I was essentially begging him to reconsider. I *did* have some dignity.

"It's more complicated than that," he said. "If I fail to deliver what they want, they could sue me for breach of contract. I came to North Carolina for the express purpose of getting away from anything that might serve as a distraction."

"And I'm a distraction." I tried to stand, but he reached over and grabbed my hand.

"You're the very best kind of distraction. There's just so much on the line. I have to be extra careful."

I really wanted to believe his reasons were legit, and I for sure wasn't going to whine about it, but rejection was still rejection. I pulled my hand away. "It's okay. I get it."

"Please don't say that. I swear I'm not just feeding you a line." He lifted his hands and almost reached for me but then seemed to reconsider, running his fingers through his hair instead.

"Line or not, you're still telling me to stay away."

He sighed. "Maybe not completely. It was fun having you here tonight. But I think we need to keep things simple and stay just friends. At least until I get my album finished."

It felt ridiculously unfair that we were even having this conversation. That kiss was the most amazing thing I'd ever experienced, and now he was saying that was it? I understood dedication to career and craft, but *just friends*? I couldn't decide if it would be worse to stay away or worse to still see him but not kiss him.

I stood and walked to the kitchen, picking up the ice cream bowls he'd rinsed and left on the counter. He followed me to his front door.

"I'm sorry it has to be so complicated," he said.

I gave him a sad smile. "It's okay. I'm a musician too, remember? I know how important it is to stay focused."

We said good night, and I slipped into my apartment, leaning against the closed door behind me. The entire evening felt surreal—from Elliott's impromptu composing to the confession of his feelings to the *taking back* of his feelings—it was hard to make sense of it all.

But I could make sense of one thing. I'd never experienced anything like that kiss.

I was still leaning against my apartment door when a knock sounded right behind my head—short, quick raps with a frenzied, frantic edge.

I swung it open.

"Elliott, what's wrong—?"

He cut off my words with a kiss, his hands cradling either side of my face. I hesitated only a moment before wrapping my arms around him and pulling in close against his chest. Our first kiss had been gentle, but this was different, charged with a fervency that left me breathless. A moment or two longer and he broke the kiss but stayed close. I leaned in, savoring the feel of his arms around me. He leaned his forehead against mine.

"What was that?" I asked.

"Feast before famine," he whispered, then leaned in to kiss me again.

Chapter 18

OVER THE NEXT COUPLE WEEKS, my schedule was totally swamped, which I guess was a good thing. It made it easy to just be *friends* with Elliott. We hardly even saw each other. I had back-to-back symphony weeks, the first for our Beethoven concert and the second for a series of daytime education concerts for the local schools. With all the rehearsing and performing, my visits with Mom were pushed into the early-morning hours or after my afternoon lessons, so it felt like I was constantly coming or going.

I did see Elliott at church and then outside on the front porch and in the entryway between our apartments a few different times, but I never had time for more than a quick hello. Even in those brief moments, the tension and heat still flared between us. He looked at me with an intensity that made me feel like he was seeing all the way into my heart. He didn't even have to say anything more than "How are you?" It left me hungry for him, not just for his touch but for his conversation. He'd said feast before famine, and he was totally right. No Elliott in my life definitely felt like famine.

By the time Friday rolled around—the Friday I was having dinner with Blake—I was missing Elliott in a bad way. So bad I wasn't even sure I could make it through dinner with another guy. Only Lilly's scolding kept me from calling to cancel. "You said yourself it's just dinner. You already said yes. Just go and have a good time," she said.

Pretty sure she was just sick of hearing me whine.

A few hours before my date, just after my last afternoon lesson, my cell phone rang. Mom called me all the time when things were fine, but since moving home, my heart lurched whenever her picture appeared on my screen, a tiny moment of panic when I knew she'd fallen and hurt herself or gotten bad news from the doctor . . . or *something*. Whenever I heard her cheerful voice on the other end of the line, I breathed a sigh of relief. But this time, she didn't sound so cheerful.

"Hey, Mom, what's up?"

She sighed. "Are you sitting?" I could hear the strain in her voice.

"Oh no. What is it? What happened? Are you hurt?"

"Calm down, Emma. I'm fine. Everything's fine."

"Then why do I need to be sitting?" I perched on the arm of the couch in the living room just to be safe.

"I just caught your sister trying to dub the audio of you playing the Barber concerto into her own video."

I immediately stood back up. "She what? Is that even possible?"

"Possible and almost finished," Mom said. "If I hadn't walked into her room when I did, she might have gotten away with it."

I started pacing around the room. "Why would she, Mom? She's smarter than that."

"I don't know, sweetie. Honestly I'm so frustrated with her right now, I could just . . . I don't know what I could do. Your father and I are going to talk about it tonight and decide how to handle things. I just wanted you to know in case she tries to come to you for support."

"Why would she come to me? It was my recording she was trying to steal."

"She actually argued that to her favor, said she could have stolen audio from any number of performances on the Internet. She used yours because she figured if she got caught, you'd be the least likely to turn her in."

"How comforting."

Mom kept talking, relaying the justifications Ava had given her, but I was already stomping around my room, looking for my shoes and car keys. I didn't want to hear Ava's reasons filtered through Mom. I wanted her to tell me to my face what she was trying to prove.

"Is Ava at home right now?" I asked Mom. "Is she there?"

Mom's voice sounded heavy, tired. "She's at the high school. There's a pep rally before the football game tonight."

"A pep rally? She pulls a stunt like this, and she gets to go to a pep rally?"

"Don't tell me how to parent, Emma. Your sister is grounded after tonight, but she had responsibilities at the school—committees she's worked on. And she's covering the game and the rally for the local paper. It's an important day for her."

It sounded like my mother was speaking a different language. Pep rallies and football games? When had Ava ever been interested in stuff like that?

"Fine. I'll just go see her at the school." I flew out of my apartment and down the porch steps, my anger growing hotter by the second.

"Please don't go to the school. A confrontation isn't what Ava needs right now."

"A confrontation is exactly what she needs. Is she even thinking about what that video means? If my professor were to pull strings to get her into Cleveland and then discover it's all a sham? Mom, that's my name on the line. *My* credibility. Why would she do this to me?"

"I don't really think she was thinking about you."

"My point exactly." I climbed into my car and slammed the door. "Thanks for telling me, Mom. I gotta go." I hung up and tossed the phone onto the seat beside me.

It was possible that somewhere in the back corners of my mind I realized I might be overreacting. But the conflict between Ava and me had been building for weeks and weeks. She'd been ignoring me, belittling my efforts, refusing to recognize the importance of what I was trying to help her do. She'd never make it in the industry if she wasn't willing to work hard. I knew better than anyone. The fact that she was flouting that knowledge and trying to cheat instead? It burned.

A memory of Ava calling and asking me to come over to help her practice the Barber concerto flashed through my mind. It was the only time she'd *ever* reached out to me on her own. And she'd only reached out so she could trick me into making a recording.

I was still seething when I pulled down the long winding drive of Ava's high school. There were cars everywhere—stupid cars of stupid people who thought football was a good way to spend an afternoon. I had to park in the sophomore parking lot twelve thousand miles away from the stadium and hike my way through the crowd. The game hadn't started yet, only the pep rally, so at least the ticket guy was forgiving, letting me slip into the stadium without buying a ticket. I tried to call Ava twice, then three times, and got no answer. When I called a fourth time, her phone went straight to voice mail. She'd turned her phone off completely.

I found her just outside the concession stand at the south end of the stadium, dressed in annoying red, white, and blue, a tiny Falcon painted on her left cheek.

"Ava!" I called.

She spun around, her eyes wide.

"Can we talk a minute?"

She hefted a box from the ground at her feet and carried it through the concession stand's back door. "I'm sorta busy right now."

A tall boy with sandy hair and broad shoulders took the box from Ava's hands. "I got this, Av. You can take a minute if you need to."

She shot him an annoyed look. "It's fine," she said pointedly. "I don't need a minute." She turned back to me, her arms folded across her chest. "I don't have *anything* to talk about."

"No? Maybe I'll just talk, then. Maybe I'll just bring up right here in front of your friends what you've—"

Ava lurched across the room and grabbed my arm, hauling me back into the late afternoon sunlight. "Shut. Up," she said through her teeth.

She still gripped my arm, and I shook her loose. "You have a lot of nerve telling me to shut up. Why did you do it? You at least owe me that much. *Why?*"

"I owe you? Are you completely demented? I don't owe you anything."

Her words stung more than I'd expected. "What does that even mean? You *stole* my music, Ava. You tried to *cheat*. How could you ever stoop that low?"

"You didn't give me a choice! All you do whenever we talk is nag and harp and demand. It's practice, practice, practice all the time. It's exhausting, Emma. You're making me crazy!"

"So talk to me about it! I'd rather you yell at me and complain than try to cheat your way into Cleveland."

"You don't get it. I don't even *care* about Cleveland."

"I can't get it if you won't talk to me! Please just help me understand what's going on inside your head."

She kept her eyes down, her shoe toying with the loose gravel scattered under our feet. "I don't *want* . . ." Her words trailed off, and her shoulders slumped.

"You don't want what?" I asked. "To explain?"

"No. I don't *want* to play the concerto."

For real? That was all? "Oh. Well, you can pick a different piece. Why didn't you just say you didn't want the Barber?"

She shook her head. "You're not hearing me, Em. I don't want to *play*. It's not what I want."

I could only stare. *Of course* she wanted to play. All she'd ever wanted to do was play. "You don't really mean that."

"I do mean it. And I don't want to talk about it anymore." She turned without another word and headed toward the bleachers. It was like watching a stranger walk away. Did I know my sister at all?

I was numb driving back to Asheville. I tried to take a step back and look at Ava objectively, but it was hard to filter out my own emotions. As long as I could remember, Ava had always wanted to play violin—*just* like her big sister. It was our thing, something we shared and enjoyed together. My years in Cleveland had made it a little harder for us to really share our love for music in person, but everybody still knew music was in Ava's blood just like it was in mine. Plus, she was so incredibly talented. If she actually did quit? What a colossal waste.

* * *

Elliott was sitting on the front porch with a book when I got home. I glanced at my watch. Forty minutes till rehearsal started. *Of course.*

"Hey," he said, standing up. "You okay? You look sad."

I frowned. "I'm okay. Just got in a big fight with my sister."

"You want to talk about it?"

I wanted to talk about the price of peas in Indiana if it meant getting to stand next to him a few more minutes. Two weeks of keeping my distance had left me wanting. "It's . . . I don't know. It's dumb. Ava says she wants to quit violin, which doesn't make any sense. She's too good to quit."

Elliott folded his arms. "It's hard to know what you want at that age."

I scoffed. "I knew exactly what I wanted at that age."

He chuckled. "Lucky you."

Lucky me? "What's that supposed to mean?"

"No, sorry. I didn't mean for that to sound like an insult. I'm just saying . . . not everyone is that lucky. I'm twenty-six and still don't feel like I know exactly what I want."

"You know you want music."

"Well, yeah. But there's a lot of ways music can be a part of your life. Maybe that's what you ought to tell Ava. If she doesn't follow in your footsteps, she could still find other ways to make music matter."

There was wisdom in Elliott's words, but they still bugged. It shouldn't be personal, but I'd been so invested in Ava. Everything about what she'd done felt personal, like her quitting was an individualized attack.

I opened the front door. "I gotta get to rehearsal."

"Emma, I'm sorry if I said the wrong thing. I probably don't know enough about your sister to have an opinion."

I shook my head. "It's fine. I'm sure you're right. And tomorrow when I'm not still angry, I'll realize it and want to thank you for being so smart."

He smiled. "I'll look forward to it."

I gave him a halfhearted smile and moved inside. He was lucky I'd managed that much.

"Wait." He followed me into the entryway. "Can I buy you dinner tonight after rehearsal? Are you free?"

I raised an eyebrow.

Elliott read my expression and gave me a sheepish grin. "It's just dinner. Dinner can't hurt, right?"

Nope, dinner couldn't hurt anything. In fact, it would probably go a long way to turn my painfully awful afternoon around, even if I didn't like what he'd said about Ava. For dinner and some time spent together, I was totally willing to forgive.

But I couldn't have dinner with Elliott. I had to have dinner with Blake.

"I can't. I . . . have a date."

Elliott's face fell. "Oh."

"It's not a big deal. He's somebody's nephew at church, and he's just visiting and didn't know anybody . . . I was trying to be nice."

"It's cool. You don't have to explain."

I glanced at my watch. Thirty-two minutes to grab a snack, change, and get downtown. It was going to be close. "I really need to go. I'm sorry though. About tonight."

"Don't worry about it." He reached for his apartment door. "Hopefully we can catch up later."

* * *

Blake was sitting in the last chair of the back row of the auditorium when I walked up the aisle after rehearsal, my violin slung over my shoulder.

He stood up and smiled. "Emma?"

I nodded. "Yeah."

"It's good to finally meet you. I'm Blake." He stuck out his hand like he wanted to shake mine, then must have reconsidered, opting instead for a hug. It was almost awkward, but Blake totally saved the situation with his self-deprecating humor. "Was that awkward? I'm just going to tell you straight up I'm a complete dork. Other guys do things, and it comes off as smooth. I do it, and it's awkward and weird. Generally I do much better on dates if I just get that disclaimer out of the way up front. I am not a suave guy."

Grayson appeared beside me, and I started to feel a little panicky. Last he'd heard, I was bringing a boyfriend to his wedding. I silently cursed Bruno for staying away for so long. His super-grandpa status down in Florida was making Grayson a regular fixture in the symphony.

Grayson looked from me to Blake, then smiled. "Great rehearsal tonight, Emma. Is this him? Your boyfriend?"

I winced. "No, this is Blake. We actually just met."

"Oh! Sorry, man. I shouldn't have assumed. Though, I guess there are worse things I could have accused you of. I'm Grayson." He reached out to shake Blake's hand.

"Blake's from Utah," I blurted, my words rushed and slightly frantic. An undercurrent of please-don't-make-me-explain-where-my-real-but-not-real-boyfriend-actually-is clung to every syllable I spoke. "He's in town visiting his aunt, and she's a friend from church, so . . . yeah. We're just going to go get something to eat."

It was awkward. *Totally* awkward. I didn't want Blake to think I had a boyfriend, because it would have been rude of me to say yes to his date if I did, which meant I really needed Grayson to be cool and not say anything else incriminating. If I kept flinging unnecessary details at him, maybe he'd just hurry and leave.

Fortunately Grayson *was* a suave guy, so he handled my detail flinging with grace. "Welcome to Asheville," he said to Blake. "Emma knows all the best places to eat. I'm sure you won't be disappointed." He touched me lightly on the elbow. "Later, Em. Good night to you both."

I turned my attention back to Blake. "Sorry. That was . . . weird. He's an old friend."

"An old boyfriend?"

I shrugged. "Yes. But it was a long time ago. He's actually getting married in a few weeks."

"Yeah? I guess that's cool. And, hey, now I can mark 'Run into your date's ex' off my dating bucket list."

"That is so not on your bucket list."

"Sure it is. I just added it," Blake said.

He was adorable—great lines when he smiled and killer brown eyes that got all bright and happy as he talked. I was generally one to go for the dark, brooding, artistic types, and this guy was definitely not *that*. But there was something appealing about the openness and genuine friendliness of his face.

"See? That guy?" He motioned in the general direction Grayson had gone. "That guy's smooth. You can just tell by the way he carries himself. He's never going to be embarrassed on a date or worry he'll say the wrong thing. He will never go anywhere and get caught with his fly down. He probably has specially engineered pants so he's never at risk for fly exposure."

I laughed. "Sometimes being smooth isn't all it's cracked up to be. I think your honesty is more impressive."

"Phew. I'm never sure about that first impression. My mother told me once I act like an overeager puppy. No matter how much I try to be cool and calm, it's those words that plague the first ten minutes of every single first date."

"That makes it sound like you've had a lot of first dates."

His cheeks colored. "No! I mean, enough I guess. Enough that I think I've finally figured out what I'm looking for."

His comment hit me right in the gut. It sounded like this guy was playing for keeps. I didn't want to hurt him, but every second I was with him just cemented the fact that my head was not in the same game. I tried to go for cool and casual, maybe even a little indifferent. "It must be nice to know what you want."

We walked out of the auditorium and through the lobby.

"You don't know?"

Yeah, I did. And his name was Elliott. "I don't know. I thought I did. Maybe I still do."

Blake chuckled. "That's the most unconvincing statement I've ever heard." We hit the sidewalk, and he pointed to the lot across the street. "I'm over here. Want to ride with me?"

"Yeah, that'd be good. Are you hungry?"

"Absolutely. Where are we headed?"

"I was thinking we could stay downtown and go over to the Chestnut. Great food, and they serve dinner late so we won't have trouble getting a table." I glanced at my watch. "Actually, do you feel like walking? We could drive in five minutes . . . probably walk in fifteen or so."

"I'm up for a walk," he said. "You want to put your violin in your car? Or my car, if it's closer."

My eyes went wide. No way, no how was I leaving my violin in any car anywhere.

Blake held his hands up. "Or we can just keep it with us. That's cool too."

"Sorry. It's . . . Violins aren't cheap. I'd rather keep it with me." I pulled the strap of my case over my head and settled the instrument comfortably across my back. We turned and headed down Haywood Street into the heart of downtown.

"I was reading up on the inner mechanics of the symphony while you were finishing rehearsal."

"Yeah? What'd you learn?"

"I read about the conductor. He's the most important one, right?"

"That's Dr. Williamson. He's our music director and conductor and is definitely the most important one."

"And then there's someone called the concertmaster? And he's like the next guy down, sort of second in command?"

"He *or* she," I added.

"Oh, yeah, absolutely. Wait—is it you?"

"Yes, but it's not that big a deal."

"Sure it is. It sounded like a pretty big honor. You have to be the best one to do all that jazz."

I shrugged. "I guess so, yeah."

"That's pretty sweet," Blake said. We moved around a street magician wowing a small crowd with a deck of cards, the top card hovering in the air above the others. A woman passed her hand under the hovering card and gasped as the crowd started to clap.

Blake smiled. "This is a great city."

"It's never boring, that's for sure." Though it was just past ten, people were everywhere, gathering on street corners, spilling onto the sidewalk in front of the bars and restaurants that made Asheville famous. "The city is mostly about food and beer," I continued. "That's what people come for."

"I read something about all the microbreweries in the area."

"They're everywhere. But the food is great too. Lots of farm-to-table and eat-local stuff."

We crossed the street to the next corner, and Blake turned and grabbed my arm. "Do you hear that?" he asked. "What is it?"

I smiled. "That's the drum circle at Pritchard Park. Come on. We're almost there."

"The drum circle?"

"It happens every Friday night. People just bring their drums and jump in." We moved across the street and stood right on the edge of the park. The circle was probably twenty people strong, a mash-up of rhythms that shook into the ground, then reverberated up through the sidewalk and into our feet.

"This is seriously the coolest thing I have ever seen." Blake started swaying, his shoulders bouncing to the rhythm of the drums pouring out of the park.

"Welcome to Asheville," I said with a smile.

"Have you ever done it? I totally want to do it."

A Jamaican man standing beside us turned. "You want to try? Here. Use my drum. There's a spot for you right there."

"For real? Do you want to do it?" Blake turned and looked at me, his eyebrows raised in question.

"No, this is all you. Go ahead."

He grabbed the drum and jumped into the circle like a, well, like an overeager puppy. His mom was totally right. I moved to an empty park bench and sat down, my violin case lying across my lap, and pulled my cell phone out of my purse. I had a text from Elliott. *Remember when I said you on a date with someone was cool? I didn't mean it.*

My heart started to race, and I glanced up at Blake as if he would know just from looking at me I was texting another guy. He was fully engaged in his drumming so I turned back to my phone. *You sound a little like a jealous boyfriend.*

I was going for more of the older-brother vibe.

You spend much time kissing your sister?

No. No, I don't.

I shouldn't have brought up the kissing. No way I was keeping my head in the game with Blake if I was reliving my make-out session with Elliott.

I think about that night all the time, he wrote.

I read his text, then quickly turned my phone over, dropping it into my lap. This was so totally not a while-dating-another-guy kind of conversation. But, then, it wasn't like I could just leave Elliott hanging. I scooped my phone back up, flexing my fingers as I tried to figure out what to say. Finally I keyed in a response. *That's breaking the rules. You're only supposed to think in music notes.*

His response was almost immediate. *The rules are stupid.*

You're the one who made the rules.

Permission to reconsider? Staying away from you is only making things worse.

You're only saying that because now I'm out with someone else.

That's not true. It's why I wanted to take you to dinner. Because I wanted to tell you I was wrong about being just friends.

Oh my holy cow. I snuck another peek at Blake. Much to my relief, he was still facing away from me, not noticing my insta-grin or trembling hands.

Well then, I guess that's different, I wrote.

Is he a nice guy?

He's a very nice guy.
Name?
Blake.
Last name?

I rolled my eyes. *Blake Johnson. Mormon. Attorney. From Ogden, Utah. Visiting his aunt and interviewing for a job with an Asheville firm. About six feet, blond hair, brown eyes. Anything else you want to know?*

Sorry. I'm being rude.
I'm willing to forgive if your reasons are good enough.
Blinding, maddening jealousy?

"Emma!" I looked up. Blake was standing at the edge of the drum circle next to the Jamaican man from earlier and a kid in a backward baseball cap who had been dancing his way around the park. "You got to see this kid! Come watch what he can do."

"Just a sec," I called. I glanced back at my phone. *Gotta go. Call you later?*

Yes, please.

It took all my willpower to put my phone away and give my full attention back to Blake.

We spent a few more minutes in the drum circle, watched the crazy dancing of a kid we decided for sure was going to be famous someday, then headed to the restaurant and had a nice dinner. It was *nice*. Blake was *nice*. And funny and charming and thoroughly entertaining. And it was a good thing because had he not been all those things, there was no way I would have made it to the end of the night without bailing and heading to Elliott's.

It was just after midnight when we made it back to the concert hall. Blake leaned against the side of my car while I unlocked the door and put my violin inside.

"I had a nice time tonight," he said.

"Yeah, me too."

"Really?" He shoved his hands into his pockets and scrunched his eyebrows.

"Yeah, really. It was fun."

"Hmm. I'm not sure I believe you."

Okay. Weird. "Do I sound like I'm lying?"

"No, I was just trying to figure out if what my aunt said was true."

Uh oh. "What did she say?"

He grimaced. "Only that you might not be interested in going out with me since you're hung up on someone else."

My cheeks flamed red. "I don't . . . There's not . . . Why would she say that?"

"I wasn't trying to make it sound like a bad thing. Sorry if I embarrassed you."

"It's fine. I guess I just forget how observant my fellow ward members are. I don't always understand their persistence in wanting to marry me off."

He chuckled. "It's a cultural thing, I think. They just want you to be happy."

"I guess so."

"So *are* you interested in someone else?"

There was only one way to answer his question. I'd tried to have an open mind about Blake, but it was hopeless. I couldn't get Elliott out of my head. "Blake, if I had a single friend, you would be at the very top of my list of guys she should date."

"But I'm not on *your* list."

"I'm sorry. This thing with this other person—I didn't really know what was going to happen when I agreed to go out with you. Things are still kinda new, but . . . I think I have to give it a chance."

"Oh, I totally get it." His tone shifted. "I mean, it's not like I could really compete with the glitz of fame and fortune anyway. If that kind of thing makes you happy, I guess I wish you well."

My eyes narrowed. Guess dear old aunty hadn't held back. "Okay, that was an entirely inappropriate thing to say. You don't know anything about what makes me happy."

He huffed. "Right. You girls are all the same."

We girls? Blake's demeanor had changed so suddenly I felt like I was looking at a different person. Not five seconds ago he'd been apologizing for embarrassing me, and now he was smug and judgmental? And for what? Because he was jealous of a guy he didn't even know? I resisted the urge to defend myself and insist my feelings for Elliott were based on way more than money or fame. But I didn't owe Blake an explanation. I didn't owe him anything. "You know what? I really believe you're a nice guy. Don't say something stupid and ruin it."

"You know the last girl I dated had a poster of him on her wall?"

Wait? What? "A poster of Elliott?"

"Yeah. She talked about him all the time. How stupid ironic is it that two dates in a row both girls have a thing for the same famous guy. How am I supposed to compete with that?"

My brain was having a hard time moving past the whole poster-of-Elliott comment. Did people even still do that? Buy actual posters of people and hang them on their walls? Better question: did grown women buy posters and hang them on their walls? I'd joked about them when I was determined to show Elliott I wasn't really a fan, but I was just being facetious. I didn't really think posters were still a thing. "I guess that is sort of a weird coincidence," I finally said. "But, Blake, Elliott and I have a lot in common. This isn't a poster-on-the-wall kind of thing. I don't own *any* Elliott posters. We're just getting to know each other like normal people do."

He heaved a sigh. It sounded like defeat. Or maybe just resignation. "Man. Dating stinks."

I leaned against the car beside him, rubbing my hands up and down my arms. The temperature around us had dropped, and a chill crept through the thin fabric of my jacket.

"I agree," I said. "Dating absolutely stinks. But only until it doesn't."

"For real? That's your take? It only stinks until it doesn't?" At least he was smiling again.

"So maybe eloquence isn't exactly my strongest skill," I joked. "I'm just saying, one day you'll meet somebody, and suddenly dating won't stink anymore. And all that time that stuff felt rough won't matter because you'll realize the timing with this new person is just what it's supposed to be and everything makes sense. You just have to wait for it."

"You make it sound way easier than it is."

"It's not easy. More like awful. I moved to Asheville and thought I'd committed dating suicide."

"But then you met somebody."

I shrugged. "I hope that's the way things are going." I stifled a yawn, and Blake smiled.

"Sorry. I know it's late." He gave me a hug. "Thanks for tonight, and I mean that for real. I swear I'm not actually a jerk."

"I believe you," I told him.

We said good night, and I drove home preoccupied with the idea of Elliott posters plastered all over America's walls. It wasn't so much that it bothered me. It was just . . . weird. I wondered if it bothered Elliott—the idea of women fixating on him, staring at his picture, imagining conversations, kisses, relationships that wouldn't ever actually exist.

I texted Elliott as soon as I was in the driveway. There was a light on in his window, which I hoped meant he was still awake. *You still up?*

Waiting for you. Want to come over?

He was standing in his doorway when I made it inside. He gave me an appraising glance but kept his distance.

"How was your date?"

"It was fine, thank you."

"I'm glad you had a nice time."

Ha. Right. "Are you really?" I gave him a playful smile that he returned with a little half grin and a cocky shrug of his shoulder.

"It's possible I was hoping the night was a total bust." He crossed the entryway, *finally*, and stopped right in front of me, hooking his pinkie finger around mine and sending my heart into an annoyingly obnoxious frenzy.

"It wasn't a bust. He was nice. I just couldn't stop thinking about you."

He slipped an arm around my waist, and I leaned in, breathing him in. "I was hoping you'd say that," he said softly.

Every ounce of me wanted to stay right there in Elliott's arms and forget about the conversation we'd had about timing and careers and albums and focus. His text had said he'd been wrong about staying away, and by the look in his eyes, he really meant it. But my doubt was still there like a heavy piece of jewelry I didn't want to wear. "Elliott, what are we doing?" I finally asked.

"Come on." He motioned to his apartment. "Let's go sit, and we'll talk about it."

I followed him into his living room, where he pulled me onto the couch.

"I think I finally understand what you mean when you say people don't see you," I said. "They only see your fame."

"Where did that observation come from?"

"Blake's aunt told him I was hung up on you, which I don't know how she would even know. But then he got all defensive, saying garbage about how he couldn't compete with the glitz of fame, and if that's the kind of thing that's important to me, then good luck."

"You're hung up on me?"

I swatted at his arm. "Stay focused."

"Sorry. You're right. That's lame." He held my hand, his thumb tracing small circles along the top of my wrist.

"It made me mad. Because I'm more than that. And you're more than that. And . . . Elliott, I don't care about your career. I don't care that you're famous or rich or whatever. It doesn't matter to me."

"I know."

"Do you? I don't want you to think I'm here for the wrong reasons."

"I don't always know. With some people, I can't really tell. But you? I've never worried about you."

I shot him a look, and he grinned. "Okay, after I figured out that my first impression was completely off base, *then* I didn't worry about you."

"I guess I just feel a little violated on your behalf. There will always be someone with an opinion, won't there? Right or wrong, someone will always have something to say."

"But it's like that for everyone, isn't it? Maybe not quite on the same scale, but I think everybody has to decide how much they let the opinions of others bother them. To some extent, at least."

"Did you know there are people with posters of you on their walls? The last girl Blake dated had a poster of you in her apartment."

"For real? Was she twelve?"

"I wondered the same thing."

He sighed and leaned back. "Does it help for me to say you get used to it? I mean, yeah. Sometimes it stinks that there are so many people who . . . *care*. But . . ." He shrugged.

"It's white noise. Like you said before."

He nodded. "In a perfect world, it's white noise. Sometimes it cuts a little deeper than that."

Thinking about him dealing with the media and crazy fans and all the extra demands of his stardom made me want to touch him, to reach out and smooth away the worry and the stress his career brought on. He'd dropped my hand while he was talking, so I reached for his again, weaving my fingers with his.

"So you were saying earlier . . ." I hinted.

He smiled. "I was saying I thought staying away from you was actually a really stupid idea."

"What about your album?"

"I've been working on my album."

"And?"

"And the song I started two weeks ago when you were with me is the best thing I've written in months. I don't think you distract me. I think you inspire me. You make me feel like I can write the kind of music I'm really passionate about."

"I thought you didn't know what you wanted out of your music," I said playfully.

He grinned. "Maybe with your help, I'm figuring it out again."

"So . . . you want me around so I can be your muse."

"Not my muse. It's more like you give me the courage to be my own kind of musician rather than just playing what everyone else tells me to."

Now that was a role I was good with. "Did you finish the song? I want to hear it."

"Not yet. But I've started two others, and they're good. I feel really good about them."

"That makes me happy." I stifled a yawn. I wasn't very good at after midnight. "What now? Have you talked to your label? Because I'm pretty sure if we spend time together in public, they'll find out."

"We probably ought to lie low until I've got a few songs I can send over, but I don't want to hide. I'm trying to be true to myself here, and this is what I want. *You* are what I want."

I'd never really considered what it would mean to hear those words. I'd danced around the idea, but it was always something that wasn't going to happen. Even our first kiss was followed by a conversation about how we couldn't actually be together. All it did was reaffirm the idea that he really was too good to be true. But then he wasn't. Suddenly he was open and willing and right in front of me, and he wanted *me*.

He leaned forward and kissed me, trailing from my lips down to the corner of my jaw, the stubble of several days' beard growth rough against my skin. I closed my eyes, my heart running a marathon, and tried to keep my wits about me. But it wasn't easy.

I was falling.

Hard and fast.

Chapter 19

Come up for air, Emma. There are people who love you and would appreciate a call every now and again.

I winced when I read Gram's text. She was right, but I'd hardly had time to notice. I was committed to two days a week with Mom and obviously couldn't skip out on rehearsals or lessons, but for two straight weeks, every second of free time I'd had, I'd spent with Elliott. Even Lilly complained that I'd completely abandoned our friendship.

The only person glad about my new boyfriend distraction was probably Ava. We hadn't spoken since our pep-rally fight, and I was almost too preoccupied to care. No, that wasn't true. I did care. My anger and frustration over her behavior were still simmering in the background, but Elliott was just so much fun.

I made sure to carve out time for a call to Grandma and made a batch of brownies for Lil. Otherwise, I willingly gave in to Elliott's pull. We played together. We laughed. We kissed. We ate takeout from every restaurant in West Asheville.

Late Wednesday afternoon, I sat on the front porch steps waiting for him. My last three lessons of the afternoon, all siblings who had come down with some sort of stomach virus, had cancelled, giving me an unexpected two hours of freedom, so we were walking to the burger place down the street to pick up some dinner. Elliott was on the phone with his agent, so I waited outside, enjoying the bright October sun.

My phone dinged with an incoming e-mail, and I opened it. My stomach lurched when I saw the sender. Greg McKenzie. *Again.* I opened the message with a sigh. It wasn't the first one I'd gotten that week. Greg had sent two others and left a voice mail the day before. This message was a little shorter, but the gist was still the same. "Emma, have you gotten my messages? The board of directors met again, and they're convinced it can't be anyone but you. They want you back. We all do. Cleveland just isn't the same without you. Please call me. Or call *someone*. David or Sandra . . . anyone. Don't miss this opportunity just because you aren't comfortable calling me. Please? Greg."

Well, that was annoying. Fine, I hadn't answered his e-mail, but it didn't have anything to do with him. Kissing Greg wasn't my proudest moment, but it wasn't that big a deal, certainly not big enough to keep me from returning his calls. I was just preoccupied with Elliott and Mom and . . . Elliott.

Plus, what he was asking was kind of a big deal. Joining the Cleveland Orchestra for a four-month-long European tour?

Yeah. Huge.

The front door opened behind me. "You ready to go?" Elliott was wearing dark sunglasses and a hat. He always wore the hat when we went out. It was a minimal disguise, but most of the time it kept people from looking too closely.

"Yeah." I stood and shoved my phone into my back pocket.

"You okay?" Elliott asked.

"Yeah, I'm good. Sorry, I just got an e-mail about symphony stuff, and I was . . . puzzling some things out."

"Anything you want to talk about?"

I didn't really have a reason not to tell him, but I also didn't love the idea of complicating what was happening between us. Things were *so good*. Anything that might threaten that goodness felt easier left alone. And really, it wasn't like I could even consider going back to Cleveland, especially not if Cleveland actually meant an entirely different continent. Not with Mom's current condition.

"No, it's nothing. It's not a big deal. How's Brian?"

"Brian is happy I'm composing. Not so happy I'm not scouting out locations for a new video."

I had a hard time deciding if Elliott really liked his agent or just merely tolerated him. He seemed like a nice enough guy, but it didn't seem like he cared much about Elliott's creative vision.

"He knows what sells," Elliott had explained once. "It doesn't matter what my creative vision is if it isn't going to make him any money. It's his job."

I got that part, but there had to be a line somewhere, and I worried Elliott was skating dangerously close to it. Things had improved—clearly I was an amazing muse—but I could still see tension while he worked. It was never just about what he wanted for his music. His agent, his record-label people, they were always in his head.

We reached the restaurant and went inside. We weren't staying to eat, just picking up our orders to take back home. Sometimes that was easier. Elliott's phone rang—again—so he stepped outside to answer it. I handed the waitress behind the register a twenty.

She looked toward the door where Elliott had left just moments before. "Is that your boyfriend?"

I smiled. "Yeah."

"I swear he looks exactly like Elliott Hart. The pianist on YouTube? Have you ever seen him?"

"Funny, you're not the first person to tell us that. We'll have to go look him up."

"For real. They could be brothers."

"That's crazy." I took the bags she handed me across the counter. "Thanks!"

Elliott was waiting for me on the sidewalk. He took the bags, and we turned down Haywood, heading back toward home.

"Did you know there's this guy who plays the piano on YouTube?" I asked him. "The waitress back there says the two of you could be brothers."

He smiled. "That's crazy. I wonder if he's any good."

"Mmm, I don't know. I've seen a few videos. It's torture what he does to classical music."

He scoffed and held up the bags of food. "I'm pretty sure this is a cheeseburger in here that you ordered. No steak in these bags."

"Fine, fine. You figured me out. I love cheeseburgers."

As soon as the words were out of my mouth, I froze, heat blazing on my cheeks. I hadn't necessarily intended a double meaning, but it sounded like there was one. Elliott only smiled and reached for my hand. "So what's going on this weekend? You have any gigs?"

I shook my head. "No, just the wedding on Saturday night."

"You're playing a wedding?"

Oh sheesh. "No, it's Grayson's wedding. I'm going as a guest."

Elliott stopped in his tracks. "I totally forgot."

I tucked my hair behind my ear. "It's not a big deal."

"It is a big deal. Did you find someone to go with you?"

Of course I hadn't found someone to go with me. I'd been a little preoccupied the past couple of weeks. But I also hadn't mustered up the courage to ask Elliott to go *again*. It felt weird to bring it up. We'd seen movies and gone out to dinner a few times, and we'd sat together at church the past couple of weeks, but a big fancy wedding at the Grove Park Inn felt significant. And public. And . . . *public*. I wasn't sure I wanted to put Elliott in that position. I'd already worked out my lie to Grayson about why my boyfriend wasn't there after all. It involved bad sushi and food poisoning and was completely plausible.

"I was just going to go by myself."

"What? No! You can't go to your ex-boyfriend's wedding alone. I'm going with you."

"You don't have to do that."

"I want to." We reached our front porch, and he motioned to the chairs in the corner. "Do you want to eat out here? It's almost warm in the sun."

"Yeah, but it's freezing in the shade. Let's go inside." The weather had taken a chilling turn at the beginning of the week, and my wardrobe was still trying to catch up. I'd been perpetually cold for days. "Mine or yours?" We'd been splitting our time pretty equally between his apartment and mine. He had the better studio for music, but I had better food.

"Let's go to my place. Oscar's coming over in an hour."

"How's he doing?" I loved how much Elliott saw of Oscar. The kid was my only competition for Elliott's time.

"He's amazing." He unlocked his front door. "He's already reading music, and he's got a great ear. Everything I say to him just clicks. Teaching him is easy."

"I've got one of those. She's got the most beautiful tone, especially for being so young. And she makes it seem so effortless. It's fun to teach kids like that."

"So why didn't you mention the wedding?" Elliott asked. "I'd have been mad had you really ended up going alone."

"I don't know." I sat at his kitchen table. "Honestly I can't believe I even asked you when I did. I hardly knew you, and I was asking you to pretend to be my boyfriend at my *old* boyfriend's wedding. That's crazy talk."

Elliott pulled the takeout containers out of the bag and handed mine over. "You didn't say anything about pretending to be your boyfriend. That's part of the gig?"

When I explained my conversation with Grayson that led to the fabrication of my imaginary boyfriend, Elliott couldn't stop laughing. "I think I would have ended up doing the same thing. Telling you to beg your cousin to come? That's a low blow."

"See? I thought so too! I acted on impulse. A fake boyfriend seemed way easier than admitting I'd be going alone."

"But now you won't be attending alone. You'll have a real boyfriend with you—in the flesh and *not* pretending."

"A real boyfriend, huh?"

He grinned. "If you'll have me."

Fifteen minutes later, my cell phone rang.

"Hey, Mom. What's up?"

"Emma? I need some help. Are you busy?"

"Not at all. What do you need? What can I do?"

Elliott looked up from his food, concern on his face.

"It's so stupid," Mom said. "I drove myself to the mall to get some shoes, but now that I'm finished, I'm not sure I can get back home. My hands and feet are completely numb."

"Mom, why didn't you ask me to go with you? I'll be over in the morning. I could have taken you."

"I know you could have, but I was feeling fine when I left, and . . . Emma, don't fault me the opportunity to do something on my own."

I hated the strain laced through her words. I understood her desire for independence, but she couldn't have it. Not anymore.

"I tried to call your father," she continued, "but he's in a late meeting, and I don't want to pull him out of work. He'll probably be done in an hour or so . . ."

"You can't wait that long. I can come. I'll be there in ten minutes."

The resignation in Mom's voice was clear. "Thank you. I'm in front of Barnes & Noble. You'll see the car."

I hung up the phone and looked at Elliott.

"Is everything okay?" he asked.

"I have to go get my mom. She drove to the mall, but her symptoms have flared up, and now she can't drive herself home."

"Okay, I'll go with you."

"You can't go with me. Oscar's coming over."

He glanced at his watch. "I'll have to call Laney and reschedule. You'll need another driver to get your mom's car home, right?"

I sighed. "I guess you're right."

"It'll be fine. Laney will understand."

We found Mom sitting in the driver's side of her car, her head pressed against the back of her seat and her eyes closed. I opened her door.

"Hi, Mama."

Her eyes opened, but otherwise, she didn't move. "Hey."

"You okay?"

She shook her head no. I could see the pain building behind her eyes. "Everything just stopped working." She held up her hands awkwardly. "I can't even wrap my fingers around the steering wheel."

"Can you stand? We're going to try to get you into my car, okay?"

Her eyebrows went up. "We?"

"I brought Elliott with me. He's going to follow us back to the house in your car."

Elliott crouched down so Mom could see his face. "Hi, Sister Hill. It's nice to finally meet you."

She smiled through her pain. "I wondered when Emma was going to bring you over."

Between the two of us, Elliott and I managed to maneuver Mom from her car into mine. It seemed easier than moving her all the way around to the passenger side of her car. I buckled her in, and Elliott shut the car door, dangling Mom's keys from his hand. "We make a good team."

"Yeah, we do. Though I'm a little worried about who's going to need our rescuing next. First Trav, now Mom . . ."

"If your dad calls with a flat tire tomorrow, we'll start to worry." He kissed me on the cheek, then moved to Mom's car. "I'll follow behind you."

"Okay. I'll try not to speed."

Inside the car, I reached over and squeezed my mom's knee. "It's going to be okay. Once you're home and off your feet, you'll feel better."

"*Stupid* feet," Mom muttered.

It wasn't alarming that Mom was having a bad day. She'd had many bad days before. What felt alarming was seeing the balance suddenly weighing far more bad than good. It had always been the other way around, but the past few months, not so much. The potential for mobility loss had always been real and likely, but seeing it happen was more difficult than I had anticipated. If Mom moved into her wheelchair full-time, the importance of being close enough to help felt more significant than ever. At the same time, I couldn't be there every day, not with my existing teaching schedule. If I moved in full-time and found a location for my lessons that was a little closer to Hendersonville, I'd be able to do more. I'd never given the possibility any thought, but maybe it was time.

I pulled the car onto the highway, checking my mirror to make sure Elliott was still close behind.

"Did he kiss you before you got in the car?" Mom asked.

I blushed. "Only on the cheek."

"If he's willing to do that much in front of your mother, there's definitely more going on when you're alone. Is it serious?"

I glanced sideways, trying to read her face, but it was useless. Her eyes were closed again, her lips pressed into a thin, tight line. There wasn't room in her expression for anything but pain.

"Yeah, I think it is serious," I finally answered. "At least, I think it's headed that way."

"You really care about him?"

"I do."

"And he cares about you?"

"I think he does."

"That's good, Emma. It makes me happy to see you happy."

A minute more and my phone rang. "Hey, Dad," I answered.

"Hey. Are you with your mom?"

I filled him in on our whereabouts.

"My meeting just wrapped up," he said. "I'll be at the house when you get there."

He was standing in the driveway when we pulled up, where, with the ease of experience and familiarity, he lifted Mom out of my car and carried her through the house and into the living room, where he situated her on the couch. Dad was always a pretty gentle guy, but there was a tenderness that surfaced whenever he was caring for my mom that hit me all the way down in my gut. Mom was lucky to have him. *I* was lucky. My parents were pretty incredible people.

"He looks like he's done that a few times," Elliott said.

I nodded. "Yeah. Even more lately. He's worried about her. We all are."

"So her fingers just stop working?" Elliott asked.

I motioned for him to follow me inside. "Some days they go completely numb; other days they just feel stiff—too stiff to bend or manipulate anything. She calls them her sausage fingers. It happens to her feet too."

Elliott looked down at his hands. "I can't imagine."

"I know. I can't either. Mom used to play the piano, actually, but . . . it's been a few years since she could manage."

Dad emerged from the hallway and crossed to where we still stood just inside the front door. He reached out and wrapped an arm around my shoulders in a half-hello-hug, then extended his hand to Elliott.

"Dad, this is Elliott Hart. Elliott, Jacob Hill."

Dad nodded. "Thanks for your help today." He looked in my direction. "Listen, you two want to stick around a while? I can order us something for dinner."

"We already ate. Besides, do you really think Mom's up for the company?"

He smirked. "I think now that you've finally brought Elliott over, she'll be disappointed if you don't stay. We'll do dessert instead."

"But she needs to rest, Dad. She was in a lot of pain today." *Also, Ava and I still want to kill each other.*

"What she needs is to feel like life isn't going on without her. We'll keep things low key, let her take it easy, but I think she'd like you to stick around."

"Where's Ava?"

Dad gave me a pointed look and glanced at his watch. "On her way to church, I expect. She'll be home in a couple hours."

I looked at Elliott, eyebrows raised in question. He nodded. "Of course. I'd love to stay."

Dad was right. Mom seemed genuinely happy to have us there, despite her confinement to the couch. After dessert, Elliott sat at the piano and entertained us with on-the-spot composing. He'd ask us to name a handful of notes and then write a melody around whatever we listed. We tried to make it hard on him. Mom and I had enough musical knowledge to pick notes we knew would sound awful together. But even the most inharmonious chords turned into something magical in his hands.

Dad watched from the kitchen, a dish towel flung over his shoulder. I moved to stand beside him, pulling the towel off and heading toward the kitchen. "Can I help you finish up?"

"There are just a few things left," he said. "You can dry those plates and put them away if you like."

We worked in silence a few moments until I caught Dad staring at me, his head cocked to the side and a weird, distant look on his face. I paused. "You okay, Dad?"

He smiled. "Sorry. I was just thinking about you."

"What about me?"

"Just how grown up you are now. Seeing you with Elliott, thinking about you getting married . . ."

"Dad, marriage? I think you're getting a little ahead of yourself."

"No, no, I know. I don't necessarily mean to Elliott. Just in general. You're all grown up, Emma. There's a man in there, a full-size man with a job and a car and a life, and he's falling in love with my baby girl. It just makes me feel old and . . . old."

"It didn't make you feel old when *I* got a job and a car and a life?"

"Of course it did. But this is another big step. I'm proud of you. Elliott seems like a good man."

"Thanks, Dad." I crossed the kitchen and gave him a hug. "Is Mom going to be okay?"

He sighed, his arms still wrapped around my shoulders. "I think so. I don't think she's ready to accept what this means."

"The doctors told her last week she needed to mentally prepare herself for the idea of her wheelchair full-time, but they made it seem like it could still be a ways off."

"I don't think it's a ways off at all," Dad said. "I think we're pretty much there. Otherwise, she's going to end up hurting herself.

What if she'd been halfway home when her feet had gone numb today? She can't keep driving."

"I'll come over more," I said. "I can shift some lessons around to free up a couple of afternoons, and I could probably make it over earlier in the mornings on Tuesdays and Fridays. Or"—I realized it was time to give voice to my earlier thought—"Dad, do you need me to move home? If I were here full-time, there would be so much more I could do to help."

Dad took my chin in his hand and tilted my face upward. "Listen to my words, Emma Grace. If you move back into this house, your mother will never forgive herself. Do you understand me? It's already killing her that you're here as much as you are."

"What do you mean? She's not happy that I'm here?"

"She's happy. She loves seeing so much of you. And she's thrilled now that you've met Elliott because we both think this is a good thing between the two of you. But she knows you left Cleveland for her. And every time she hears you play, she berates herself for it—for the career you aren't having because of your commitment to her."

"I didn't move because of Mom."

Dad raised an eyebrow.

I glanced at the floor. "At least not completely. Besides, it's been a good move for me. I'm okay. I'm happy. Mom doesn't need to feel guilty."

"It's not guilt so much as it's sadness over missed opportunity."

"So no moving in?"

"No moving in," Dad repeated. "Just as long as you're minding your manners living across the hall from your boyfriend."

"Dad. Seriously?"

Laughter echoed out of the living room, Mom's voice loudest of all.

"Come on," Dad said, giving me a playful nudge. "Let's go see what's so funny."

Ten minutes later, Ava materialized in the hall, her bag and keys still clutched in her hands. Elliott's hands fell from the piano, and an awkward silence filled the room.

"Hi," I finally said.

"Ava, come in and meet Elliott," Mom said from the couch. "He's been playing for us, and it's been so wonderful."

"I've got homework." Ava turned and walked in the opposite direction, disappearing down the hallway without a backward glance.

Mom sighed. "I'm sorry, Elliott. That was rude of her."

"It's my fault," I said, standing up. "It's me she's trying to avoid, not him. I'll go talk to her."

Elliott reached out and squeezed my hand as I passed the piano.

I knocked on Ava's door. "Hey. Can I come in?"

She didn't answer, but I heard the lock click open. I figured that was as much of an invitation as I was going to get. I eased the door open. Ava was stretched across her bed, her biology textbook open in front of her.

"Can we talk a minute?" I asked.

She didn't look up. "It's not like I unlocked the door so you could stare at me while I study the Krebs Cycle."

"Ugh. Krebs Cycle. I remember." I turned her desk chair around and sat.

"Actually, I really like it. It makes sense to me." Her words were more defensive than they needed to be, like she felt she had to justify her enjoyment of science.

"You've got a better brain than me," I told her. "I never could wrap my head around it."

She rolled her eyes.

"Ava, come on. Can we please just talk?"

"There's nothing to talk about."

"Of course there is. We can't pretend like nothing happened here."

"What do you want me to say? You want me to apologize? Fine. I'm sorry I tried to cheat."

"It stinks that you did it, but I'm more concerned about why."

"I already told you why. You're the one choosing not to hear me."

"I *do* hear you. You don't want to play. But I think that's probably my fault. I've been pushing too hard and pressuring you. I'm going to back off, but I can't accept you just throwing all your talent away. I think you'll regret it if you do."

She didn't look up from her book. In fact, she hadn't looked me in the eye once since I'd entered the room.

"Ava, do you have any idea how talented you really are? You're better than I was at your age. You've been given this amazing gift, and I just don't understand why you don't want to embrace it. So you like science too. What's the big deal? Something like 30 percent of Ivy League medical students get their undergrad degree in music. You don't have to pick one or the other."

She finally dropped her pencil and looked up. "You say that, but you don't mean it. Because people who do both can't be the best at both. And that's the thing with you, Em. There's no acceptable standard but perfection. If you're going to play, you're going to be the best. And anything less will never be good enough. You're trying to turn me into you, and you're *not* hearing me. I *don't want* it."

I stood and walked to the door, afraid of what I might say if I hung out too much longer. "What I'm hearing is that you're throwing away something amazing just to spite your sister. I'm sorry I've put pressure on you, but I'm not sorry I believe you're capable of truly being extraordinary."

"Then brace yourself because you're going to be disappointed. And I'm not sorry about that." She stood and crossed the room, nudging me into the hall before slamming the door in my face.

In the car on the way back to Asheville, Elliott stayed silent for quite some time, maybe sensing my frustration. Maybe just waiting for me to be ready to talk. He finally reached over and touched my knuckles, still white from the tension I held in my shoulders and hands, my fingers curled tightly into fists. "Ready to share?" he asked.

"I just get so frustrated with her," I told him. "It feels like she's rubbing it in my face, you know? Almost like she's giving it up just so she doesn't have to be like me."

Elliott was quiet, which was a little unnerving. I wanted him to agree with me and validate how ridiculously stupid my sister was being. But he didn't say anything at all.

Chapter 20

I STOOD IN THE MIDDLE of Asheville Mall and wished for a fairy godmother who could wave a magic wand and dress me for Grayson's wedding. Though, to be real, Lilly wasn't such a bad choice for a fairy godmother. She knew fashion. She'd also let me whine about my sister problems all the way through dinner. The least I could do was take her wardrobe advice. "Are you sure I can't wear black?"

Lilly rolled her eyes. "You're going to a wedding, not a funeral. Tell me again why we're just now shopping for a dress?" She stared up at the mall directory.

"Because the dress I was going to wear is absolutely not worthy of a date like Elliott."

"Which one? The pale green? With the little brown belt?"

"Yeah. I mean, it's pretty, but it doesn't exactly say *wow*."

"So that's your only requirement?" Lilly said. "A dress that says *wow*?"

"If you're not going to let me wear black."

"Whatever. I've seen your closet, Em. You can't pretend like you don't care about fashion."

"I care about practical, reusable, long-lasting fashion. I don't know how to do fancy dresses unless I'm performing."

"Fine, fine. I'll have mercy on your pitiful soul." She latched onto my arm. "Come on. I know just where to start."

* * *

My faith in Lilly was not ill-placed. When I stood the following afternoon in front of the full-length mirror in my room, delicate folds of deep purple gathering around my waist, hugging my curves and flattering my figure in just the right way, I was sure I couldn't have found a prettier dress had I tried on everything in the entire mall. Lilly had pulled my hair over to the side and pinned it up loosely, giving me an understated look that was elegant without being flashy. It was perfect.

I stepped into my shimmery silver peep-toe pumps and turned to face Lilly. "So I'm good?"

She smiled. "You look beautiful."

Trav was in the kitchen when I passed through to the living room. "Wow. You look amazing."

"Thank you very much." I did a little spin.

"Geez, are you sure I can't take you to the wedding?"

"Stop hitting on my roommate." Lilly joined us in the kitchen. "She'll never say yes, not when her date is way more attractive than you are."

"Good thing your standards aren't quite so high." He wrapped his arms around her, and they kissed.

I moved into the living room just in time to hear a knock at the door. I swung it open to find Elliott wearing the light-gray suit I loved and a deep-purple tie. He looked amazing. And also a little stunned.

"Holy smokes," he finally said. "You look beautiful."

"Thank you." That compliment alone felt totally worth the price of the dress. "Shall we go?"

* * *

We pulled up to the front entrance of the Grove Park Inn just before seven. Valets lined the drive, waiting to assist wedding guests out of their cars and into the luxurious hotel. Elliott tossed the keys to the valet and joined me on the other side of the car, where he offered me his arm.

A couple standing outside the hotel pointed at Elliott, then turned to each other, the woman whispering something to the man. "Are you missing your hat and sunglasses?" I nudged him with my elbow as we followed the signs pointing us through the lobby to the Skyline Room, where the wedding was to be held.

"I considered wearing them but figured with you on my arm, no one's going to pay me any attention."

I blushed. "Did my mother pay you to say that?"

He nodded without skipping a beat. "She slipped a twenty in my pocket before we left your house on Wednesday. My delivery was good though, don't you think? So perfectly timed I think maybe she owes me a tip."

I laughed and earned a reproachful glance from a man looking very much like a stern butler, checking a list of names at the door of the Skyline Room.

"Name?" he asked with dour dignity.

"Emma Hill," I said. "And guest."

His pencil slid down the list with precision and purpose until it landed on my name. For a moment, I panicked, wondering if Grayson had forgotten to add me, but then the butler, who I decided I wanted to call Jeeves, made a tiny check mark with his pencil and motioned for us to enter the room.

Floor to ceiling windows surrounded the space, showing off incredible views of the Blue Ridge Mountains. The rich fall colors of the changing leaves were bright as the sun sank into the horizon. The outdoor terrace to the left of the room was set up for the reception and looked both elegant and magical all at the same time. Large swaths of fabric were elaborately draped from the pergola overhead and an abundance of greenery and flowers and tiny sparkly twinkle lights covered the tables and wrapped around every exposed beam. The Rockwells hadn't held anything back. When coupled with the natural impressiveness of the inn and the winding walkways and manicured gardens, it was a wedding you might expect to see photographed in the pages of a magazine.

I'd never dreamed of an elaborate wedding. My parents had once told me they could drop a fortune on an impressive venue and buy me a butter dish as a wedding gift or give me a reception in the church cultural hall and make my wedding gift the cash they would have spent on a fancy wedding. For me it was a no-brainer. I'd take cash over glamour any day. But in that beautiful room, wearing a beautiful dress, sitting next to a man who was, well, yes, even he was looking pretty beautiful, it was hard to resist the pull.

I distracted myself from my worsening case of bride envy by scanning the faces in the crowd and wondering who I might recognize. I saw Grayson's parents sitting on the front row and his aunt Pam right behind them with her husband. Bruno was two rows ahead of me with his wife, and just beyond him sat several friends from high school, who waved when they caught my eye. They held my gaze a moment longer, looking pointedly from me to Elliott, then back to me again. If Elliott noticed, he didn't acknowledge it, and I wondered if that was something he'd had to practice: how to function normally, as if no one was staring at him, when half the people in the room actually were.

He leaned over. "Can I tell you a secret?"

"Of course."

"I just did a pretty thorough examination of everyone here, and I'm ready to declare a winner."

"A winner?"

"*You* are the winner. Without a doubt, you're the most beautiful woman in this entire room."

I smiled a little half smile. "Well, the bride isn't here yet. I'm pretty sure *she'll* be the most beautiful woman in the room."

A hush fell over the crowd as Grayson walked down the aisle and took his place in front of the pastor at the head of the room. A moment later, the first strains of "Pachelbel's Canon" filled the space, and every head turned.

Jane looked . . . overwhelming? There wasn't really a better word. She was a tiny person, probably not five foot three wearing heels, but her wedding dress literally made her as broad as she was tall. The princess skirt filled the entire aisle as she passed, the train extending at least ten feet behind her. I couldn't imagine how they would ever bustle that thing. Elliott leaned over, his mouth just beside my ear, and whispered, "Not even close."

* * *

Five minutes after the dinner plates were cleared, one of the bridesmaids approached Elliott. We'd been lucky with our dinner companions, an older couple who were neighbors to the Rockwells, and Bruno and his wife. They hadn't seemed to care who Elliott was. But the bridesmaid had a look of hunger in her eyes, and I found myself reflexively reaching for Elliott's hand.

"I, um, so, I wasn't sure it was really you at first, but, oh my word, I'd know your face anywhere, and I just . . ." She waved her hands in front of her face. "I just want to tell you how much I love your music." She was visibly trembling, which kinda made me feel sorry for her. It wasn't like I'd managed to have all that much grace the first time *I'd* talked to Elliott. "I voted for you every single time you played on *Talent Hunt*," she continued. "And it was the most amazing thing when you won."

"Thank you," Elliott finally said. "Tell me your name?"

She beamed. "I'm Jenna."

"Jenna, I really appreciate your support."

Oh, he was good.

"Do you think maybe I could get a picture with you? Would you mind?" Jenna looked at me, a question in her eyes. Elliott shot me an apologetic look.

I shook my head ever so slightly, just enough for him to know I didn't mind. It was actually kind of entertaining. "Here. I can take it for you." I stood and took Jenna's phone, feeling more than a little glee when Elliott didn't put his arm around her but instead kept both his hands pushed deep in his pockets. It was entertaining, sure, but that didn't mean I wanted someone else snuggling up beside him. I opened the camera app on the phone, took a couple of photos, then handed it back.

"Thank you so much," she gushed. "For real, it is such an honor to meet you." She turned to me before she left. "Are you a friend of Jane's?" She was likely trying to figure out just how far removed she was from Elliott's circle.

"I went to high school with Grayson," I answered. "I'm Emma."

There was no trace of recognition in her eyes, and I was glad. I had no desire to be the subject of Jane's or her bridesmaids' conversations. Jenna thanked Elliott again and hurried across the room to her fellow bridesmaids, who received her with open arms and huge smiles.

"You were very gracious," I said to Elliott as we sat back down.

"I can usually manage. As long as no one asks me to sign their bra."

"And that's happened before?"

"More than once."

Across the table, Bruno's eyebrow went up. "Exactly what line of work are you in, son?"

"Emma."

I turned to find Grayson standing behind me. I stood and gave him a quick hug. "Congratulations," I said. "Everything's been really nice."

"I'm glad you came." He gave Elliott an expectant look.

"Grayson, this is my boyfriend, Elliott Hart. Elliott, Grayson Harper." I did a little internal victory dance that I'd managed not to trip on the *boyfriend* part of my introduction.

"Elliott Hart?" Grayson said. "You were on that TV show, right? You play the piano?"

"That I do." Elliott extended his hand. "It's nice to meet you."

"Man, had I known you were coming, I'd have made sure there was a piano in the reception hall. Jane's a big fan."

"I appreciate that," Elliott said. "I hope you'll introduce us before the night is over."

"Grayson, what on earth has taken you so long?" An older woman I immediately pegged as Agnes Rockwell descended upon our little circle. She wore an elaborate gold dress complete with a high-standing collar, a la Queen Elizabeth II, and a cape. As in a for-real, I-could-be-a-vampire *cape*. The cape was attached to the sleeves of her dress so when she held her arms out, putting one arm around Grayson and the other around me, I had a sudden vision of a pointy beaked vulture landing next to a smear of road kill, its wings flapping as it came down on its prey. "Where is the enchanting Emma Hill I've so much wanted to meet?" She pushed on my shoulder, turning me so she could see my face. "Oh, it's really you, darling. Greg told me you were even prettier up close, but even that doesn't do you justice. You're stunning!"

Greg?

Grayson finally spoke up. "Agnes, this is Emma Hill and her date, Elliott Hart." He looked back at us. "This is my mother-in-law, Agnes Rockwell." He managed the fancy pronunciation, *An-yez*, without a single pause. I wondered if Jane had made him practice when they'd first met.

"It's nice to meet you," I managed. "I'm sorry, did you say Greg?"

"Of course! Once Greg knew there was a possibility you'd be here, I told Grayson he simply couldn't let up until you'd promised to come. Greg's an old friend. All he had to do was express a desire to see you, and I was determined to make it happen."

I could only think of one possible Greg who might have any interest in seeing me, but I was having a hard time fitting him into the Rockwell/Harper wedding. "Greg McKenzie?" I finally asked.

"Who else?" Agnes said, like it had been clear all along. "Now you must stay right here while I find him." She turned and scanned the crowd. "I wish I knew when this wedding turned into such an elaborate affair. I honestly have no idea who half these people are. Oh, wait. There he is. He's coming this way. Emma, be a dear and spend some time with Greg, won't you? He's had such a desire to see you; he's hardly talked of anything else. Grayson? You're with me, darling. I have someone else I want you to meet."

As quickly as she had arrived, she was gone. Grayson glanced over his shoulder, his eyes apologetic, then allowed himself to be dragged off across the terrace. I watched as Agnes flapped her cape wings over to Greg, pausing long enough to kiss his cheeks and point him in my direction.

"So . . . Greg?" Elliott asked.

I spoke as I looked up and caught Greg's eye. "Greg McKenzie is an assistant conductor in Cleveland."

"The jilted lover assistant conductor?"

I winced. "The very one." Greg was only a handful of steps away, but I knew he would bring up the spring tour. It had to be the only reason he wanted to speak to me, and I couldn't fathom Elliott hearing about it from him instead of me. "Um, also? Don't be mad. I should have told you before now, but Greg has been e-mailing me all week. Cleveland invited me to tour Europe with them this spring . . . as concertmaster. They want me to come back."

There wasn't time for Elliott to respond.

"Well, if it isn't the lovely Emma Hill." Greg leaned forward and kissed me on the cheek. "You look beautiful, as always." He gave Elliott a once-over, then turned back to me, his eyebrows raised.

"Greg, this is my boyfriend, Elliott Hart." They shook hands but didn't speak. It almost felt like they were sizing each other up. "What are you doing here?" I finally said to Greg.

He shrugged. "The Rockwells are old family friends. Jane's father and mine grew up together."

"How did you even know I would be at the wedding?"

"Nothing but luck. An overheard conversation between my mother and Jane's. Fortuitous though, isn't it? That we both happen to be here? Maybe now you'll finally answer my question."

I sank into my seat. This wasn't anything close to what I'd expected from Grayson's wedding. Elliott moved some chairs around so there was room for both him and Greg to join me at the table.

"I'm sorry I didn't respond to your messages," I said. "It's been a busy week. And I wasn't sure how to respond."

"You're considering it though, right?" Greg stuck his finger in his collar as if to loosen it, then glanced over his shoulder at the bar. "I could use a drink. Do you want anything?"

"Let me get the drinks," Elliott said. "What are you having?" He waited for Greg's answer, then headed to the bar.

Greg sat back and crossed one leg over the other. He studied me with such quiet intensity I felt uncomfortable under his gaze. He motioned to Elliott with a light nod of his head. "Is he the reason you don't know how to respond?"

"No." My answer was immediate. "He's a musician too. He understands things like this, but I did have my reasons for leaving, Greg. And none of those reasons have changed."

Greg pulled a sheet of paper out of his suit pocket and unfolded it before sliding it across the table. The paper was a full-page ad for the spring tour, with a list of tour dates and locations, all superimposed on a close-up of *me*. I remembered the photo; it was from a final concert with Cleveland. It was taken in that moment of perfect stillness after the endnotes of a piece, when the vibrations of sound are still humming through your body, and though you can't hear the music anymore, you still feel it. My eyes were closed, my face revealing every ounce of emotion I'd felt while I'd played.

Elliott returned just in time to see the ad. "That's an amazing photo."

"Magical, isn't it?" Greg said. "They want you to be the face of the tour, Emma. This is just a mock-up, but it's all the board can talk about."

"Why me? It's not like there's a shortage of talented violinists in Cleveland."

"But it's more than just your talent as a musician. It's your ability to lead a section, to communicate with others, to inspire people both on and off the stage. You're also young, attractive, and an alumnus of CIM, which makes you extremely marketable. Let's be real. The past few years, Cleveland's audience has gotten, well, *old*. Ancient, really, and if we're going to pull in a younger demographic, we need a fresh face to show the world."

It was flattering—beyond flattering, even—but there was too much to consider. I looked up. "Why is this invitation coming from you?" It hadn't occurred to me to wonder until then, but it didn't actually make sense that Greg, an assistant conductor, was the one responsible for wooing me back to Ohio. "Why not Sandra or Dr. Hamilton?" Sandra Richards was executive director, and Dr. Hamilton the music director. The invitation would have made a little more sense coming from them.

"It was my idea to bring you back." He glanced at Elliott. "They thought I might have the most luck convincing you to say yes."

I motioned to the advertisement. "So this is all because of you?" I didn't mean to sound accusatory, but I also didn't want to make a major career decision (or not make a decision because, hello, I wasn't going back to Cleveland) based on motives that weren't 100 percent musical in nature. If Greg had asked only because he hoped the one kiss we'd shared would turn into something more, the offer wasn't even worth consideration.

"It's the right move for the symphony. I promise my motives are pure."

I couldn't say it wasn't tempting. But I'd worked too hard to make peace with leaving the first time around. Going back couldn't be an option. I shook my head. "I can't do it. I can't leave the life I've created here for a marketing campaign. I have students and a quartet. I have a symphony here now." *Also Elliott*, my brain supplied. *And Mom.*

"This is about more than a marketing campaign, and you know it. We want you to play for a symphony that is worthy of you. It's where you belong."

I looked Greg right in the eye. "You know it's not that easy."

He took a deep breath, forcing it out through his nose in a noisy huff. "It should be. I can't fathom how your priorities could place anything over an opportunity like this. Just promise me you'll think about it. Take a few months. Rehearsals won't start until February, so there's still plenty of time to decide. You have to at least give me that." He picked up the paper and folded it into thirds, then reached for my hand and pressed it into my palm. "You're destined for great things. Don't squander all you're capable of." He gave my shoulder a gentle squeeze, then disappeared into the crowd that filled the dance floor.

"You okay?" Elliott put a hand on my back, giving me reassurance I didn't realize I needed until it was there.

"Not at all. I'm feeling a little overwhelmed."

"Are you thinking about going? Is that why you didn't tell me?"

"No. I didn't tell you because I *wasn't* thinking about going. I mean, it's Europe. I'd love to go, but . . . I can't. I can't ignore all the reasons I came back home in the first place."

He motioned to the ad I still gripped tightly in my fist. "Musicians dream of that kind of face time with the press. You'd be *the* face of the tour. That'd get your name out there in a big way."

I dropped my hands into my lap. "Last week I found Mom in her bedroom, where she'd been working for more than twenty minutes just to put on her socks. Her days of mobility are dwindling, Elliott. How can I leave when she's at such a critical point with her health? She needs people around her who can help."

"Emma, I believe you. But you said it yourself: if your mom knew you were sacrificing your career for her, she'd never forgive you. More than she wants your help, she wants you to be happy and successful and fulfilled."

"But I'm not unhappy. Europe would be nice, but I like my life here."

He hesitated but eventually nodded his head. "Okay. I believe you." He leaned forward and kissed me softly. "If it matters, I like your life here too."

I unfolded the ad Greg had given me and looked at it one more time.

"What can I do for you right now?" Elliott asked. "Do you want to sit here and make a list of all the reasons why staying in Asheville is a good idea? Or we could dance, maybe? Go for a walk?

Bust out of this joint and go get some cheeseburgers? Tell me what you need."

Despite the turmoil I was feeling inside, I couldn't help but smile. "No lists," I said. "I don't want to think about this anymore. Not tonight anyway. But dancing sounds fun."

He shrugged out of his suit coat and hung it on the back of his chair, then offered me his hand. "Your wish is my command."

The next forty-five minutes were filled with the most fun I'd ever had at a wedding reception. Elliott was a great dancer. No, that wasn't the right way to say it. He was a good dancer, but he was so completely unaffected by what other people thought of him his ability to cut loose turned him into a great dancer. As fancy and stiff as the Rockwells seemed, I hadn't expected the reception to take such a turn, but by nine thirty, it was a full-on dance party. I introduced Elliott to a few people I remembered from high school, one who made him promise he wouldn't leave until she'd found something he could sign for her. He also met Jane, who was much more decorous in her compliments. She and Grayson looked really happy together, something I was glad to notice.

By the time Elliott had signed the back of a catering menu for my old friend, the cake had been eaten, and the bouquet tossed—nope, I didn't catch it—I was ready to be done wearing heels.

"You ready to get out of here?" Elliott asked.

I nodded. "Absolutely."

Rather than cut back through the hotel, we left the terrace and walked through the dimly lit gardens surrounding the Grove Park. The stone walkways curved up and down and around, following the contours of the mountain that hugged the entire resort. The air was cool against my skin but not uncomfortable, a slight breeze lifting the tendrils of hair that had fallen loose throughout the night.

"It feels amazing out here," Elliott said. "I'm glad it warmed up."

I grabbed hold of his arm, bracing myself as I removed my shoes. It wasn't so cool that I minded walking barefoot. "This is much more typical of October," I said. "Last week was unseasonably cold. Normally it's just like this: beautiful fall colors, amazing views of the mountains, and nights that feel like this, when the humidity is gone and it's just . . ." He held my gaze with such building intensity I couldn't even finish my sentence.

"Perfect?" he finished for me. He wrapped one arm around my waist and pulled my hand to his chest, holding it there with his own.

"That's the word I was going for."

He smiled. "Want to hear my confession?"

"Okay."

"Every minute I'm with you I worry I'm nothing but a word away from screwing things up," he said.

"You shouldn't worry. I'm not going anywhere."

He leaned his forehead against mine and hugged me tighter.

"You know you could also just kiss me," I whispered. "I promise that'll never screw anything up."

He leaned in slowly, but the kiss was well worth the wait.

When we broke apart a moment later, we were both breathless.

"Nope, that didn't screw anything up for me," he said. "You?"

I laughed softly and shook my head. "Not even close."

Chapter 21

ELLIOTT KISSED ME GOOD NIGHT right outside my apartment. Even after all the time we'd spent together, it was still disconcerting that he only had to cross the hallway to go home. Knowing that if I wanted to see him it would only take fifteen seconds to get to his door made it incredibly difficult to get him out of my head. But after the wedding, I was happy to have him consume my thoughts. Replaying the night's events was the perfect way to fall asleep. Everything really did feel perfect.

A knock sounded on my apartment door at 8:00 a.m., when I was seconds away from jumping in the shower to get ready for church. Thinking it might be Elliott, I threw on some yoga pants and a hoodie and hurried across the living room. I swung open the door, and he stalked in, agitation clear on his face.

"Has anyone contacted you?"

"What?"

"Any press. Have you gotten any calls?"

"I don't think so. My phone's been silenced since the wedding. I haven't checked. What's going on?"

He sighed. "Where's your laptop?"

"It's right there on the desk. Is everything okay?"

I watched as he opened the computer and navigated his way to an Internet browser. Curious to know if I really had received any calls, I raced back to my bedroom and grabbed my phone. I pressed the home button, lighting the screen, and my heart started to pound. I had fourteen missed calls. I walked back to the living room.

"Elliott, please tell me what this is about."

He pushed back from my desk and collapsed onto the couch, motioning to the computer with a jerk of his head. "Read it."

He'd pulled up some sort of Hollywood gossip site where the feature photo was a close-up of Elliott and me kissing in the garden at Grove Park Inn. I felt sick. I hadn't bothered to sit, but I suddenly needed to. I reached for the rolling chair behind me and pulled it forward, gripping the armrests as I read through the article that accompanied the picture.

Just weeks after an announcement from pianist and Talent Hunt *winner Elliott Hart's camp that he was stepping away from the Hollywood scene to work on his highly anticipated third album, it appears Elliott's finding ways to spend some time outside the studio as well. This picture was snagged while the superstar attended a wedding at the Grove Park Inn in Asheville, North Carolina.*

"This wasn't even twelve hours ago," I said. "How? Did someone follow us into the garden?"

"Apparently so." Elliott sounded exhausted. "Keep reading. It gets worse."

I scrolled past an ad in the middle of the article and found the rest of the text.

No word on how Elliott knows the bride and groom of the elaborate Grove Park affair, but our sources say his love interest is a musical darling in her own right—violinist Emma Hill, who this spring will launch a European tour with the Cleveland Orchestra. No comment from Elliott's team on the photo. The Cleveland Orchestra also declined to comment. As for us, we wish the couple well and hope they'll be making beautiful music together for years to come.

Under the article was a second photograph, this one a copy of the Cleveland spring tour ad that Greg had given me.

"Oh no. Oh no, oh no, oh no." I still gripped the armrests, needing something to anchor me, to keep my head from spinning. "Who did this?" I finally managed. "Who would . . . and where did they find that ad? And how can they just print something if they don't even know it's true?"

"Websites like this don't generally care about truth."

"But who, Elliott? We were alone in that garden. Who would do this?"

"The photo credit goes back to someone named Najim Berkley. He works for *Asheville News and Culture*. You ever heard of it?"

I shook my head.

"It's some sort of online magazine. I don't know if Najim was a friend or if he was there to cover the wedding. The Rockwells seem like the kind of people who would warrant a little bit of local press coverage, but he's definitely the source."

"I must have left the Cleveland ad on the table when we went to dance. I thought I put it in my purse, but . . ." I pushed my head into my hands. "What do we do now?"

"We do damage control as best we can."

"Damage control."

"Yes. You need to call whoever is in charge of Asheville Symphony as soon as you can. Maybe they don't read celebrity gossip on the Internet, but eventually someone in the symphony will, and word will get back to them. If you talk to them first, there won't be any question about where you stand. You also need to take down your teaching website. The less people can find about you online, the better."

"But my students use my website. Parents send in their payments and record practicing sessions and send me e-mails. I can't just take it down."

"How many voice mails do you have?"

"What?"

"On your phone—voice mails and missed calls? How many have you gotten?" There was nothing gentle about his voice. His tone was edgy and harsh.

"Fourteen."

"How do you think those fourteen people got your number? Emma, you've never had to fight this kind of a battle, but I have. You have to trust me. If you leave that number up, they won't leave you alone. At the very least, strip the site of any contact information."

"For how long?" It was a stupid detail to cling to, but I felt like my entire world had been flipped upside down. "What's the point of even having a website if people can't use it to contact me?"

Elliott looked beaten. "For as long as you're with me."

"So, what? I'm just supposed to go underground? What about Facebook and Twitter? Should I delete that stuff too?" I sounded defensive—more defensive than I felt, but the reality of what dating Elliott actually meant was like a cold slap in the face. I'd never felt like my privacy was in question, but suddenly strangers were trolling my website, stealing my contact information for nefarious purposes. What was next? Would they show up at concerts? Call my family? The next time Elliott did something newsworthy, how far would the media attention extend? To me?

He pushed his head into his hands. "I'm sorry, Emma. I'm sorry about all of it. My people are working to get any mention of you removed from the website. But honestly it's an uphill battle. Other sites will pick up the article, someone will blog or tweet about it. Fighting the spread of Internet gossip is like trying to fight a forest fire with a watering can. There's no way we'll be able to contain it all."

"People. You have people?"

"Yeah. My agent and my publicist. They're good at what they do, and they'll try their hardest to squelch this. I'm just trying to be honest with you about it. There's never an easy, instant fix with rumors."

It was frustrating that I was going to have to explain myself, probably multiple times, to the people in my symphony, to the board, to the personnel manager, even to my fellow musicians. But more than that, it was embarrassing that a moment so intensely personal was now fodder for public speculation. My career, be it in Cleveland or Asheville, was only interesting because I was the girl Elliott Hart had decided to kiss. And that was a realization that struck me all the way down to my core. If I had any kind of a future with Elliott, *everything* we did would be cause for public discussion.

"Don't answer your phone for the next few days," he continued. "Not unless you know the number. There's no reason for you to talk to any press at any time. You *can't*. If they think you like the attention, even for a second, they'll run with it, pumping you for information about your personal life and our relationship."

"Do I need to worry about someone trying to find me in person?"

"I don't think so. Najim what's-his-name, since he's local, may try to track you down. But I don't think anyone from the tabloids will. If they do, though, you can't give them an inch. Do you understand?"

I didn't answer. I was barely holding back tears, images swimming through my mind of paparazzi and grungy tabloid journalists pouncing at me from behind the bushes in front of the house. It was like the disgusting guy at the beer festival all over again, only this time STUD guy had my phone number.

"Emma, do you understand?" Elliott repeated.

I looked up. "I get it, all right." A single tear fell. "I get it. You don't have to yell at me."

"No, no. I'm not trying to yell." He crossed the room to where I still sat in the chair and reached for my hand. He pulled me up and wrapped his arms around me, whispering into my hair. "Please don't cry." He took a deep breath. "I hate that they've done this to you. I hate that I've pulled you into a place where you're under such scrutiny. I don't want this. I don't want them to hurt you."

I looked up and met his gaze, a question in my eyes. He didn't want this? Or he didn't want me?

He answered me with a kiss, soft at first, then with the same stupid heat that always flared between us. Even frustrated and upset, tears falling down my cheeks and onto his face, kissing him was still enough to threaten my sense of reason. He intensified the kiss, bracing his arm against the wall behind me, making me curse the fact it was just past 8:00 a.m., I was wearing yoga pants, and I still hadn't brushed my teeth.

I clung to the one logical thought pulsing through my brain and willed away the fire flowing through me. Kissing wouldn't solve anything. Maybe it made his intentions clear, but what about mine? I realized with sickening clarity: I had no idea what I wanted.

Him? Yes. But all that came with him? Twelve hours before, I would have screamed yes without hesitation. But now? Yes felt scarier and heavier than ever before.

I broke the kiss and leaned into his chest, pressing my forehead against him. "Elliott, I need some time."

I could hear the resignation in his voice. "I know you do."

"Everything just happened so fast. I'm feeling a little overwhelmed."

He gave my arm a final squeeze and moved to the door. "I'll check on you in a little bit."

* * *

Five hours later, Lilly found me on the couch, a list of symphony board members in front of me, half the names crossed off.

She dropped her bag on the chair by the door. "Hey. What are you doing here? No church?"

"I kinda had a crisis. Where have you been?"

"I was at Trav's. What happened? What crisis?"

I was too overwhelmed to explain. "Go Google Elliott. Better yet, Google me."

Lilly sat at the open laptop and keyed my name into the search engine. "Oh my word," she said as she scrolled through the hits. I looked over her shoulder. It hadn't taken long for the one news story from this morning to morph into more than twenty, gossip sites and blogs reposting the picture over and over. Some just posted the picture, eliminating the details of who I was and what I did for a living, but others went the opposite direction, digging up details about my current position in Asheville, speculating about my planned move to Cleveland in the spring, and projecting how I fit into Elliott's picture.

Lilly shut the laptop without even closing out of the browser. "You don't need to be reading this stuff."

I sighed and collapsed onto the couch, rubbing the back of my neck. I was stiff from sitting still so long, from making phone call after phone call, trying to smooth any feathers of Asheville's symphony board. Only our personnel manager, Chloe, had heard the news. "I can assure you," I told her, "I don't have any plans to leave Asheville. Cleveland made me an offer, but I haven't accepted it. This is all just a misunderstanding."

She accepted my explanation right away but then proceeded to grill me with questions about Elliott. How did we meet? Was my relationship with him serious? It just illustrated what had hit me so hard earlier that morning. It wasn't so much that my career was the story. *I* was the story—and only in the context of what I meant to Elliott. I felt both sensationalized and trivialized at the same time.

Lilly moved to the couch and sat next to me. "So, big night, huh?"

"I don't even know what to think."

"You wanna tell me if I'm gonna need a new roommate in the spring?"

"Oh! No. Greg McKenzie was at the wedding. He's one of the conductors in Cleveland, and he offered me my job back. Actually he's been e-mailing me about it all week, but I'm not going to take it. The ad was just a mock-up of what they want."

"He's been e-mailing you all week, and you didn't tell me?"

"Don't be mad. I didn't tell Elliott either. I didn't tell anyone."

"Are you not even considering it?"

"No. You know I can't. But even if I would have considered it before, I especially can't now. I've been calling symphony board members all morning, assuring them I have no intention of leaving Asheville. I feel like I have to backpedal and downplay the whole situation just so everyone doesn't hate me."

"No one would hate you, Em, even if you did go on tour. It's just business. Have you called your parents?"

I nodded. "I called Mom first. I didn't want her to hear anything from anyone but me."

"I'm so sorry." She reached over and gave me a one-armed hug. "This totally stinks. How did the trashmags even get the ad?"

"Greg gave me a copy. I must have left it on the table or dropped it somewhere. I guess when Elliott Hart is your date, people pay attention."

"That's what upsets you most of all, isn't it? The extra attention Elliott brings."

"Lilly, everything about being with Elliott last night was amazing—the mood, the dress, the location, that kiss in the photo. It was all perfect. And now it feels cheap."

"But it isn't cheap. It's still your moment. All the gossip about it doesn't have to mean anything. It doesn't change anything between you and Elliott."

I shook my head. "How can it not? He's famous. Everything he does, people watch. He wears a disguise when he goes out to dinner. People follow him to take pictures of him with his date. I mean, I'd thought about all of that, but thinking about it and experiencing it firsthand are entirely different things."

"But there's an upside too, right? Think about all Elliott is able to do because of his celebrity. He has a voice he can use for good. He has money he can donate to charity. He has organizations he can work with and resources he can use to make a difference."

"*He* can do that, but being that exposed is not the life I would have ever imagined for myself."

"Do you care about Elliott?"

"You know I do."

"Then maybe he's worth it. Just give it some time. Things will settle down, all this Cleveland business will blow over, and then you can really sit back and think about what this means for the two of you."

I was huffy, my voice edgier than it should have been, but I was weary and worn and completely overwhelmed. "What it means is that if we're together, every important decision we make will be the subject of a press release. It means magazines buying the rights to photos of our wedding, of our first kid. It means scrutiny and gossip and attention and . . ." I tried to keep the panic out of my voice, but it was creeping in, stressing my words, making my hands shake. "I don't know if that's what I want."

"Oh, honey. That's the very reason Elliott fell for you so hard. Because you don't care about any of that garbage. You're exactly what he needs to stay anchored."

"But what about me? What do I need?"

She shook her head. "That's something you gotta decide. Is he worth it?"

A heavy silence settled between us.

"I don't know."

The words left a bitter aftertaste in my mouth. Of course he was worth it. I couldn't let my fear get the best of me. I needed to see Elliott, to hear him tell me everything was going to be okay. "I'm gonna go find him."

I knocked and waited only a moment before he yelled from inside, inviting me to come in.

"Where are you?" I called from his living room.

He appeared in the hallway, holding a shirt. "In here. Come on back."

I followed him into his bedroom. There was a suitcase open on his bed, half filled. He gave my hand a quick squeeze and kissed me on the cheek. "How are you?"

"I'm . . ." *Not fine*, I wanted to yell. Especially if he was packing that suitcase for himself. "Are you leaving?"

He sighed. "I have to go back to L.A."

"Why?"

"To try to fix stuff with the label, I guess. They still aren't happy." He picked up a pair of shoes and dropped them onto the bed.

"I don't understand. Because of the wedding? Why does it matter how you spend your Saturday nights?"

"It only matters if it looks like I'm partying in Asheville instead of working on an album."

"But you *have* been working. You're composing, writing stuff they're going to love. Isn't that what they want?"

"What they want is an album they think they can sell, and that's not what I'm giving them."

"But how do you know? They haven't even heard your new music."

He scoffed, dropping a stack of T-shirts into his suitcase. "They have heard it. And they don't love it."

My heart sank. That definitely made things worse. But any record producer who didn't love what Elliott had been working on wasn't worth his time. His compositions were brilliant. He shouldn't have to compromise. "Elliott, why are you trying to fix things with a label that clearly doesn't understand what you're capable of? Let them be mad. You're better than the music they're asking you to produce."

He turned his back to me and ran his fingers through his hair, then faced me, his hands on his hips, his shoulders tense. "You have to stop saying that. The music they're asking for is the kind of music that made me famous. And it's still mine. I realize it isn't what you love, but that doesn't make it bad."

This wasn't at all how I'd expected our conversation to go. "That isn't what I meant. I know it isn't bad, but I just thought . . . You've talked about doing an album of your own music, and you've been working so hard. I thought you wanted to do something different."

"And it's that easy, right? Just because I want it I can make it so?"

I didn't want to sound simpleminded, but *yeah*. When you want something bad enough, you work to make it happen. "I'm just saying you should fight for what makes you happy, for what you really want."

"You gonna give that same advice to your sister?"

What the . . . what? "What is that even supposed to mean?"

"Is your sister allowed to fight for what makes her happy? Because she's tried to tell you more than once, and you're not willing to accept it. She doesn't want to play. You're telling me to stand up to my label, to just tell them what I want, but you're not letting Ava tell *you* what she wants. You can't have it both ways."

His words stung *bad*. "I don't understand what my sister has to do with any of this."

He sank onto the bed like someone had drained the energy from him. It was horrible to realize that person was me. "I'm just saying it isn't always black or white. And it isn't as easy as you make it sound. You knew what you wanted from the very start, but most of us aren't that fortunate. Success isn't just about talent or wants or passion. It's such a carefully crafted balance of opportunity and luck, and I'm not sure I'm ready to toss what I've built just on principle. If I can fight to keep things good, then I have to fight."

"But what exactly are you fighting for? Fame? YouTube views? The right to have a record label tell you they don't like your music? That shouldn't be what your music is about. Why does that stuff even matter?"

"That *stuff* is my career."

"I know. And I don't mean to diminish that. But is it really the career you want?"

He froze, his glare cutting into me like a thousand tiny knives. "Asks the girl who's hiding behind her mother's illness so she doesn't have to tour Europe?"

The shock of his words pushed me backward to the door, the silence between us deafening. I took a deep breath, willing the tears to just stay in my stupid eyeballs already. "You don't . . . I can't . . . I need to go."

His shoulders dropped, and he stood. "Emma, wait. I didn't mean—"

I held up my hands to stop him. "No. You know what? It's better this way. I just spent all morning trying to erase myself from the Internet so people will just leave me alone. I've had to apologize to my colleagues, make explanations to my parents and my friends, and it's all because of you. I don't need that kind of extra stress in my life." I shook my head and took another step back. "It's not worth it."

I left his apartment, my heart lodged somewhere in my throat, and crossed the entryway to my door. I tripped on the threshold, stumbling in before I slammed the door behind me. I slid down, still leaning against the door, until I sat on the wide planks of the wood floor, my knees pulled close to my chest. My hand caught on a loose sliver of wood between the old boards, and I flinched, a large splinter digging into the pad of my thumb. A single drop of blood beaded up on the surface of my skin. I whimpered. I stuck my thumb in my mouth and sucked away the blood, then picked at the splinter, trying to pull it loose. It was hard to see through my tears, which only made me want to cry harder.

Stupid splinter.

Stupid Elliott.

Stupid Najim Berkley.

Stupid *me*.

Lilly lowered herself onto the floor beside me. "Hey."

I sniffed and held up my finger. "I have a splinter."

She smoothed my hair away from my face. "What happened?"

"It's over," I said. "I've ruined everything."

Chapter 22

BREAKUPS ARE HARD ENOUGH. BREAKING up with a famous person just after a picture of you kissing floods the Internet? Yeah. Definitely harder.

The following week was a symphony week: Monday through Thursday rehearsals, with performances on Saturday and Sunday. I was glad to be busy but was not glad to have the extra scrutiny and questioning regarding the entire kissing-Elliott/Cleveland debacle.

Most people were pretty cool about it. A few of my fellow violinists looked like they'd love for me to pack up and take the job in Cleveland. A few others couldn't spare a second thought on my career but were all about dishing about my kiss with the famous Elliott Hart. Which I really didn't want to do. Especially not with people I'd never had a nonmusical conversation with.

At the end of rehearsal Thursday night, I hung back, taking my time packing up, waiting for everyone to clear out so I could leave in peace. When I reached the back of the auditorium, Grayson startled me when he stepped out of the shadows.

"Good grief, Grayson!" My hand flew to my heart. "You're going to give me a heart attack."

"Sorry. I didn't mean to scare you."

"What're you doing here? Shouldn't you be on a honeymoon?"

"We leave next week. Jane had a work thing come up, so we had to push it back."

"Oh, that's too bad."

"I wish I'd known," he said. "If I had, I'd have signed on to play this concert. It's great music."

He walked with me through the lobby of the concert hall and out onto the sidewalk. "Where are you parked? Can I walk you to your car?"

"Sure. I'm across the bridge. Did you just come to hear the rehearsal?"

He shook his head. "I came to check on you."

I stopped and turned to face him. He looked sincere, genuine concern radiating from his dark eyes. It was almost enough to make me cry. I took a deep breath. "So I guess you heard what happened."

He nodded. "I saw the picture on Twitter. Then Greg filled me in on the Cleveland ad."

"You saw the picture on Twitter. I still can't wrap my head around what that sentence means."

"Emma, I feel responsible. I had no idea Agnes was going to spring Greg on you like that. I thought he just wanted to say hello, to catch up. He made it sound like you were good friends."

"We are friends, and that was fine. I didn't actually mind seeing him. He was maybe a little pushy, but I can forgive him that. He's just trying to do his job." I started walking again. "I don't love that any of this happened, but Greg wasn't the problem. I don't hold that against you at all."

"No, Emma," Grayson said. "It's more than that."

"What do you mean?"

He frowned. "Najim Berkley is a friend. I invited him to the wedding."

I spun to face him. "Okay, I am going to hold that against you. Why would he do such a thing? Spy on us after we'd left? Is that what he aspires to be? A sneaky paparazzi?"

"It's awful, I know. And if it makes you feel any better, I reamed him out over it. I made him promise he wouldn't try to contact you and that he'd stay away from Elliott too now that he knows he's in Asheville."

"He's not in Asheville anymore."

"No?"

"He's back in L.A."

"Oh. Well, just the same, Najim won't be bothering you again. I can promise you that."

"How much did he make off that photo? I'm sure he sold it. That's what paparazzi do, right?"

Grayson hesitated. "I don't know exactly. But I know it was more than what he's making writing for *Asheville News and Culture*."

I shook my head in frustration. "I'm so glad someone was able to profit from my shame and humiliation."

"Now, wait," Grayson said. "I get that it's a little embarrassing. And the whole thing with Cleveland complicated it all even further. But what are you ashamed of? You and Elliott are adults who happened to be caught on camera enjoying what looked to be a pretty consensual kiss." His question was sincere, not judgmental, so I gave it real consideration, ignoring the semi-awkwardness of talking about kissing someone with my newly married ex-boyfriend.

"But it's not just that it was caught on camera. I've had to explain to ten different members of the symphony board why my career path suddenly became worthy of national attention, and the only reason I can give is that I decided to make out with Hollywood's most eligible pianist. It was a private moment, and now everyone is talking about it. *That's* humiliating."

"What's funny is not everyone would feel that way. Some people would eat up the extra attention or bask in the knowledge that they'd made out with someone so many people are interested in."

I cringed. "Ugh. I can't imagine."

He chuckled. "That you can't imagine is what makes you such a paradox."

"Why am I a paradox?" I was growing weary of the conversation and really wanted to just go home, but he also had me curious.

"You're a performer, Emma. Most stars are only stars because they want to be in the limelight. And when you're on stage performing, you shine brighter than anybody. You demand the attention of every single ear and eye in the room. And yet, once you drop your bow, it's over. You don't want the attention at all, which is incredibly rare in this business."

"But it's not me that demands the attention when I play. It's the music. I'm just . . . the vessel."

"That's why you're so good. But I also wonder . . ."

"What?"

He shook his head. "When I think about you in that context—as a performer—it makes sense that you wouldn't want to go to Europe. You've never liked extra attention."

"How did you know I didn't want to go to Europe?"

"Greg told me you turned him down. He's hopeful you might reconsider."

I huffed. "Being concertmaster is hard enough." I heard myself say the words before I really understood what they meant. I'd always loved the anonymity of the symphony, that it wasn't about me and my instrument but about all of us working together to make a whole that was so much greater than each of our individual parts. But Grayson had just defined my feelings about performing in ways I'd never been able to quantify. And he was right.

I'd trained myself to be the best, and with that came certain responsibilities. I played the solos. I sat as concertmaster. But that was never what it was about for me. Which meant Elliott was also right. I was hiding. Because who would believe a musician who didn't want to be the face of a European tour? Not wanting that kind of opportunity didn't jibe with what I'd been working and striving and studying and practicing for for years. I couldn't admit to anyone it wasn't what I wanted. I hadn't even been able to admit it to myself. Mom *had* been a great cover story.

Grayson leaned down to catch my eye. "Hey, you okay?"

I managed a smile. "Yeah, just . . . I don't know that I've ever realized that about myself."

I clicked my car unlocked, and Grayson opened the back door, reaching for my violin to put it inside. "I'm glad I could help out."

"Thanks for checking on me," I said. "It was nice of you. And I appreciate you calling off Najim."

He reached out and gave me a hug. "Things will be all right, Emma. Just hang in there. Tell Elliott I said hello."

I didn't tell him I couldn't tell Elliott hello.

I couldn't tell Elliott *anything*.

* * *

As the days passed, life without Elliott became dull and achy and just plain miserable. I thought about him all the time, replaying the last moments we'd had together over and over again. I became the worst kind of Internet stalker, trolling gossip sites for any mention of Elliott like a mouse looking for crumbs. I was annoyingly aware of the irony, turning to gossip sites for the exact information I resented everyone else for wanting. I even stooped so low I called our landlord to see if he knew anything about Elliott's intentions. Even just a glimmer of hope that he might return to Asheville would have been enough to keep me going.

"He paid six months in advance," Julio had said. "As long as he's paid, who really cares if he's living in the house? He's paid up through February. That's all I know."

I kept feeling the sting of the accusations Elliott had thrown in my face and the shame of the ones I'd thrown at him. The worst part was recognizing just how right he'd actually been. I'd already admitted his shrewdness in defining my motivation about Europe, but the more I considered his thoughts on Ava, the more I realized he was right in that regard too. It wasn't fair for me to push Elliott to pursue his dreams but not give Ava the same courtesy. I'd always claimed I wanted her to be happy, but I'd been pretty adamant about defining that happiness for her. She and I were due for a hard conversation. I just wasn't sure I had the emotional stamina to go through with it. At least not yet.

* * *

"Momma?" I pushed the back door open with my hip and hauled two large grocery bags into Mom's kitchen.

"In here," she called from the living room.

"I brought groceries," I called. "I'll be there in a minute."

After putting everything away, I joined Mom in the living room, where she was resting on the couch, a book open on her lap. I sat beside her and pulled my feet up, leaning into her side. She wrapped her arm around my shoulders.

"Any news?" It had been almost two weeks since Elliott had left.

I shrugged. "Nothing new. I still miss him."

"Your grandma is worried about you. Are you avoiding her calls?"

"No. I don't know. Maybe? I just don't know what to say about it anymore. I've found a kind of numbness where I'm managing to exist at least semifunctionally. But talking about it makes the numbness go away. It's too hard."

"I wish talking could make *my* numbness go away."

"Oh, geez, Mom. I'm sorry. That was totally lame."

She chuckled and reached over to pat my hand. "It's fine. I was trying to be funny."

"How are you feeling?" I asked. "Any different?"

She waved away my question. "Don't change the subject. We're talking about you right now."

I scoffed. "Uh-uh."

"Don't uh-uh me. I don't think this is complicated. You're miserable without him."

She was right, and I'd made peace with some of the things he'd said to me when we'd argued. But I was still scared, worried that my final words—those ugly, awful final words—actually held a tiny sliver of truth. The media inquiries and unwanted calls and texts had slacked off after a couple of days, and by the end of my concert week, everyone with the symphony had pretty much decided they believed I wasn't going anywhere. But the comments and speculation about who I was and what I meant to Elliott were still rampant on the Internet. Entire message boards were dedicated to discussing the long-term potential of our relationship. The amount of information they'd managed to unearth about my life was frightening, everything from my high school graduation photo to news articles about my scholarships to CIM and my time at Juilliard to my time playing with the Cleveland Orchestra. It was crazy.

I didn't need to be reading any of it. It jaded my thoughts about Elliott and interfered with my ability to listen to my own heart. But I was having a hard time looking away.

"Emma." Mom squeezed my hand. "Don't throw this away. He makes you happy. That's all that matters."

It wasn't like Mom to give such specific advice. She was queen of "I have faith in you," a firm believer in giving her children the tools they needed to make good decisions, and then a master at stepping back and letting us make our own choices. To actually tell me what she thought I ought to do? It was a little unprecedented. And kind of annoying.

I sat up. "I need to get back to Asheville. I have lessons in forty-five minutes." It was pretty rotten as far as dismissals go, but I was trusting Mom's ability to forgive and love me anyway.

She patted my hand again. "Okay. Thanks for the groceries. Do you want to come over on Sunday?"

"Yeah, probably. What's Dad grilling?"

"The chicken you just bought," Mom said. "Come early. It might be a good time to talk to your sister." She gave me a knowing look.

"Maybe," I said.

"You should ask her to play for you. She's been working on some fun stuff. Last night it was Michael Jackson."

"For real? On her violin?"

Mom murmured her agreement. "It was quite good. *Thriller*, I think."

So it wasn't so much that Ava didn't want to play. She just didn't want to play like me. "Too bad *Thriller* won't get her into CIM."

Mom shrugged. "She'll make her own way. We've had some long talks the past couple of weeks. She isn't exactly sure what she wants to do, but she's pretty certain what she doesn't want to do. We have to support her in that. *We*—as in me, your father, and *you*."

I heaved a sigh. "I know. I'll talk to her."

Mom raised her eyebrows. "That's it? You know?"

"Don't act so surprised. I'm not too prideful to admit when I'm wrong."

"Are you too prideful to admit you're in love with Elliott?"

My jaw dropped. "What's gotten into you today? Call me out a little more, why don't you?"

"Okay, I will. I think you're making a mistake. I know Elliott's fame is overwhelming, but you'll get used to it. You'll find a new normal together and adjust."

"You make it sound too easy. And it isn't just about his fame. It . . . We said some stuff. It wasn't pretty."

"So fix it. Life is too short to waste on misspoken words and wounded feelings."

I kissed her on the cheek and stood. "I really gotta go. See you Sunday."

* * *

I barely made it through lessons. I was irritable, still a little bugged from my conversation with Mom. That I managed to make it through without making any of my students cry felt like a small victory.

After lessons I stopped at the grocery store to pick up a gallon of milk. In the checkout line, a woman approached me, a timid smile on her face. "You're her, right? Elliott's girlfriend? I recognize you from the picture."

I gave her a tight smile but didn't say anything in return.

"Do you think I could get a picture with you? Just really quick before you go?"

Seriously? A picture with me just because I'd been Elliott's girlfriend? "You know?" I finally responded. "It's been a long day. I'd really rather not."

The woman's expression changed, like she finally realized what she'd been asking. "Oh. Okay. Sorry for bothering you." And then she turned and walked away.

I couldn't stop thinking about her as I made my way home. It wasn't even a fifteen-second conversation, and yet somehow I felt like everything had changed. Because I realized the woman in the grocery store wasn't in control of me. She could ask to take my picture, ask about my personal life and my relationship with Elliott, but I didn't have to respond. I didn't have to let her in.

Elliott had tried to tell me I couldn't play their game. I couldn't let them get to me, but that was precisely what I'd been doing. Every time I opened a browser and looked for new comments or new blog posts or new articles about our relationship, I was feeding the monster that was eating me alive.

But I didn't have to play.

Elliott was right. Grayson was right. Mom was right. Everyone had me figured out. Everyone but me.

Except, not anymore.

Chapter 23

I FOUND LILLY IN THE kitchen, still wearing her scrubs, her hair pulled back in a loose ponytail. "Hey. Are you just getting in? How long did they make you work?" I asked.

She nodded. "Twenty-five hours straight. It was crazy. I've never seen so many babies on the floor at one time."

"Is it even legal to make you work that long?"

"Not technically. I slept in the on-call room for a couple hours. But I couldn't leave. Seventeen deliveries in twenty-four hours. We set a new record." She collapsed onto the couch, grabbing the blanket hanging over the arm and spreading it over herself. "How are you? Any new Elliott sightings?"

I hesitated. "I don't know. I haven't checked today."

"For real? That's progress, I guess."

"Yeah." I dropped onto the desk chair and pulled my legs up, wrapping my arms around them and burying my face in my knees.

"You know what's different between you and all those women who look for pictures of Elliott on the Internet?"

"What?" I asked, my voice muffled.

"You actually have Elliott's phone number and can call him and talk to him anytime you want."

"I can't call him."

"Why not?"

"Because I have no idea what I would say. Plus, I hurt him. I don't know how to fix things."

"Hi, Elliott. This is Emma. I know I hurt you. I'm sorry. You're worth everything. I love you. Please come home." Lilly fired her words at me in rapid succession, though in her tired state, they hardly sounded convincing. She yawned. "See? Easy."

"Not easy. Maybe you can call him for me."

"Yeah. Not happening. So have you decided that's what you want? You want to call and work things out?"

I moved to the couch and sat beside her. "Someone stopped me in the grocery store tonight and asked if she could take my picture. Said she recognized me from the photos online."

Lilly pushed herself up. "That's it? She just asked for a photo?"

"Yeah."

"You know what? Big hairy deal!" She turned sideways so we were facing each other. "I'm gonna speak the hard truth to you here. I think you're maybe being a little selfish. So what if people want to take your picture. You can say no. You can choose to be a private person even if your boyfriend has a public career. You don't have to play the game. I mean, yeah, sometimes stuff will happen and you'll have to ignore it, but that's just it. You can ignore it. If you like this guy, I mean really, truly like him, and you think he's a good fit for you, you can't be so selfish that you cut him out just because you don't want some girl in the grocery store to take your picture."

"Um, I guess there's no question about where you stand on the issue. Are you finished?" I asked after waiting patiently for her tirade to end.

"Yes," she huffed.

"Good. 'Cause I think you're right."

"I am right. Wait. I'm right?"

I nodded. "So she asked for my picture. I declined and kept walking, and she went away, and it didn't matter. I was in control, not her."

"Good girl," Lilly said.

"And maybe there will be some stuff I have to get used to, things about our life together that will be different, but different isn't a bad thing. Different can be a good thing, right?"

"Yes, yes, right! So if you realize this, why are we still sad? Why aren't we calling Elliott and telling him how stupid we've been?"

My shoulders fell. "Because I don't just like this man, Lilly." Mom would be so proud I was willing to say it out loud. "I really love him, and I'm afraid I've ruined everything. I'm scared."

"Oh, honey. Don't let fear win."

"What if he went back to L.A. just to get away from me?"

"His suitcase was already packed when you insulted him. Try again."

"What if he got to L.A. and realized he was wrong about me and he really loves his record label and wants to live in L.A. covering boy-band music forever?"

"Then he's not the man you thought he was, and it's a moot point."

"What if he's fallen for someone else?"

"In two weeks? You think?"

"What if he's decided I'm not worth it?"

"But you are. And he's told you that enough times you have to believe it."

"What if he can't forgive me?"

"What if you never ask him to and you live a lonely, miserable, Elliott-less life and die a spinster? You want to keep playing this game?"

"But he's in L.A., and I'm here. What if we can't make that work?"

"People make long-distance relationships work all the time. Why are you making things so complicated?"

"Because it is complicated. This is my future we're talking about. I don't want to screw it up."

"Oh my word! I swear you Mormons make everything so serious. Why are we talking about your future? Why can't we just talk about here, now, what you're feeling this minute? You don't have to be able to see the future clearly. You don't have to see this perfect rose-colored path to your wedding day. You can just let stuff happen and see where you end up. You're overthinking, Emma. You just said you love him. Why are you being so stupid about all of this?"

"Me? I'm being stupid? You want me to just let stuff happen, but I'm not like you. There's a reason we Mormons make everything so serious. It's because relationships *are* serious. We can't just try one on for size to see how it fits. You may take it to the bedroom on the first date just to see how it'll go or be fine waiting around for your juvenile boyfriend to decide if he's going to grow up, but I'm not like that. It's not what I want."

"Did you seriously just say take it to the bedroom? Is it 1937 inside your brain?" She stood and flung a throw pillow back at the couch, missing my head by mere inches. "At this rate, you're not going to make it to the bedroom *ever*, happily Mormon-y married or not, if you're not willing to risk a little bit. And I didn't even *kiss* Trav on our first date. You're tired, and you're stressed, and I know you've had a bad couple of weeks, so I'm gonna forget you just insulted me and my boyfriend. But I'm not going to apologize for calling you selfish. Because that's what you are right now. Maybe Elliott deserves something better." She stomped down the hall and slammed the bathroom door with a thud that echoed through the apartment.

I didn't want to admit she was right, but the second the words were out of her mouth, I knew she was. I wasn't trying to be selfish, but I was scared. I knew what I wanted. I wanted Elliott. But I had no idea how to get him back, and fear was winning big time. Every single thing I'd said was colored by that one emotion. I pounded after her. "Fine. You're right. What am I supposed to do differently?"

"Pick up the phone, genius," she shouted through the door. "And stop being such a whiny . . ." The water turned on, and the shower rings slid across the rod, so I couldn't hear what she called me. But I had a pretty good idea. I leaned against the wall across from the bathroom and slid to the floor. I was a mess. A stupid mess saying stupid things that I didn't really mean. I stayed in the hallway until Lilly emerged from the bathroom wrapped in a towel, her dirty scrubs tucked under her arm.

I followed her to her room and stood in the doorway, blocking her from shutting the door.

"You know I'll drop this towel and get dressed in front of you if you don't let me close my door."

"I'm sorry," I said.

She turned, tossing her laundry into the hamper by the wall. "For what?"

"I'm sorry I accused you of having loose morals, and I'm sorry I called your boyfriend juvenile. I was a jerk, and I didn't really mean it, and I really love you both, so I hope you'll forgive me because I can't stand life without you, and I don't want you to be mad at me."

She rolled her eyes. "Oh, whatever. I might have loose morals if I didn't have a Mormon best friend to keep me in line. And Trav totally is juvenile. But he's juvenile with potential, so I'm not giving up hope yet."

"Thank you for being my friend," I said. "And for not staying mad."

"Blah, blah. Go call Elliott."

I smiled. Lilly and I had had our share of fights. We couldn't be friends from fourth grade on and not get into it every once in a while. But we'd never stayed mad at each other longer than five minutes, a reality I was grateful for every time Lilly forgave me so readily.

It took twenty minutes of pacing up and down the hallway to muster enough courage to just call already. Lilly was dressed and standing across from me when I finally dialed the number, my hands shaking the entire stupid time. I listened to the ring—two, three, then four—then breathed out a sigh of relief when his voice mail picked up. The sound of his voice made my heart swell. Oh, I missed him. I dropped the phone from my ear like I was going to hang it up, then caught Lilly's eye.

She shook her head angrily, motioning the phone back to my face. "Leave him a message!" she whisper-yelled just as I heard the beep.

"Hi. Um, hi. So I know it's been . . . I don't really know what to say. I just was hoping we could talk. Sorry. This is lame. Gah—me and words. I'm so not good at this. Okay. I just wanted to say . . . I miss you. And, well, the thing is, I can't figure out . . . I just know there are some things that I should say. That I want to say. But how?"

Lilly slowly reached for the phone. "You're all done. Just say good-bye," she whispered.

"Okay. So yeah. Call me back. Bye." I looked at Lilly. "How was that?"

She grimaced. "It's possible I pushed you into that a little too quickly."

I groaned. "Was it awful? It was really awful, wasn't it?"

"What if you just play something for him?"

I scoffed. "Why do people keep suggesting that? I can't play an apology. Uggh. I'm hopeless."

"You're not hopeless. And if this guy loves you, that message will mean something to him anyway. It's not like he hasn't witnessed your unique mastery of the English language before."

Ha. Ha. Ha.

"Thanks, Lil. Thanks for that."

She put on her serious face, placing both of her hands on my shoulders. "Listen to me. You're strong enough for this. You're strong enough to say the right thing. You're strong enough to tell this man you love him. And you're strong enough to deal with what life with Elliott will bring. It's time to put on your big-girl pants and just do it already."

Chapter 24

Elliott called three days later. I was teaching, so my phone was turned off, but he left a message.

"Hi. Thanks for calling. I'm sorry I missed you. Things are just crazy right now. My schedule is insane . . . but yeah. I'll call you again soon. Listen, can you find out how Oscar's doing? I miss that kid. I guess that's all for now. Take care, Emma. Bye."

After listening to his message, I felt like my insides had been hollowed out. I'd been hopeful, waiting for him to return my call, but everything about his message, from the tone of his voice to his bringing up Oscar, screamed that things would never be the same.

He didn't call again. When I texted him a video of Oscar playing a piece he'd been working on, Elliott responded with one word: *Thanks.*

By the end of November, my mood matched the muddy brown of the leaves collecting in the gutters of Maple Crescent. I mean, I was fine. I was teaching and smiling and playing and going out with Lilly on Friday nights and eating dinner with my family every Sunday. Life was good. But I wasn't happy. I felt like a symphony without a violin—utterly incomplete.

* * *

A couple of weeks before Christmas, I spent a week getting ready for a conversation with my sister that I'd put off for way too long by practicing the second part of a slightly frenzied, mostly chaotic, but totally hip rendition of Imagine Dragons' "Radioactive"—for two violins.

I pulled out the sheet music after dinner one Sunday afternoon and handed it to her across the table. "Want to give it a try?" I asked her.

She gave me an odd look. "You want to play this with me?"

I shrugged. "It might be fun."

It *was* fun. More fun than I'd had in weeks. We played until our fingers hurt, then we collapsed on the couch, gratefully accepting the warm mugs of hot chocolate Dad brought us from the kitchen. I looked at Ava across the top of my mug.

"You know I'm going to love you no matter what, right?"

She looked down. "I know."

"I mean, you can go to the University of Montana and study cattle ranching for all I care. I just want you to be happy."

She took a sip of hot chocolate, then set her mug on the coffee table in front of us. "I was so afraid you'd be disappointed. I didn't know how to tell you. And it isn't that I don't like to play. It's just not what I want to do full-time."

"Which is so totally fine. I shouldn't have been so hard on you. It was our thing, you know? What we did together. I think I was afraid that if you quit, we wouldn't have anything to keep us together. But you don't need to go to CIM to be my sister. I'm trying to do better at remembering that."

"Emma. You just played an Imagine Dragons song on your violin. You're doing *way* better."

* * *

The Wednesday before Christmas, I packed an overnight bag to head to my parents' place. I wasn't sure at first that I'd stay overnight, but my grandma was in town, and I wanted as much time with her as possible.

Lilly knocked on my bedroom door. "Hey. You heading out?"

"Yeah. I'm almost finished. Is Trav here?"

"He will be in ten. I hope you have a good holiday."

I opened the door, and she followed me down the hall. "Thanks," I said. "You too. Call me after Trav proposes."

She smiled. I'd been placing bets for weeks on the day Trav would finally drop the question. My money was on Christmas Eve night. "He's so not going to propose," she said.

"Then why are your eyes all sparkly and excited? Do you know something for real?"

She shook her head. "No, but . . . he's definitely different. Something's coming. I can tell that much."

I gave her a hug. "I hope you say yes."

"Yeah, yeah. Still no word from Elliott?"

I shook my head.

"Stupid man. He said he'd call again. Why hasn't he?"

"I'm sure he's got a lot going on."

"That's not an excuse. If he's in love with you, he'd find time to call."

My eyebrows pulled together, and I frowned.

"Oh, no. That's not what I meant," she said quickly, trying to backpedal. "I'm sure there could be reasons why he hasn't called. I just meant that . . . When you said he had stuff going on, he can't use that as an excuse. There's gotta be something else that's making him keep his distance."

Yeah, there was something else. Me. "It's okay. You might be right. And maybe it's time for me to realize that. It might be time for me to move on."

"You're gonna be fine. You'll bounce back."

Maybe, but I really didn't feel like bouncing.

* * *

"Hello? Is anyone home?" I stood in my parents' noticeably empty kitchen. At least the food for tomorrow's Christmas Eve dinner was there. Sweet potatoes lined the counter, and all the ingredients for a broccoli salad looked prepped and ready to assemble. Two pumpkin pies sat on the kitchen table, along with Dad's famous skillet apple pie. If all that wasn't convincing enough, I'd passed the turkey brining on the front porch. Christmas was absolutely, for real happening. So where the heck was everybody?

"Emma? Is that you?"

"Grandma?"

"I'm in here."

I followed her voice to the living room. "Where is everybody?"

"Your father's at a church service thing. And Ava drove your mom to the grocery store. Something about needing cream cheese." She stood and gave me a hug. "It's good to see you. You look good."

"Thanks. You too. How's Ohio?"

"A little dimmer without your presence, but we're getting by. Have you heard from Elliott?"

"Not a word." I shrugged. "I think it's really over."

"Of course it isn't over. This is just an issue of timing, nothing more. Sometimes it takes awhile to get it right." She patted my cheek. "Want to sit with me? I'm actually glad to get you alone for a moment."

"Sure. What's up?" We sat together on the couch.

"I had a long conversation with your mother last night."

"Yeah? She seems like she's been doing a little better lately."

"That's true, but we weren't talking about her health." Gram reached over and patted my hand. "We were talking about you."

"What? Why me?"

"You don't give her enough credit. I know you told her about that silly kiss with your conductor and convinced her it was the reason you moved, but she's not buying it anymore. She knows you're here for her, and she hates it. That you're turning down an offer to tour Europe is the worst kind of thorn in her side."

I breathed out a heavy sigh. "Dad said something similar before I even knew about the tour. I don't want her to feel unhappy about it though. I really am happy here. And I like being around to help."

"I believe you do. But I also think your heart is longing for something different." What my heart was longing for was Elliott.

And I wasn't going to find him in Europe. "I don't need to go to Europe," I said. "I know I'd love the music on a tour like that, but I'm not so sure I'd love all the attention." It was the first time I'd admitted as much out loud, and it felt strangely liberating. "I don't like being a spectacle, and that's what I would be if I agreed to go. It may look like I'm sacrificing so I can stick around and help Mom, but truly, I'm happy here. Some sacrifices are worth it."

"But you're young, Emma. Opportunities like this won't come along every day. I think your mother would really love for you to go."

"It's just not that important to me, Gram."

"Truly? You aren't interested in going at all?"

It was a difficult question to answer. Had I not left Cleveland at all and the tour was just another responsibility in a symphony I was already a part of, I would have done it. Things about it would have made me uncomfortable, but yeah, I would have gone. But I'd spent a lot of time thinking about what Elliott had said and what Grayson had said and even more time reflecting on what was nestled in my own heart. Europe wasn't enough of my dream to give up what I had in Asheville. I shook my head. "It's not my dream."

"What if I said you aren't needed here?"

I slumped back into the sofa and folded my arms across a throw pillow in my lap. "I'd say you're crazy. The last three months prove how much I'm needed. I've been over two, three, sometimes four times a week helping out."

"I know you have been. I know your mother needs the help. That's why I'm moving in. I'm leaving Ohio. It's time I be with your mother full-time."

"What? Gram, you can't leave Ohio just because you want me to tour Europe. It isn't that important."

"Emma Grace," she scolded, "don't be so self-centered as to think these decisions only have to do with you. Karen is my daughter. I want to be here."

"But I've been trying to take care of her. I even offered to move back in, but Dad wouldn't let me."

"Do you know how proud your mother is of you?"

I nodded.

"Do you know how happy it makes her to hear you play?"

I nodded again. "I do, but I'm not going to pretend my playing is more important than Mom's health. It's not. Nothing is."

"Bug, if you don't want to go to Europe, that is absolutely your prerogative. But you owe your mother a conversation. I know you're trying to spare her the guilt you think she'll feel if you discuss the career choices you *aren't* making, but your distance is only hurting her more. The two of you are long overdue for a conversation where you can bare your heart about what you really want and give her the chance to do the same."

The reality of Gram's words settled on my shoulders hot and a little heavy. She was right. I was trying to protect Mom. Whether I wanted to go on tour or not, Mom deserved to know my true feelings on the subject. "Are you really moving?"

She nodded. "Just after the first of the year. There's nothing left for me in Ohio, not with your grandfather gone, your uncle moved to California, and you down here. It doesn't feel like home anymore, not when all my family is so far away."

"And Mom needs you." I couldn't hide the hurt in my voice. I'd made a lot of sacrifices to be around for Mom, and while I wasn't necessarily hurt by the idea of Gram's moving in, I was a little disappointed that I'd failed.

"You've done beautifully the past few months, Bug. But she does need me. She needs someone who can be here full-time. And that's too much to ask of you right now when your wings are just beginning to stretch."

I pulled my feet up under me and leaned into Gram, resting my head on her shoulder. "Do you think I should go to Europe?"

"It might kill some time till that man of yours gets his emotions in order."

Before I could answer, my phone dinged in my pocket, and I pulled it out. There was a text from Lilly. *Turn on the TV NOW. Channel 13. They're going to talk about Elliott after the commercial. Hurry!*

I dropped the phone and scrambled across the living room to the television. "Where's the remote?" I said to myself. "Where's the stupid remote?"

"Calm down. It's right here," Gram said. She held it up.

I lunged back across the room and scrolled through the channels until I found the right one.

"Fans of the *Talent Hunt* sensation Elliott Hart are going to have to wait a little longer for his highly anticipated third album. We've just gotten word from Blue Bridge Records they've parted ways with the pianist, citing creative differences and a lack of shared vision for future projects. No word on whether any new record deals are in the works for Elliott. But for anyone listening, here at Inside Hollywood, we sure do hope so. Elliott's team has declined to comment on the split."

I sank back onto the sofa. "Poor Elliott," I said more to myself than to Gram.

"He's lost his record deal? Did I hear that right?"

I nodded. "I can't believe it. He must be devastated."

"Maybe you should call him? See if he's okay?"

It was a terrifying thought, but she was right. I did need to call him. I stood. "I'll be right back."

Grabbing my phone off the corner of the couch, I raced down the hall to my old bedroom, shutting the door behind me. I sank onto the bed and pulled out my phone, my hands already shaking.

Maybe because it was all I'd gotten the last time I'd called, I expected his voice mail. But he picked up on the second ring. When he did, I barely managed to choke out a response. "Hi," I finally stammered. "I . . . sorry. I wasn't sure you'd pick up."

"You caught me at a good time. How are you?"

I closed my eyes and savored the sound of his voice. "I'm okay, I guess. I'm at home for Christmas."

"Me too," he told me. "The whole family is here."

"Uncle Elliott, then."

He chuckled. "Yeah. It's been pretty fun."

"I heard about your split with Blue Bridge. I'm sorry, Elliott."

He breathed out a sigh. "Thanks."

"What happened? Do you mind if I ask? The news called it creative differences."

"Is that all they said? That's a pretty kind explanation of what really went down."

"Do you want to talk about it?"

"The short version is that I kept pushing to at least get some of my original songs on the album. I was fine doing some covers and some mash-ups, but I wanted a few tracks that were mine alone."

"And they wouldn't do it?"

"We went back and forth for weeks, but then Brian brought over the final track list, and it was all covers, all from the same album."

"They wanted you to cover an entire album song for song?"

"You ever heard of Starting Over?"

"The boy band?"

"It was their last album. I guess they wanted to piggyback off their success. They wanted piano versions of all their songs, and that was it—my entire album."

"That's completely unfair."

"I thought so too. So I walked."

"Wow. Are you in trouble at all? Are they bugged about you breaking your contract?"

"They're not. My attorney put some pressure on, and they agreed to just let the agreement dissolve, which is nice, but at the same time, it doesn't send much of a message to the rest of the industry."

"What do you mean?"

"They're basically saying it's easier to cut me loose than actually work with me." He hesitated, his next words a little quieter. "They're saying I'm not worth it."

Pain sliced all the way to my core. Those were *my* words—my slimy, awful, untrue words. I swallowed. "So what happens next? Will you sign with a new label?" I pushed my forehead into the heel of my hand. Why couldn't I just apologize? Why couldn't I just tell him how wrong I'd been?

"I don't know. My agent is looking, but I'm a hard sell these days."

A beat of silence passed between us, heavy with all the words I wanted to say but had no courage for.

"Elliott, I'm sorry I hurt you," I finally blurted. It wasn't the apology he deserved or even the apology I wanted to give. It sounded too final, like I was sorry I hurt him, but now I was happy to be moving on. But it was all I could manage through my nerves.

It took so long for Elliott to answer I almost wondered if he'd hung up. When he did finally speak, his voice was so soft I almost didn't hear him. "I have to go. Thanks for calling."

He hung up before I had the chance to respond.

I collapsed back onto my bed and pulled a pillow over my face. Stupid words. Stupid, stupid words that never worked and never said what I wanted them to say.

Mom found me in my room an hour later, curled up under the covers, reading a worn copy of James Herriott's *All Things Bright and Beautiful*.

"Can I come in?" she asked from the hall.

I nodded.

She steered her motorized chair through the doorway and stopped just beside my bed.

"You're really starting to cruise in that thing," I said.

"I know! Didn't hit the wall or a doorjamb once coming down the hall." She pushed herself up onto wobbly legs and motioned with her hands for me to move. "Come on. Scoot over."

I scrambled to make room for her, grabbing an extra pillow to prop behind her once she settled beside me on the bed.

"Gram said you were going to try to call Elliott," she said.

"I did call him. We talked."

"How's he doing?"

I closed my book and dropped it onto the nightstand. "I don't know. We were talking about things and work and his music, but then I apologized for hurting him, and he said good-bye. No explanation. He was just gone."

"So he's still convinced you don't think he's worth it."

"Or maybe he's just decided I'm not worth it either."

For nearly an hour, we rehashed every detail of my history with Elliott, from our awkward first encounter to the beer festival to our monumental kiss at Grayson's wedding. Somewhere about halfway through, Gram joined us on the foot of the bed, then Ava wandered in, surprising us all when she curled up right next to me. I kept talking anyway. I was sharing far more personal details about my life than I'd ever thought I'd want my sixteen-year-old sister to know, but there was something magical about the circle of women on my bed—three generations who cared about me and loved me and wanted me to be happy.

Eventually I got all the way through to the end of my Elliott history: the phone call I'd ended not two hours before. "And then he just said he had to go, and that was it."

"That's so dumb," Ava said.

"What?"

"You love him, and he loves you. But you're here, and he's there. And neither one of you is going to say anything to the other that would just fix all of this."

"I don't know that he loves me," I said.

"Oh, whatever. Of course he does."

"You need to tell him," Mom said. "Plainly, clearly. Just tell him you love him. He won't be able to argue with that."

"But I tried! Just now on the phone, I tried to tell him. You know how bad I am with words. Stuff never comes out right."

"But you didn't try to tell him," Ava said. "'I'm sorry I hurt you' is not enough to undo 'You're not worth it.' And that's the last thing he heard."

It was a surprisingly astute point from someone with so little experience.

"Have I ever told you the story of how I met your grandfather?" Gram asked.

I nodded. "He drove a delivery truck, right? He brought something to the house . . . a new refrigerator or something."

"That's right. My mother was there too when he came walking into the house, pushing that big old box, and she never liked him. She didn't love the idea of me marrying a working man. She'd rather I found someone with an education who would work with numbers and books. I was too good for a blue-collar worker like your grandfather."

"What did you do?"

"I married him anyway. It was four years to the day before I had my first baby—your mother. And four years and three weeks before my mother stepped foot inside my house."

"She didn't come see you for four years?" Ava asked.

"She didn't even talk to me for four years. She was hurt," Gram said. "In her eyes, I'd made a mistake marrying someone so different from her family. I'm not sure she ever changed her mind about Charlie, even up to the day she died, but I'll tell you this much: I'd make the same choices all over again. I loved your grandfather, and that's what we do for people we love. We make sacrifices. We move mountains if we have to."

"So I need to tell him how I feel."

"Yes!" all three shouted at once.

I knew they were right. All I needed was the courage to do something about it.

Chapter 25

Four days after Christmas, a package arrived on my doorstep—tiny, wrapped in brown paper, and postmarked from Colorado.

I pulled off the paper to find a small white box wrapped in silver ribbon. There was a card taped to the outside of the box with a note only one sentence long.

No regrets. Love, Elliott

I opened the box and pulled out an iPod, knowing immediately what I would hear as soon as I pushed play. I raced to my room and grabbed my headphones, plugging them in as I settled on my bed.

I recognized the melody from the very first notes—the same first notes I'd heard Elliott pick out all those weeks before on the night of our first kiss, when they were nothing more than the shadow of a melody. The piece continued, lilting and light but with undertones that added a depth that spoke of something more. It was joyful but not exultant-joyful. More like humble-joyful. The first time I listened all the way through, I sat on my bed and cried. I mean, I was there when Elliott had picked out the very first notes on his piano. To hear it whole and complete, with depth and movement and harmony—it was perfect.

Hours later, I'd listened to it enough times I could pick up my instrument and play the violin part without missing a note. Elliott's note, *No regrets*, might have read like it was a final statement, like he was moving on and he wanted me to move on too, but that song didn't sound like no regrets.

It sounded like hope.

* * *

Thursday morning, I was in the kitchen eating breakfast when my phone, still charging in my bedroom, started to ring. I scrambled across the apartment, trying to reach it before my voice mail picked up. I made it just in time.

It was a number I didn't recognize.

"Hello?"

"Emma, it's Ron Williamson."

"Oh. Hi."

"Listen, we've had a slight kink with the January concert. Baronovsky can't make it."

"Oh no. What happened?"

"It's the most dreadful thing. He closed his hand in one of those antique rolltop desks and broke three of his fingers. It'll be months before he can play again."

I balled my hands into fists at the thought. Broken fingers were every musician's worst nightmare. "That's terrible."

"We can't do the Prokofiev, not with Baronovsky out, so I was hoping you'd have something in your repertoire we could feature. We'll just headline you as the soloist instead. What about the Bartok Concerto you played when you auditioned?"

"Sure. Cleveland even owns the parts if we need to borrow the music. I could do the concerto."

"Good, good. I hate to lose the Prokofiev. It's one of my favorites to conduct, and it goes so nicely with Dvorak's Seventh, but I think the concerto will be an acceptable replacement."

A sudden thought buzzed through my brain, a rush of adrenaline filling my veins and my heart and every ounce of my being. Elliott knew the Prokofiev. He'd told me as much when we'd talked about Baronovsky coming to play. Who better qualified to replace

Baronovsky than one of his own students? "Ron, what if I can find us another soloist?"

"For what? The Prokofiev?"

"Yes. I know someone. He's a friend and a brilliant pianist, and I know he can play the piece."

"But is he soloist quality? Lots of people can *play* Prokofiev. He would need to be capable of more than that."

"He is. He absolutely is. He even studied with Baronovsky in Russia. I wouldn't recommend him if I didn't think he could do it."

"Well, I guess it wouldn't hurt to at least give him a listen. Can you bring him in to play for me?"

So maybe I hadn't thought through all the details. "You'll have to give me a few days. He's not in town right now, but . . . yes, I think I can."

"It will have to be soon if we're going to have time to get programs printed. Plus, we'll need time to get the music from Cleveland if we end up doing the Bartok. When can you get him here?" Ron asked.

"I'm not sure. By the end of next week?"

"That's not quick enough."

"Please, Ron. You're going to love him. He's perfect."

He paused, then sighed. "Fine. Wednesday next week, but that's the longest we can wait before we have to make a decision."

"Wednesday." That was less than a week away. "Okay. I'll see what I can do."

I couldn't call Elliott. I needed to call Elliott, but calling him for this, when I still hadn't managed to call him to say, I don't know, hello and I love you, felt lame. Like I wasn't really calling because I wanted to talk to him, only because I needed him to save our concert. But I couldn't get him to Asheville if I didn't call and explain, which meant I was utterly and completely stuck.

When Lilly came home an hour later, I was still standing at the counter, staring at my phone like maybe it would figure out what to do and just do it for me.

"What are you so stressed about?" Lilly asked.

"I'm not stressed," I said. "Okay, no, I am stressed. I need to get Elliott to Asheville, and I don't know how."

"You need him like you need a make-out session? Or you *need* need him for real?" *Both. Definitely both.* "I need him for real. The symphony needs him." I told her about the call from the symphony's music director.

"And you can't just call Elliott and explain all of this?"

My shoulders slumped. "I can't. The next thing Elliott hears me say needs to be 'I love you.' I can't call him about this when I haven't figured out how to say *that*."

"So call him and say I love you, then wait twenty-four hours and call him back about the concert."

"No! Even a day later, my motive would still be suspect. He'll think I was only saying I love you so he'd agree to come."

"For real, Emma? You gotta give the man a little more credit than that."

"What if I really just want to say it in person? I don't know that I can fix stuff over the phone, but if this gets him here, I'll have the opportunity to try. Face-to-face."

She leaned against the counter and nodded her head. "Okay. I see your point. So why don't you call his agent? If you didn't know Elliott personally, the agent is who you'd call to set up stuff like this anyway, right?"

Call his agent. It was an incredible idea. "Yes! I need to call his agent! Brian. What's his last name? Brian Jenson. How do I get ahold of Brian Jenson?"

"Emma, take a breath. Google will help us. Just chill."

Five minutes later, I had the main office number for Spectral Media, the agency Brian worked out of, written on a sticky note beside my phone.

"So what are you going to say?" Lilly asked. "You're going to have to be pretty convincing to get his agent to help. I mean, this is Asheville. It's not like playing with the symphony here is going to help his career or anything."

I looked at Lilly, my eyes wide, my brain already hatching the beginnings of a plan. A big, amazing, probably impossible plan. "That's it," I said.

"What's it?"

"I have to make the concert help his career."

"Slow down, turbo. Give me the how."

"I don't know exactly, but if I can just get a few key people into the audience, a record producer who does classical music, maybe, or I don't know, a conductor from a big symphony, once they hear him play, they'll know what he's truly capable of. They'll want to sign him."

She looked skeptical. "It's a nice thought, but again, this is Asheville. Not L.A. What kind of record producer is going to hop on over to North Carolina for a concert with the Asheville Symphony?"

"I haven't figured that part out yet." I pushed my hands through my hair and willed my thoughts into some semblance of order. "But this is Elliott Hart we're talking about. Surely his name has some kind of pull, even if he doesn't have a current record label. Plus, I have a few connections I can reach out to. My time in Cleveland has to mean something." Then the biggest piece of my plan fell solidly into place. I *did* have connections in Cleveland. And I knew exactly what I could do to get them to help me out.

I left a message on Brian Jenson's work line, stressing the importance of his getting back to me as soon as possible. Then I sent an e-mail through the generic *Contact Us* link on the agency's website, providing the same information and practically begging for a response. After that, there was nothing else to do but wait.

By Sunday night, three days later, even though I'd sent two more messages to Spectral Media and called the front desk once more, I was positive there was no way Elliott would be in Asheville by Wednesday. If I didn't hear anything by Monday night, I decided I had no choice but to call Elliott and explain everything myself.

Monday morning at seven, Brian finally returned my call.

"I'm looking for Emma Hill," he said when I answered.

"This is Emma." I sat up in bed, trying to sound like I hadn't been asleep. I glanced at the clock, noting with mild curiosity that it was 4:00 a.m. in California. Regular business hours for Brian?

"Emma, Brian Jenson with Spectral Media. You called about an opportunity for Elliott Hart?"

"Yes. Yes, I did."

"I want you to know I only called you back as a courtesy. It was you, right? That was in the photo with Elliott at the wedding? I'm sorry about what happened to you career-wise. Elliott said you took quite the beating."

"No, it was fine. It wasn't a problem in the end."

"Good, good. Glad to hear it. So listen, Elliott is free to play wherever he chooses at this point. There's not a label anywhere that cares where or what he plays, so it's fine by me. You go ahead and set everything up, whatever you need to do." His voice was clipped, not harsh but definitely no nonsense.

More than ever before, I wanted my words to work. I needed to say the things that would convince Brian he wanted to help me, and that wouldn't happen if my stupid nerves kept my tongue tied in knots. I closed my eyes, imagining myself on stage, violin at the ready, and tried to will the peace and confidence I felt into my voice. "Actually, it's not that simple. I think this opportunity could be more than a concert. I think it could be Elliott's ticket to another record deal, except this time, for the kind of music he actually likes."

"Why's that? What's so special about this opportunity?"

I'd been thinking about how to answer all weekend. Asheville was a small city with a relatively obscure symphony. It wasn't the kind of place where anyone who would further Elliott's career as a classical pianist would just happen to be. But it had taken only two simple phone calls to give me the confidence I needed to make Brain a guarantee. "Asheville Symphony is a great orchestra," I began. "And it's a wonderful piece of music that I know Elliott can play. Playing this concert would be good for him."

"Good for him? My job is to care about what's good for his career."

"But if we could get a record producer into the audience, someone who would see this is the kind of music he needs to be playing . . ."

"Listen, if I had the ability to get a record producer into a concert hall to hear Elliott play, don't you think I'd be doing it? He's a contemporary artist with a little bit of YouTube fame that just got dropped by his label. He's not exactly on everyone's list of favorites right now."

"But he should be. He's so much more than what people are giving him credit for."

"Maybe so, but I'm not sure it matters now. Sure, he's had a good run, but it's over. He can retire on what he's made so far. He needs to celebrate that and move on."

"Please don't say that."

"You must be a good friend to reach out like this, but I'm just not sure I see the point."

I closed my eyes. Brian was going to make me play every card I had. "If you can get Elliott to Asheville to play with the symphony," I said, "I can get Richard Schweitzer into the audience to hear him."

Brain paused, the beat of silence before his words straining my nerves almost to breaking. "Schweitzer? With Academy Records?"

Schweitzer wasn't the only name I was hoping to pull in, but he was definitely the most impressive. "He worked with the Cleveland Orchestra a few years ago on an album of Beethoven's favorites. He does a lot of classical recordings."

"And he'll be in Asheville?"

I hope. I pray. If I'm lucky. "Yes."

He paused, and I held my breath, the weight of all that was in the balance hinging on his next words.

"Have you talked to Elliott about this? Is he willing to come?"

I collapsed back onto my pillow. I didn't exactly want to get into the finer points of my relationship with Elliott, but I really needed Brian to be on my team.

"I haven't talked to him. We aren't exactly speaking right now. But I don't want this to be about us. This just needs to be about getting his career back on track so he's making music he actually loves. That's all I want from this. Just for him to find his music again."

He sighed and mumbled something about lovers' quarrels. "Which is why you're calling me. So his big, bad agent can boss him into flying back to Asheville."

"By Wednesday afternoon."

"Wednesday, day-after-tomorrow Wednesday?"

"The concert isn't for two more weeks, but he needs to perform for the conductor by Wednesday." I crossed my fingers.

He sighed again, this one a little longer, a little more pronounced. "Agggh, all right. If you can promise Schweitzer, I'll get Elliott to Asheville by Wednesday. I can't make him talk to you though. You're on your own in that regard."

"Thank you," I said, relief flooding my chest. "This is going to work," I told him. "I promise this is going to work."

As soon as I hung up, I texted Greg.

If you can help, I'm in for the tour. Let's make this happen.

Chapter 26

WEDNESDAY MORNING I GOT A text from Brian with Elliott's flight information. He landed in Asheville at three twenty, which gave him just enough time, if he drove straight to the performance hall, to play Prokofiev for Dr. Williamson before the conductor had to leave for dinner at five.

"I can't be late for dinner," he told me. "If this friend of yours is going to play for me, he better be here by four."

I debated whether I should be there for Elliott's audition. He had to know I'd been involved in bringing him back to Asheville. I had no idea how much his agent had told him, but even if he'd been told nothing, he was smart enough to piece everything together. Asheville was my symphony. He was invited to play because of me.

In the end, I hid in the shadows offstage, watching as Elliott entered the auditorium, shook my conductor's hand, then moved to the piano. He rolled up the sleeves of his dress shirt and sat down, his eyes focusing on the keys. To see him after so many weeks apart made my entire body tense, every nerve ending on high alert. I ached to touch him, to breathe him in. Once he began to play, the feeling only intensified.

He was incredible. I was biased. Of course I was biased; I was completely in love with the man. But his ability to turn music into a living, breathing, feeling thing was beyond anything I'd ever experienced before. And I'd been around a lot of musicians.

I slipped out the side stage door and walked to the back of the auditorium so I could sit in the last row. Through the first movement and into the next, Elliott played the Prokofiev with unwavering skill. That he'd had so little notice and was still able to walk up and power out twenty-plus minutes of a piano concerto with no music and no orchestra to back him up was mind-boggling. He was the consummate professional. Truly, he was the best I had ever seen.

When he finished, I held my breath, hoping Dr. Williamson agreed.

The conductor stood from his seat in the front row and clapped his hands, the singular sound of his acceptance echoing through the empty room. "Bravo," he said simply, nodding to Elliott. "Bravo."

I waited for Elliott at the back of the auditorium. He stopped a few feet in front of me, his hands shoved deep into his pockets. "Hi." He spoke without smiling.

I swallowed. "Hi. You sounded really good." *Understatement of the year, but fine.*

"Thanks." He was uncomfortable, which only made me more uncomfortable. All I needed were some words, some good ones that made sense and were clear and concise and easy to understand. But there was no mental violin strong enough to channel peace and confidence into this conversation. I was a complete wreck. My tongue felt like rubber wrapped in Velcro, my head full of sentences there was no way I would ever have the courage to say. I stared at the floor, my cheeks flaming red, frustrated by my inability to just talk already.

"So thanks for setting this up for me." He motioned over his shoulder to the piano. "I guess my agent is bringing in a producer from Academy Records to hear the concert, so . . . I don't know. Maybe something good will come of it."

Wow. I was annoyed at first that Brian would try to take the credit for getting Schweitzer to the show, but after a moment's consideration, I decided it was probably better if Elliott didn't know I was involved. At least not beyond the effort I'd made to secure him an invitation to play. I wasn't trying to buy his affection or earn back his good opinion. I loved him. I wanted him to be happy, and I really, really hoped he was in love with me too. But even if he wasn't, if there wasn't a single hope of us ever winding up together, I wouldn't change anything. I'd still be doing the very same thing.

"It was nothing," I said. "I was happy to do it." I looked toward the door. "Can we talk for a minute? Want to go for a walk?"

He glanced at his phone. "I only have an hour or so. I have to get back to the airport."

I tensed. "You're leaving?" He wasn't supposed to be leaving.

"I'll be back in time for the concert. Before that, probably, so I have time to pack everything up at the apartment."

No, no, no, no! Tears sprang to my eyes, and I turned so he wouldn't see. I headed out the door of the auditorium and through the lobby, making it several paces down the sidewalk before he finally caught up.

"Emma, wait. Please!"

I stopped walking, but I couldn't look at him. I knew the minute I did every bad, sappy sentence filling my brain would find a way to escape. *Stupid words.*

"Emma," he said again. He spoke from somewhere just over my shoulder, his tone gentle, his words soft. "I meant it when I said no regrets. I wouldn't take back a single minute of the time we spent together."

"But?"

"But you were right. It's not worth it. I can't ask you to sign up for a life that makes you uncomfortable."

"So you're leaving instead?" I could feel him moving closer, close enough that if I turned and reached out, I could touch him, feel him, breathe him in.

"It wouldn't be good for either of us if I stayed. I can't live across the hall and see you every day. It wouldn't be fair."

I scoffed. "When is life ever fair?"

"But it doesn't have to be this kind of unfair. I care about you, and I want you to be happy. Even if that means letting you go."

It sounded like a canned speech, like a stupid line from a stupid movie where a stupid therapist tells some stupid guy what to say. *If I really love you, I have to let you go.* No. If he really loved me, he'd stop the crazy talk about moving out of Asheville and just kiss me already.

"I didn't mean it," I whispered. I turned to face him. "Elliott, I didn't mean it. I was scared and overwhelmed, and I didn't know what I was saying. You are worth it. You're worth everything."

He took several paces away from me, then turned, his arms folded tightly across his chest, his jaw clenched. "Don't say that."

"But it's the truth. I'm not proud of what I said, and there were some things I definitely had to figure out. But I realize now my life only has to be ruined by a meddling media if I'm willing to let it. I don't have to. I don't have to play their game. In hindsight, the only significant fallout from that stupid photo was that I lost you. And that's way harder than anything the media could ever throw at me."

He breathed out a frustrated sigh and shook his head. "No. It took me weeks to get my head in a place where I could even think about standing this close to you without it killing me. I told myself I had to let you go, that it was the best thing for you, and I did. I did let go. Please just let me do that."

"But it's not what I want. It's never what I wanted."

We weren't exactly fighting in the middle of the sidewalk, but we were definitely having an emotional conversation, the kind that would draw attention regardless of celebrity status. But Elliott was a celebrity. Which meant we didn't just get attention. We got people turning our conversation into a photo op. A camera clicked and flashed from across the sidewalk, the woman behind it not even making an attempt to hide her curiosity.

Elliott reached for my arm and pulled me down the sidewalk in the opposite direction. "But you don't want this either." He motioned behind him to the woman with the camera.

"Shouldn't that be a decision I get to make myself? You're not even asking me what I want. You're telling me. Why don't you stop and ask me how I feel." A sharp wind tossed my hair into my face and made my breath catch. I'd left my coat inside the performance hall, and the chill cut right to my bones. I wrapped my arms around my middle, my shoulders hunched against the cold.

Elliott shrugged his coat off and held it out. "Here."

I shook my head. "I don't need it."

"Please, just put it on."

I jerked it out of his extended hand, annoyed that even in the midst of our argument, he still had to be so nice. He watched until I'd pulled the coat tightly around my shoulders, my hands pushed into the pockets. It was almost enough to kill me—wearing his coat with the smells and the lingering body heat. It was the worst kind of unfair.

"You just don't understand, Em. You're too good to be pulled into the world where I've built my career. I don't want to expose you to the ridicule and curiosity. I saw how that photo hitting the tabloids affected you. And if you're with me, I am powerless to stop the same thing from happening over and over again. I hate that I wouldn't be able to protect you from all of that."

"Did you hear anything I just said? What if I don't need protecting? Shouldn't I be the one who gets to decide? Shouldn't I get to decide if I think you're worth it?"

"It's easy to say as much when you've only been through it once. But I've seen it wreck people. I've seen this business wreck relationships and ruin families."

"So, you're just going to be alone forever? Because you're so self-sacrificing and magnanimous that no one should ever have to endure the chore of loving you because it might mean some stranger snaps a picture with their cell phone?"

He scoffed. "If that's what it takes, then yeah."

"Boy, you are jaded, aren't you?"

"You can call it jaded. I'll call it realistic."

I took a step back, pain flaring in my chest. "What's realistic about that? Making your decisions based on how the media treats you? You want to talk about what's real? Our late-night composing was real. Oscar was real. *We* were real. Every minute I spent with you was real for me."

"And then you looked me square in the face and said it wasn't worth it."

I took a step closer. "I was angry. And I was scared. And you said some hard things to me. You were right, by the way. About Ava, about Europe—all of it. But I didn't know that then. I was speaking out of a place of hurt and confusion, and I was wrong."

"I don't know." He shook his head, moving away again. "I don't know if I believe you."

Now, Emma. Say it now. "Elliott, I'm in love with you. I love you, and I don't care who takes my picture because of it. I want to be with you. It's my choice, and I choose *you*." *I love you.* The words echoed inside my head, blatant, bold, completely un-take-backable. I'd just given Elliott every ounce of my heart. By the look on his face, he didn't want to take it.

His shoulders hung low like there was an invisible line pulling them down, a force he had to fight to keep his body from sinking into the concrete beneath us. Even his eyes stayed down, glued to a spot somewhere to the right of my left shoe. "I've got to catch my flight," he finally said. "I'll see you in a couple of weeks."

I stood there rooted in place for what seemed like an eternity, watching him walk away. He didn't look back.

Chapter 27

With Elliott gone again, it was harder to follow through with my original plan. Everything I'd planned to do was for him. After his rejection, I wasn't feeling all that altruistic. But I'd made a commitment to make this concert count, and I was too far in to back out now. I gave myself a couple of days to wallow; wore Elliott's jacket, which he'd left *on my person* when he'd walked away; cried on Lilly's shoulder through a therapeutic night of chick flicks and comfort food; then forced myself back into the land of the living and functional. Time was growing short, and I had to check off the few remaining things on my list of concert preparations. The first and most important item was the heart-to-heart conversation I promised Gram I'd have with Mom.

Gram was in the kitchen making bread when I arrived. She smiled at me over the bowl of dough rising on the counter and wiped her hands on her apron. "What are you doing here in the middle of the day?"

"I need to talk to Mom. Is she around?"

"She's reading in her room. Everything all right?" She shot me a knowing look.

I nodded, then headed straight for Mom's room.

She was reclined on the bed with her eyes closed, her book open and resting spine up on her chest. I climbed gently onto the bed.

"Hey, Mama," I whispered.

She opened her eyes. "Hey! What are you doing here?"

I sat beside her, my legs crossed. "Can we talk about Europe?"

Her eyes turned up, and she gave me a faint smile. "I thought you'd never ask."

* * *

Richard Schweitzer wasn't the only person I wanted in the audience to hear Elliott play. I wanted someone who could write about his performance and get his name into the symphony circles in New York and Chicago. I started my research by writing the names of every person in the past twelve months who had written a review of a symphony performance for the *New York Times*. It wasn't that long a list. There were tons of reviews, mostly of those symphonies local to the northeast—the New York Philharmonic, Boston Pops, the National Symphony Orchestra in Washington, D.C.—but some reviews were farther reaching. I found one on The Los Angeles Philharmonic and one on Cleveland, which, it was exciting to realize, mentioned me by name. The articles were written by several different writers, but one woman kept popping up more than all the others—Jeanine Whitaker.

I tried calling the *New York Times* directly, but they weren't particularly obliging, saying they didn't give out personal information about their staff writers. They suggested I write her an e-mail using their online contact form, an annoying repeat of what I'd been through with Spectral Media. Luckily newspapers were better at correspondence than talent agencies. An hour after I sent the e-mail, Jeanine responded with her cell phone number.

"So you're telling me you'll fly me to Asheville and all I have to do is write a review?" Jeanine hadn't been hard to convince. It was more like she thought I was bluffing, like the deal I was offering was too good to be true. It probably was, but I couldn't afford her not coming.

"An honest review," I told her. "That's all I need you to do."

"You've got yourself a deal, honey."

An hour later, I e-mailed Jeanine her flight and hotel information and convinced myself I could more than handle charging $973 to my credit card to cover her trip. It was only money. And life wasn't about money. Life was about people. And zero percent interest for eighteen months.

After confirming plans with Jeanine, I got in the car and headed to Biltmore Forest. Grayson had given me pretty good directions, but I still managed to drive past the imposing English Tudor that was the home of his brand-spanking-new in-laws. I backtracked and finally found the large stone pillars he'd mentioned, a lion perched ceremoniously on each one, the name Rockwell carved into the imposing stone. The house was surrounded by huge trees and sprawling yards, with a circle drive that wrapped around a gurgling fountain. I shouldn't have been surprised by the opulence of the house. When I'd talked to Grayson, he'd been in Hawaii, still on his honeymoon. His eight-week-long honeymoon. People who could afford to fund an eight-week honeymoon—it had been their wedding present, I remembered Grayson telling me—could definitely afford a family estate in Biltmore Forest.

Agnes Rockwell was wearing a silk robe and bedroom slippers when she opened the door. "Oh, Emma, I'm just so glad you called. Greg told me everything."

"Thank you for seeing me. I realize this is a lot to ask, especially when it's so last minute."

"Nonsense. This is the kind of thing that makes life exciting!" She led me into a large sitting area at the back of the house, faint winter light streaming in through large floor-to-ceiling windows. She motioned for me to sit but stayed standing herself, her hand resting on the marble mantel above the fireplace. "Now, I've already begun to make some calls," she said. "Greg tells me he's bringing Schweitzer, which is just perfect. And you said on the phone you've got a *Times* reporter coming?"

I nodded. It was Greg's idea that I call Agnes. With her clout as a big-time symphony donor, she'd be able to get the tickets I needed for the concert—actual *good* tickets, not just the comps I was planning on begging off of friends. He'd mentioned her name within minutes as soon as he heard what I was trying to do.

"She's a huge patron of the arts," he had said. "She has an apartment in New York and flies up at least three times a year to hear the Philharmonic. She's very well connected in the city. Plus, she loves this kind of thing. She's just the person for the job."

I'd been hesitant to be honest with Greg about what I was trying to do, remembering the almost tense moment when he and Elliott had been sizing each other up, but Schweitzer in the audience was only going to work if Greg was on my team. Luckily telling him the truth had been a good call.

Agnes walked across the room to a table behind the sofa and poured herself a large glass of orange juice. "Would you like some?" She held up the glass.

I glanced at my watch. 11:30 a.m. Still early enough to be wearing silk pajamas and drinking orange juice, right? I nodded, silently hoping it was just juice. "Sure."

She handed me the glass and sat beside me. "I have another idea if you're open to it."

"Um, sure."

"I met Yvonne Spzilmann at a dinner in New York a few months back, and we just really hit it off."

"Yvonne Spzilmann, as in married to Jakob Spzilmann?"

"Oh, lovely. You know who they are! They're both the most wonderful people. Yvonne talked of wanting to visit Asheville, but we've just never gotten around to doing it. It's a shame, really, now that the leaves have all fallen. I should have had her down months ago, but there's nothing to be done for it now. I suppose the mountains are still pretty, even in January. Anyway, I've given her a ring and asked her if she'd like to come down for the weekend, and she's delighted to come. She and Jakob are both coming. Won't that just be lovely?"

I hardly knew what to say. "You're bringing Jakob Spzilmann to the concert." Jakob Spzilmann was a cellist, a senior professor at Juilliard, and an emeritus conductor for the New York Philharmonic.

"It's all but official. I told them about you and your pianist. They're looking forward to the show. Have you ever met him?"

"Once, a long time ago, at a series of workshops I attended while still in school. He's phenomenal."

"I do so love the work he did with the Philharmonic. He always put on such lovely concerts."

I was completely overwhelmed. I thought I was asking Agnes for help securing extra tickets to a sold-out performance. I had no idea she would go so far as to bring one of the nation's finest conductors to the concert. "Agnes, I don't know how to thank you. This is so generous of you."

"Well, I've always believed one good turn deserves another. You made Greg a very happy man."

I looked at the floor.

"Plus, if this young man is as good as you say he is—"

"Oh, he is. I promise he is."

"Then let's hope he doesn't disappoint. It looks like he's going to have quite the audience. Now. Let's talk about tickets. We need two for the Spzilmanns, one for the *Times* reporter, one for Greg, and one for Richard Schweitzer. Is that all?"

I shook my head. "One more if you can spare it. There's someone else I'd like to bring as well."

She nodded. "So six total? No problem. I'll make some calls. I'm sure I can manage that many."

After Grayson's wedding, I'd looked up the Rockwells' name on the list of symphony donors. They were season underwriters, which meant annual donations of ten thousand dollars or more. I was more than willing to trust her connections and her influence. That she was even willing to use her influence on my behalf was a tender mercy I hadn't expected.

Agnes fed me chicken salad sandwiches and lemonade, which felt so much like a rich-person meal I almost laughed when she brought me my plate, then sent me out the door with kisses on each cheek and a promise to wear her best for the concert because "surely it was going to be an event to remember." I honestly didn't even know what hit me until I was back in my car, my head reeling from everything that had happened in such a short amount of time. My plan was actually going to work.

Before heading home, I stopped by the box office at the performance hall to drop off a check for an undisclosed amount from Agnes—"Don't open it, child. It hardly matters to you what's inside"—and to pick up a press pass and a concert ticket Agnes promised would be waiting for me. From there, I went back downtown to a tiny basement office on the south side of Broadway in between a dry cleaner that specialized in leather restoration and a used electronics shop with a sign in the window that said "Scooter repair. We'll get you going again."

I opened the glass-paned door etched with the words "Asheville News and Culture" and headed down the narrow wooden staircase. At the bottom of the stairs, a small reception area opened into one room, two rows of desks lined up in the middle. There were eight desks total, but only three were occupied. Everyone looked up, surprise on their faces. Apparently they didn't get many visitors.

I recognized Najim Berkley from his online profile picture, so I walked past the empty reception desk and stopped in front of him. "Are you Najim?"

He grinned. "For you? Absolutely."

I rolled my eyes. "Do you want to sell another story about Elliott Hart?"

His eyebrows went up, recognition dawning on his face. "Ah, I remember you. That was a good sale."

It was all I could do not to punch the guy or even just scold his glaring lack of decency. I'd debated whether I should turn to Najim for help. I mean, I had someone from the *New York Times*. I didn't need bottomfeeders like this guy. Except, I did. Because he was the one who would sell to gossip columns, and the gossip columns were the ones that would get Elliott's name trending. And that was what I wanted.

I wanted to believe Elliott's brilliance as a performer would be enough to wow Richard Schweitzer into signing him on the spot, but seeing that his name still had star power and still generated online interest couldn't hurt. For once, I actually wanted the paparazzi to help me out. And Najim was the closest thing Asheville had to paparazzi.

I took a deep, steadying breath, forcing it out through my nose before dropping a list of names and phone numbers onto his desk, along with a ticket to the Prokofiev concert and the press pass I'd wrangled from the concert hall that would allow him to bring his camera to the show.

I motioned to the ticket. "A week from tomorrow, he'll be there. It's . . ." I hesitated. "The concert is a really big deal. And that list is every single reporter or tabloid that contacted me after you sold the wedding photo, some with a lot bigger names than the trash column you sold to last time. If you get some good shots, I'm sure they'll be interested."

He looked at the list with interest. "*Celebrity Weekly*, huh? Not bad."

"Will you do it?"

His eyes ran up and down my body in such a blatant way I felt like I needed to shower to get the feel of him staring off my skin. How had he and Grayson ever become friends? "You play too, right? Will you be on stage?"

I sighed. In reality, with the position of the piano and my seat as concertmaster, I'd likely be in the background of most of the photos he took of Elliott. "I'll be there."

Najim shrugged and picked up the ticket. "All right, you've convinced me. I'll see what I can do."

It wasn't a perfect answer, but I was out of time. It had to be good enough.

Chapter 28

"So really, truly, you think it's over for real?" Lilly paced around the living room while I sat on the couch and folded a basket of towels. "I think you need to talk to him one more time."

"Lilly, I said I love you, and he walked away. I think he made his feelings pretty clear."

"Does he know you're going to Europe?"

I shook my head. "When would I have had the chance to tell him? Plus, I don't want him to know."

"Why? Because then he might realize just how much you actually love him?"

Well, yeah. "I don't want to put him on the spot like that—like, now, because I've done this big thing for him, he's obligated to, I don't know, love me back."

"You're completely crazy."

I put the last towel on top of the stack and stood to carry them to the linen closet. "No, I'm trying really hard to not be crazy. I need to be a grown-up about all of this." Also, I needed to not cry. And if I let my guard down even for a second, the tears came hard and sure and fast. Any little thing set me off: seeing (or wearing or sleeping in) his jacket still hanging in my bedroom, listening to the song he'd written just for me. A constant "I am a grown-up" inner monologue was the only way I was keeping myself together.

"I wish you didn't have to leave," she called down the hallway.

"It's not like you wouldn't be leaving this summer anyway. Unless you were planning on having Trav move in here with us after the wedding." I stored the laundry basket on top of the washing machine in the hall closet and went back to the living room, where Lilly sat admiring the diamond sparkling on her finger.

"I still can't believe it's actually going to happen," she said.

"I can, and it's going to be great."

A knock sounded on the door, followed by Trav's deep voice shouting a greeting. "Hello! I'm coming in!"

Lilly smiled but didn't move from her seat on the couch. "Hi."

Trav bent down and kissed her hello. "You ready to go?"

"Yep. You sure you don't want to come, Em? It's supposed to be a good movie."

"Um, so I've got a big concert this weekend? Have you heard? We actually have to practice if we're going to be any good, so rehearsal tonight."

"Don't be getting all sassy. We know about your concert." Trav pulled a pair of tickets out of his pocket and waved them around. "In fact, I just picked up these puppies today. It's a good thing I ordered them ahead of time. They're saying the performance is sold out."

"Look at you planning ahead and being all thoughtful. You really are a changed man, huh?"

He beamed. "I'm doing my best."

I smiled. "I'm glad you guys are coming."

"Are you kidding?" Lilly said. "We wouldn't miss it. We'll probably be downtown after the movie if you want to meet us after rehearsal. Want me to text you where we are?"

"No. Ava's coming over to watch the rehearsal, and then we're heading to The Chocolate Lounge."

Lilly gave me a quick hug good-bye. "I'm happy you and Ava are on Chocolate Lounge terms. Bring me home a macaron?"

* * *

It was past eleven when Ava and I finally made it back to my apartment. Ava carried a big box of French Broad truffles, while I hauled two to-go cups of steaming hot chocolate, a piece of pumpkin torte, six salted caramel macarons, and two different kinds of brownie. It was more than we could eat on our own, but choosing had been impossible. Also, a night out with my sister, free of the tension that had plagued our relationship for almost a year, felt like a good reason to celebrate. Dropping thirty bucks on dessert was nothing.

Ava giggled while I tried to pull my keys out of my purse without toppling one of the hot chocolates. "I'm not sure we got enough," she said. "I think there's an extra inch of space in our box. We should have had them put in another brownie."

"Shut up and take these so I can get my keys."

She put the truffles on the floor of the entryway and took the cups of hot chocolate. "Where's Lilly? Can we just kick on the door so she'll let us in?"

I kept digging, but my keys were inexplicably absent from my purse. "She's out with Trav. Seriously, Ava. I cannot find my keys. They have to be here. I just used them to drive us home."

"Did you leave them in the car?"

It had been a bit of an orchestration getting us both out of the car with all our chocolate, plus Ava's overnight bag. It was possible my keys had gotten lost in the shuffle. "Wait here. I'll go check."

Two minutes later, I returned to the entryway completely disheartened.

"No keys?" Ava asked when she saw my face.

"No, they're there. Right on the center console. But seeing as how the car is locked, they aren't much use."

"Oh no! Do you have a spare key?"

"Sure I do. Inside my apartment."

"So we're locked out of everywhere. Can you call Lilly?"

I pulled out my phone. "I'll send her a text. Dang it, I feel like an idiot."

"It could be worse," Ava said. "Your front door could have been locked. Then we'd be locked out *and* freezing. At least the entryway is warm."

Lilly responded to my text almost immediately. *Ended up seeing a late movie. Done in an hour. Can you wait?*

I sighed. "Lilly can be here in an hour." I keyed out a response. *Yeah, we can wait. Thanks.*

Knock on Elliott's door. He's there. Saw him arriving on our way out. His couch is better than the floor.

So Elliott was back. I knew I'd see him at rehearsal the next morning, and I'd been mentally preparing for that. But right now? With my little sister along? I stood staring at his door long enough that Ava figured out what was running through my brain.

"Is he home?"

I glanced out the front door. "I don't see his car, but Lilly says she saw him come in."

Ava took two steps across the entryway and knocked on his door before I could even utter a protest. "Our arms are full of food," she said. "What guy says no to free food?"

Seconds later, Elliott opened his door. He looked from Ava to me, then back to Ava again. "Hi."

"Hi." There was something else I was supposed to say, but, *surprise*, my brain totally stopped talking to my mouth the second Elliott said hello.

"So we're locked out," Ava said, giving me a pointed look. "Can we hang at your place till Lilly gets home to let us in?"

Elliott looked my way, his eyebrows raised in question.

"Sorry. I locked my keys in my car, and Lilly won't be home for another hour."

"We have food, if that helps." Ava held up her bag of chocolate. "We just bought out The Chocolate Lounge."

Elliott looked weary, his face passive as he ran his hand across his jaw, but he finally smiled, his hesitance gone in a blink. "I've only heard about The Chocolate Lounge. I guess it's time I finally try it." He pushed the door open behind him. "Come on in."

We spread our assortment of desserts over the counter in Elliott's kitchen. *Elliott's* kitchen. Where he was standing. His hair a little unkempt. Bits of stubble lining his chin and cheeks. It was almost too much for me to handle.

"This was just going to be for the two of you?" he asked, eyeing all the options.

"It was too hard to choose," I said. "Plus, we're celebrating happy sister time." I looked toward Ava as she stood in the living room studying Elliott's bookshelf.

"Things are good?" Elliott asked.

I nodded. "Yeah. Better than they have been in a long time."

"I'm really glad."

We were being too polite, ignoring the tension humming between us, pretending like our last conversation hadn't been groundbreakingly awful. But with Ava in the room, it was impossible to say anything different.

"Are you kidding me?" Ava called. "This is signed by the author?" She held up a copy of Brandon Sanderson's *Words of Radiance*. "This is seriously one of my favorite books."

"Yeah? Mine too," Elliott said. "I met him at a charity event last year."

"This is the coolest thing ever." Ava opened the book and studied the title page, Sanderson's swirl of a signature gracing the bottom half.

Elliott crossed the room and stood beside her. "You know what? Why don't you keep it? He didn't personalize it, so you should have it."

Ava looked like she was going to melt out of her shoes. "For real?"

"I've got his e-mail. I'll ask him to send me another one."

She looked at me and held up the book, her eyes and smile equally wide. "Do you see this?" She pointed at the book. "Do you see how amazing this is?"

I laughed as she stretched out on Elliott's couch and opened the book. "Okay, don't worry about me," she called. "I'll be right here basking in the brilliance of Brandon's words."

Elliott walked back to me, genuine happiness in his eyes. He was happy for Ava and me. He didn't even have to care, but he did anyway, and it was unraveling my emotions faster than I could reel them in. When he stopped in front of me and ran his fingers through his hair, I had to turn away. I cleared my throat and crossed to the other side of the kitchen.

"I haven't seen her this happy in a long time," I managed to say.

"I'm glad you guys were able to work things out."

I leaned against the counter. "It was easy, really. I just had to ease up and let her know I loved her no matter what. She should have known that all along, which is the hardest thing for me to realize. If I'd just talked to her and listened to how she really felt . . ." I shrugged. "Live and learn, I guess."

He pushed his hands into his pockets.

"Thanks for nudging me in the right direction," I said.

He moved across the kitchen so we were standing side by side. "It was nothing. I'm thinking maybe it's advice I should have taken myself."

His words sent my nerves into a full-on frenzy. My stomach felt a little like it was trying to crawl out through my throat, and my hands started to tremble. *Stupid hands.* I clenched them into fists and crossed my arms, hiding my fists in my armpits. I swallowed, hoping I understood what he meant. "Yeah?"

Ava popped her head in the kitchen. "Sorry. Just getting another macaron."

I forced myself to breathe. "It's okay," I told her. "You can get whatever you want."

She picked up a cookie and took a bite, moaning with pleasure. "Seriously. How have I never tried these before? They're French, right? Promise when you're in Paris you'll send me some."

I closed my eyes and winced.

"Paris?" Elliott asked.

"Emma's touring Europe this spring. She hasn't told you yet? I keep begging Mom and Dad to let me fly over to see one of her performances, but they seem to think high school is more important. It's so lame."

Elliott looked my way. "So you took the job with Cleveland." He didn't sound mad exactly, just surprised.

I nodded. "Rehearsals start in February. I have to be there by the tenth."

"Wow. I mean, is that . . . I guess it's great. What about your mom?"

"Grandma moved in just after Christmas. I know I had my reasons for not going, but I guess stuff has changed. Plus, I've done a lot of really hard thinking since we . . . since you left, and, well . . . yeah. I'm going to Europe."

My explanation felt hollow. Words were screaming through my brain—explanations, assurances, promises I was ready and willing to make—but it didn't feel right to say any of them, not when as far as I knew, Elliott's feelings were no longer the same as mine.

"Are you excited about the performance tomorrow?" Ava asked Elliott. This time I was actually glad for the distraction.

"Yeah. I really love playing Prokofiev." He turned to me. "How have rehearsals been?"

I shrugged. "I think we're ready. We're maybe not as good as we should be—not good enough for you. But I think we're as good as we can be. We're doing Dvorak's Seventh before the Prokofiev. It's my favorite."

Silence stretched between us until it was almost unbearable. The awkwardness was killing me.

Ava grabbed another macaron, shoving the entire thing in her mouth in one bite.

I looked around Elliott's apartment, to the sheet music scattered across his piano, the shoes by his bedroom door, the books lining his shelves. And then I realized—I turned to face him. "You haven't started packing."

"Oh. No, I, uh, I decided to stick around a while."

It was the worst kind of feeling to know he was going to be in Asheville after all and I wasn't.

The next forty-five minutes were brutal. Awkward small talk, bone-burning tension pulsing between Elliott and me. Ava seemed completely oblivious, which was probably better. She was the one who kept us talking, asking questions about people Elliott had met, places he'd been.

Lilly finally knocked on the door just before twelve thirty. "I'm home," she called through the door. "You're officially rescued."

I started gathering the leftovers from The Chocolate Lounge and stacking the containers on the edge of the counter.

Ava grabbed the desserts. "Here, I'll take these. I'm sure Lilly will want something." She turned to leave the apartment. "You coming, Em? I'm gonna steal your favorite pillow if you don't hurry."

"I guess I'll see you tomorrow," I said to Elliott.

"Yeah," he said. For the briefest of moments, he looked disappointed, but then it was gone, hidden behind a more neutral mask of indifference. "Tomorrow."

Inside my apartment, I dropped my purse on the couch and pulled out my violin. I didn't even care that it was almost one in the morning. I might not have the words to explain to Elliott how I felt, but I did have the music. I stood close to the wall, where I knew he would hear me, and played the song he'd sent me at Christmas like it was the last song I would ever play. I knew every note, every dynamic like he'd written the music right into my heart. He didn't have any regrets? I was determined to make sure he knew I *did* have regrets. And I wasn't going down without a fight.

Chapter 29

Elliott looked up, his eyes meeting mine *again*. When guest soloists perform with a symphony, they only rehearse once, normally the day of the performance, so Saturday morning was the orchestra's first opportunity to meet him. He was gracious and charming and patient as people introduced themselves and asked for pictures and autographs. But the eye contact—he was definitely seeking me out, giving me the tiniest hint of a smile every time he caught my eye.

It was thrilling, but I was too much of a music nerd to claim it was even remotely significant compared to the exhilaration of accompanying him. I'd never experienced anything like it. After rehearsal, the energy on stage was palpable, everyone buzzing from the music. We sounded good. And that was a great feeling.

Brian arrived at the end of rehearsal, whisking Elliott away for a series of interviews with various media outlets and then a pre-concert meeting with Richard Schweitzer. Elliott and I didn't have the chance to speak even once. Instead I returned home alone to take a nap and get dressed for the concert.

I chose my best concert black, a fitted dress with a wide boat neck, three-quarter-length sleeves, and a skirt that flared at the knee just enough to give me the comfort I needed on stage. I swept my long hair into a chignon at the base of my neck, a few loose pieces framing my face, and spent extra time on my makeup.

Lilly met me in the kitchen, nodding her head in approval. "You make black look better than anyone I know," she said. "You're going to be great tonight."

I hoped.

At seven fifty-four, I stood backstage and played through a few measures of the Dvorak that would open our performance, blending in with the other musicians warming up and tuning their instruments on stage. It wasn't pretty, exactly, but I loved the cacophony right before a performance when everyone was getting ready. It was the sound of anticipation, a reminder that all our instruments with their varying sounds, from the deep thrum of the tuba to the trill of the clarinet to the resonant hum of the cellos, would soon blend into one great whole.

"The perks of being concertmaster, huh? You get your own grand entrance." I turned to find Elliott standing behind me. I'd never seen him in a tuxedo and was momentarily distracted by the sight. The man knew how to wear a suit.

"I hate it. I'm always afraid I'm going to trip."

"I'm sure you're going to be great."

"I hope so. Are you nervous?"

"More than I ever have been before."

"You shouldn't be. You know you've got this. How was your meeting with Schweitzer?"

Elliott smiled and gave me a slight shrug. "He's interested. We listened to a few demos, and he liked what he heard. If this goes well tonight, I think there's a good chance of me signing."

If the evening goes well? If Elliott played even half as well as he'd played at rehearsal, the audience was in for the concert of a dang lifetime. "That's amazing. I'm really happy for you."

He held my gaze, intensity building behind the smoky blue of his eyes. "I need to tell you something."

I gripped the neck of my violin a little tighter. "Okay."

"First of all, thank you for this." He motioned to the stage and the auditorium around us.

"Why are you thanking me? You're the one saving the concert."

"No, it's the other way around. You've given me a gift by asking me to play tonight. I had forgotten what this felt like, and it's made me doubt what I'm capable of. I should have listened to you before I went to L.A. I was running scared, afraid to be true to myself because of what I might lose. I'd stopped trusting my intuition. But not anymore. Playing like this feels right."

"You deserve this, Elliott. I'm just glad I get to be up here with you."

He took a step closer. "The other thing I wanted to say is I'm sorry."

I closed my eyes, afraid to meet his gaze. I couldn't afford tears this close to going on stage.

"I never should have walked away from you after you told me how you felt."

The noise on the stage finally quieted, serving as my cue to join the orchestra.

Stupid, stupid orchestra!

"It was stupid. I'd just worked so hard to convince myself a relationship with me meant hurt for you; it took me a few days to really process what you said."

I gave him a pleading look. I hated to leave, but the only thing holding up the start of the concert was me. "I need to go on stage," I whispered.

Elliott nodded. "Just one more thing. The song I sent you for Christmas. I never told you what it's called."

Dr. Williamson materialized beside us and cleared his throat, giving us a pointed look. "I believe you've missed your cue, Ms. Hill."

"It's French," Elliott continued. "*Le Coup de Foudre.*"

"Now, Emma. Time's up," Dr. Williamson urged.

Elliott gave me a resigned smile. "Go," he said softly. "I'll translate later."

Chapter 30

AT FIRST I WORRIED I might not be able to get into the right head space to make it through the first half of the concert without dwelling on all things Elliott. But it took only the first few notes of Dvorak's Symphony no. 7 before everything else faded into the background.

When the music was just right, something I was particularly passionate about, my brain went to this in-between space where I no longer felt the solid presence of the chair beneath me or the worn wood of the stage under my feet. I didn't see the audience or feel the heat of the bright lights overhead or notice the deep red of the heavy curtains gathered on either side of the stage. I didn't even really see anything. I only felt the music, the vibrations running through me like a heartbeat. Dvorak's Seventh? It was that kind of music.

But I did think of Elliott just moments before he joined the orchestra on stage. As I watched my stand partner move the Dvorak aside and pull forward the Prokofiev, I thought about the words Dvorak used to describe his Seventh Symphony. He said it was written without one superfluous note. In a way, it was how Elliott's performance needed to be—intentional, purposeful, perfect. Every single note he played had to ring like it was the most important note the audience would ever hear.

When Elliott emerged onstage, thunderous applause reverberated off the cavernous ceiling of the performance hall. He crossed to where I stood and shook my hand, soloist to concertmaster. He caught my eye for only a tiny speck of a moment, but it was enough for me to recognize the glint of confidence in his expression. *I got this*, his face said. *I got it.*

And he did.

Oh, how he did.

His performance was a study of opposites. One minute his notes were soulful and joyful, the next something frenzied and brusque. Whatever the piece demanded, Elliott complied, the music moving through his hands, up his arms, and into his shoulders until it was bursting from every inch of him, shining on his face like a testimony of Prokofiev's greatness.

Twenty-eight minutes later, when Elliott played the final notes of the concerto, there was a moment of perfect silence where it felt like the entire audience took a collective breath, then applause burst forth louder and more enthusiastically than anything I'd ever heard in the performance hall before. Dr. Williamson turned and bowed, then motioned for the orchestra to stand. We took our bow, and then finally Elliott stood, bowing to the audience as the applause grew even louder.

He played a Tchaikovsky Nocturne for an encore. I was impressed by his choice, both because of his crazy-good talent and because choosing Tchaikovsky demonstrated good performance sense. The nocturne was a perfect contrast to the intentional chaos of the Prokofiev. Elliott was so, so much more than what his YouTube repertoire had ever given him credit for.

When a second encore brought him back onto the stage, he carried a microphone. Just before he started to speak, he glanced over his shoulder, looked right at me, and smiled.

"Thank you." His voice was deep and resonant as it filled the auditorium and sent chills all up and down my spine. "It's an honor to be with you tonight. If you're willing to indulge me, I'd like to finish the evening by playing something I wrote myself. It's my most recent work, something I titled '*Le Coup de Foudre.*'" He glanced over his shoulder, meeting my gaze one more time. "It's a French title, but when translated into English, it means love at first sight."

Love at first sight. I repeated the words in my mind, hoping against hope they meant what I thought they meant. If he loved me then, surely he still loved me now.

Before sitting at the piano, Elliott crossed to my chair and held out his hand. "Play it with me?"

I swallowed once and nodded my head, then took his extended hand.

"Ladies and gentlemen," Elliott said into the microphone, "your concertmaster for the evening, the lovely and talented Ms. Emma Hill."

From the very first notes of the song, we were connected in a way that showmanship or bravado couldn't ever explain. It was different from anything he'd played all evening because it was his. I wasn't just playing with Elliott Hart; I was playing his *heart*. Every ounce of his emotion poured into the music like his life depended on my hearing it. Because even though we were playing in an auditorium filled with thousands of people, it was me Elliott was playing for. And when I joined in? I was playing for him.

Had I had time to really internalize it, I might have been uncomfortable with so many people having a front-row seat to my love life. Playing with Elliott was personal, almost intimate, and anyone with even slight observational skill could probably see exactly how we felt. My parents were in the audience. And my little sister. My ex-boyfriend, my ex-boyfriend's in-laws, probably my bishop. Not to mention a *New York Times* reporter, a record producer from L.A., and the slimy Najim Berkley. But none of that seemed to matter anymore. Nobody mattered but Elliott.

I was crying by the time we finished because, well, of course I was crying. There was no way I could make it through a performance like that without tears. Elliott rose from the piano and took two steps across the stage, stopping right beside me, and reached for my hand. We bowed together, the applause growing louder by the second, and Elliott squeezed my hand. He looked my way, leaning in just enough for me to recognize his raised eyebrows as the invitation they were meant to be. He might have been satisfied with a small kiss, something chaste and appropriate for our captive audience, but *I* wouldn't have been. I dropped his hand long enough to place my violin on the back of the piano, then launched myself into his arms right there in front of everyone and their in-laws.

Funny, after an evening of so much incredible music—Prokofiev, Dvorak, Tchaikovsky, and Hart—nothing had brought the house down quite like that kiss.

There was a post-concert reception at a restaurant just down the street from the performance hall. I knew as soon as Elliott was in the room he'd be consumed by those anxious to talk with him. I wished I could have even a minute alone with him first, but there were people everywhere. Any alone time with him felt a long way off. By the time I put my violin away and made it to the reception, he was already standing with Greg and a man I presumed to be Richard Schweitzer. Agnes stood off to the side with another woman and a couple I didn't recognize.

Even though Elliott was completely engaged in his conversation with Greg, I could still tell he was looking for me, glancing toward the door every few moments. I moved into his field of vision, my heart tripping over itself when our eyes locked and he smiled. The smile was an invitation, I could tell, but I didn't join his conversation. Only because I knew if I did, it would take only a matter of moments before Greg said something about my joining Cleveland for the spring tour. A part of me still hoped Elliott wouldn't figure out my involvement in upping the significance factor of his audience, but when he looked across the room, catching my gaze for a second time, I could tell by his expression he already knew.

For nearly half an hour, Elliott worked his way across the room, signing programs, talking, smiling, posing for photographs. I hung back, waiting for him, not wanting to make a scene, even though I was pretty sure quite a few people in the room really wanted us to make one.

I killed some time finding and thanking Agnes for all she had done. "Oh, the pleasure was mine," she told me. "You weren't wrong about him, Emma. He's sensational—the best I've ever seen. And, good grief, to get to stare at that face all night . . . I'd have enjoyed the evening even if he'd been awful."

"Did the woman from the *Times*—Jeanine—did she like the performance?"

"Well, you know how they are, so close-lipped about things, not sharing their opinions until they can write them up properly, but just between you and me, I saw tears during the second encore. I'm sure her review is going to be fantastic. It didn't hurt that she was sitting next to Yvonne, who was just riveted by the entire evening."

I took a deep breath. They were the words I'd been hoping to hear. "Thank you," I said again. "For everything."

I found my family next, trying my best to field the specific questions my mother tossed at me. Did you know he was going to ask you to play? Was the kiss rehearsed? Is he staying in Asheville? What happens now? Has he proposed? I laughed out loud at that one.

"It was a beautiful night," Grandma said. "Your best performance, Emma—ever." Gram had seen more of my Cleveland performances than anyone, which made her compliment feel huge.

"Thanks," I told her. I reached out and gave her a hug.

"That really was some kiss," she said.

"It was way more than a kiss," Ava said, her voice a little dreamy. We all turned in unison to look at her. She folded her arms across her chest, looking slightly panicked by her new captive audience, but then she thrust her chin out and rolled her eyes. "I mean, whatever. The kiss part was totally cheesy, but when you played together, it just seemed like it was . . . more."

"I think I'm inclined to agree with your sister." I felt Elliott's hand on the curve of my waist the same moment I heard his voice.

"See? What did I tell you?" Ava said. "He agrees with me, and he should know better than anyone."

Elliott gave me a quick squeeze, then extended his hand to my parents. We all visited together for a few minutes before my family turned to leave, Dad and Gram walking beside Mom's chair and Ava trailing behind. Finally alone, Elliott put a hand on each of my shoulders. "Want to get out of here?"

"Can you?" I asked. "Have you talked to everyone you need to talk to?"

He gave me a pointed look. "I don't know. Maybe you should tell me if there's anyone else I need to talk to." If his eyes hadn't been smiling, I might have worried he was annoyed.

"I . . . have no idea what you're talking about," I said.

"Don't play coy with me. Greg spilled it. You're busted."

"He's terrible at keeping secrets."

"You shouldn't have done it, Em."

"I should talk to Greg before we go. Have you seen him lately?" I spotted Greg and started weaving my way through the restaurant to reach him.

"Don't ignore me. I'm serious."

I stopped and looked Elliott right in the eye. "You can't tell me I shouldn't have done it. Not after how successful tonight has been."

He huffed. "But that's not fair. You put so much on the line. You didn't know if it would work. You didn't even know if I'd play."

"But I did know. And it did work. And come on—what did I get out of the deal? A four-month tour of Europe? Not a bad bargain if you ask me."

"A four-month tour you never would have chosen had it not been for me."

A flock of smiling symphony patrons descended upon Elliott, asking for autographs on their programs. A few asked for mine as well, which was slightly surreal and more than a little unnerving, but I still managed to break away before Elliott, so I was on my own by the time I reached Greg.

"Congratulations on a successful evening, Emma." He smiled and glanced back toward Elliott. "Looks like things happened just as you'd hoped."

"It wouldn't have happened without your help. Thank you for getting Schweitzer here. I won't forget it."

"I have no doubt I'm getting the better end of the deal. You'll be sensational on tour. Especially if we can get Elliott on stage beside you. He'll be busy working on an album, but I'm taking his name back to Cleveland, and I'm calling his agent. We've got to work something out. The crowds will love the two of you together."

I couldn't even process half of what Greg had said. Elliott working on an album. Elliott on tour? Elliott on stage with me? I'd had high hopes for the evening, but we'd just officially crossed into too-good-to-be-true territory.

"That all sounds wonderful."

Greg said good night with a promise to be in touch as soon as he was back in Cleveland. "I'll see you in a couple of weeks," he told me. "I'm looking forward to it."

* * *

"Do you want to come in?"

I stood with Elliott in the entryway between our apartments. I nodded. "Yeah, just give me a minute. If you leave the door open, I'll be right there." I slipped into my apartment long enough to drop off my violin and kick off my shoes. Lilly and Trav sat curled up together on the couch, watching a movie.

"How was the reception? Did everyone love him? Did he get a new album deal?" Lilly launched her questions too quickly for me to answer.

"Everyone loved him. The deal isn't a sure thing, but I think it will be soon."

"The concert was really great," Trav said. "I'm glad you and Elliott finally got your stuff together."

"Thanks. It took us long enough. I'm going across the hall."

"Ya'll behave over there," Lilly called. "You need me to come chaperone?"

"Haha. Good night."

I let myself into Elliott's apartment, pushing the door shut behind me, then headed for the couch, but he stopped me before I could get there.

"Wait," he said. "Don't sit." He closed the distance between us and kissed me with a fervency that took my breath away. One hand wrapped around my waist while the other moved to the base of my neck, his fingers tangling in my hair. I pressed my palms flat against his chest, feeling the warmth of his skin and the rapid pounding of his heart through the fabric of his shirt. He pulled his lips away but kept his forehead close to mine. His voice was low and a little husky. "I've missed you so much."

I wrapped my arms around his waist and leaned my forehead against his chest, my brain still a little foggy from his kiss. "You have no idea how much I've missed you." His grip around me loosened, but I only held tighter. "No, don't let go. Not until you kiss me again."

He seemed happy to oblige.

We settled onto the couch, and Elliott took my hand, rubbing his thumb over my fingers. "Okay," he said. "I need details."

"*You* need details? I need details. I want to know exactly what Schweitzer said. And did you talk to the Spzilmanns? I didn't get to meet them before they left."

"I did meet them. They were great. And Schweitzer loved the concert. We're meeting next week in L.A. to talk about the next step. He wants to do an album—all original, maybe a few classics."

"*Rhapsody in Blue*, maybe?" I grinned.

"Ha. For you, I'll see if I can work that one in. He does want to record '*Le Coup de Foudre*,' though. I'll need you for that one."

"For the recording? For real?"

"You think I'd find a different violinist?"

"I've never done studio work before."

He smiled. "I think you'll be able to handle it. Now, stop avoiding my question. Details. What's your commitment?"

I hesitated. "A year: the tour for the first four months, then ten concerts over the next eight months."

"Ten concerts. That doesn't seem like enough to justify living in Cleveland full-time."

"It isn't. I think I'll probably come back to Asheville and just travel up to Ohio when I'm needed."

"So everything—Schweitzer, the Spzilmanns, the lady from the *Times*—Greg set all that up just because you agreed to the tour?"

I shook my head. "Schweitzer was Greg's doing, but I brought the lady from the *Times* on my own, and Agnes Rockwell brought the Spzilmanns. Though, Agnes and Greg are friends, so I guess that was Greg too. He did ask her to help."

Elliott leaned back and shook his head, an expression of wonder on his face. "I can't believe you did all this to help me."

"I believe in your music, Elliott. And I knew others would too."

He pulled my hand to his lips, kissing the tops of my fingers. "If Greg hadn't told me about your bargain, were you just going to let Brian take the credit?"

I sighed. "I was afraid it would make you feel guilty, like I was trying to buy back your favor. And I didn't want it to be about us. Because I still would have done it. Even if we'd never worked things out, if you'd moved back to L.A. and hooked up with some blonde soap opera actress, I would have made the same deal. I needed this to work for you."

"Please don't underestimate how much I appreciate what you've done when I say this, but, Emma, I was ready to walk away from my music. To stay in Asheville and teach piano lessons and play organ for the local women's choir if that's what it took to be where you are. What makes me happy is you. I'm not sure I need anything else."

I closed my eyes, wanting to soak up his words and feel them sink all the way into my soul. It was what I'd wanted to hear all along, that there was an *us* he thought was worth fighting for. But I wasn't enough. I knew that. And if he really thought about it, he would know it too. I shook my head. "That's not true."

"What's not true?"

"You need your music. Plus, you have too much to give. I'm too well acquainted with what you're capable of to let your gifts waste away behind the organ of a women's choir."

He leaned forward and kissed me, slower this time, his thumbs brushing across my jaw line, past my ear, and down the curve of my neck. "I love you, Emma. I'm sorry it took me so long to say it."

I felt like there should have been trumpets playing a fanfare in the background, something, anything to celebrate the moment. "I love you too. I'm sorry it took you so long to say it too."

He laughed. "You need me to say it a few more times to make up for the lack?"

"Yes, please. Once an hour for the rest of forever."

He took my hand and turned it over, tracing the words onto my palm and up onto my wrist, sending shivers up and down my arm. "There you go. But that's it. I'm cutting you off until"—he glanced at his watch—"2:00 a.m. And not a minute sooner."

"Do you think Greg will make it happen? Get you on the tour?"

"If he doesn't, I'll be there anyway. I'm going to follow you wherever you go."

"You want to be my groupie? I've never had a groupie before." It wasn't lost on me that Elliott really *had* groupies, which somehow made my joke feel less funny.

"I'd rather be your boyfriend than your groupie. I hear they get better seats at performances."

He leaned back and pulled me against him, my head resting on his shoulder.

"Was it really love at first sight?" I asked.

"It was probably more like love at first note."

"When we played together through the wall?"

He nodded. "It was like a punch to the gut. Every time I heard you practicing, I realized how much I wanted you to know I was more than just crazy videos and cover songs. I wanted you to think I was good enough for you to notice."

I reached for his hand, tracing the arch of his long, graceful fingers with my thumb. "Mission accomplished."

"When you played the next Sunday in church, I was done for. That was when I knew."

"And then after the wedding . . ." My heart hurt to think of the pain I must have caused him.

He sighed. "That was a dark six weeks for me. I loved you. I knew I did. But I wanted to be what you needed, and I wasn't sure I was. I didn't want to hurt you any worse than I already had."

I sat up and pulled my hair out of its twist. It was late, and all the excitement of the evening was settling in my shoulders. I shook my hair loose. "Elliott, nothing hurts worse than thinking about those awful words I said. Please know I didn't mean them. I don't love extra attention, and I don't particularly love the limelight. But I do love you. Anything that happens, anything the media throws at us or demands of us or says about us, it won't matter. There's not a single thing in this world that will keep me from loving you. As long as you'll always love me too." Not too bad for a girl who was terrible with words.

He reached up, brushing the hair from my face. "You've got yourself a deal."

* * *

Four months later

City lights reflected on the shimmering surface of the Seine, big-band music floating out of the corner bistro in Paris where I'd just finished dinner. The tour was nearly over. Two more stops in Florence and London, then our final performance back in New York and we were finished. I hadn't seen Elliott since he'd performed with us in Amsterdam five weeks before, and it was nearly killing me. He would meet me in New York, but that was still ten days away. Ten days felt like an eternity.

I turned the corner, glimpsing the hotel lights twinkling at the end of the block. A man emerged out of the darkness that stretched between the hotel and me. I could see only his outline at first, but everything from the shape of his shoulders to the cadence of his walk felt familiar. I rushed forward.

"Daddy?"

He smiled and opened his arms. "Are you surprised?"

I wrapped my arms around him, overwhelmed by the sheer shock of seeing my father in the very last place I ever would have expected him to be. "What are . . . ? How on earth? When did you . . . ?" I couldn't figure out which question to finish first.

Dad laughed. "No questions. Not yet anyway. I'm just here to give you this." He handed me a single sheet of paper.

I looked it over. It was sheet music for piano, if I had to guess, but it wasn't labeled, and the melody wasn't something I recognized. "What is this?"

Dad put his hands on my shoulders and pointed me toward the hotel. "Keep walking, and I think you'll find your answer."

I gave him a puzzled look, but he only grinned, urging me forward with a tilt of his head.

"Are you coming too?" I asked.

"I promise I won't be far behind," he said. "Now, go on. You've got somewhere to be."

I hurried to the hotel, my heart pounding in my chest, and wondered what kind of goose chase Dad was sending me on. I had just made it through the front door when a familiar voice stopped me in my tracks.

"What? You aren't even going to say hello?"

I turned around. "Trav? Are you kidding me?"

He laughed and pulled me into a hug. "It's good to see you, Em."

I reached up and gave his cheek a friendly pat. "You shaved!"

"You like it? I'm still getting used to it, but Lilly's a fan."

Hope surged through my chest at the thought of seeing Lilly. "Is Lilly here?"

"I'm not at liberty to say. I've only been instructed to give you this." He handed me another sheet of music.

"For real, Trav. Somebody better tell me what's going on."

He waved his hand. "Keep going. You'll know soon enough."

I hurried through the lobby, looking left, then right, then left again, half expecting someone to jump out from behind one of the giant marble columns to surprise me. Finally I saw Ava sitting on a small cushioned bench in between the elevators. When she saw me approach, she stood and ran into my embrace.

"What is everyone doing here?" I asked her, my eyes wide.

"That's all the hello I get? It's nice to see you too."

I gripped her shoulders, then gave her another hug, happy to ignore her sarcasm. "Looks like you're getting to see Paris after all."

"You know it. And tomorrow you're going to get me some of those cookies. For now, this is for you."

More music. Of course.

I shook my head. "I'm not even going to question anymore. Where to next?"

The elevator dinged behind us. "Pretty sure you're supposed to get on this elevator," Ava said.

When the doors slid open, Lilly jumped out. "Surprise!" She pulled me onto the elevator, her eyes all bright and happy, and gave me a big hug. "How are you? Are you surprised? Are you happy?"

"I'm . . . I have no idea what I am. I'm a little confused, but yes, it's amazing to see everybody. Where are you taking me?"

She handed me a room key.

"What, no music?"

"Oh! Right." She pulled it out of her pocket. "I almost forgot."

I added it to the stack. Immediately I noticed something I hadn't seen on any of the other sheets. It was only one word, a dynamic scribbled in haste across the bottom of the page. *Pianissimo.* But it was enough for me to recognize the careful, measured script of Elliott's handwriting. I'd known Elliott had to be involved. I was holding a stack of piano music, after all, but seeing confirmation of what, until then, I'd only hoped to be true was enough to stop my breath, trapping the air in my lungs a beat too long.

"Emma," Lilly said. "Yo. You hear me? Breathe."

I took a breath, then grabbed Lilly's hand. "Where is he, Lil? Please just tell me where he is."

The elevator chimed and opened. Lilly nudged me off without answering my question but stayed behind herself. "Room 714," she called as the doors slid closed.

My hands trembled as I moved down the hallway and found room 714, making it extra difficult to slip the keycard into the reader affixed above the door handle. It took three tries before the little indicator light flashed green and the door finally clicked open.

"Surprise!" Mom and Gram moved forward simultaneously, pulling me into the room and wrapping their arms around me from both sides.

"We promise there are no more family members lurking in closets," Gram said.

I laughed. "That's a relief. I'm not sure my heart can take any more."

Mom lowered herself into her wheelchair, positioned by the bed, and reached for my hand. "There is *one* more surprise, but I'm pretty sure this one is going to be your favorite." She handed me a small piece of cardstock bearing the name of the hotel's glitzy restaurant, the day's date, and a time: *9:00 p.m.*

I closed my eyes and pressed the card against my chest. There was only one person left; it had to be Elliott.

"You better hurry and change," Gram said. "You've only got ten minutes."

"Change? This isn't even my hotel room."

"It's all taken care of," Mom said. "Everything you need is in the bathroom."

A dress hung on the back of the bathroom door, and my makeup bag, apparently retrieved from my own hotel room, sat on the counter. My hands trembled as I pulled on the dress. It was simple and black *(Ha! Black!)*, knee length, with a deep v-neck and shimmery sleeves to the elbow. I spent a few minutes messing with my hair, then touched up my makeup and emerged from the bathroom to face Mom and Gram.

"Oh, you're lovely, Bug. The dress is perfect," Gram said.

"It *is* perfect," I said. "Who picked it out?"

They glanced at each other and shrugged. "We're just the messengers," Gram said. "We don't know anything more than what we've been told."

Mom smiled, her eyes all misty. "I'm so happy for you, Emma."

I moved to the door. "Are you guys supposed to come with me?"

"We'll be right behind you," Mom answered. "But you go on ahead."

"And don't forget the music," Gram added. She stood, retrieved the sheet music from where I'd left it on the dresser, and handed it over. "And here." She added a final sheet to my stack. "This is the last one."

Page one. Elliott's name was listed clearly at the top as the composer, but there was no title, only a blank line drawn across the top of the page, where someone might write one in.

"Go on, then," Gram said. "You've got everything you need." She shooed me out the door with a grin.

I walked on trembling legs back to the elevator, taking it down to the main floor of the hotel. I looked for signs of my family as I passed through the lobby but didn't see anyone. My *family*. All of them. Even Lilly and Trav. They were *all* in Paris. I couldn't even wrap my head around it.

When I finally reached the restaurant, it was empty. At first I worried I'd gone to the wrong place, but then I heard the piano.

I followed the notes through the dark dining room until I found him seated behind a sleek baby grand under a large window in the corner, the city lights beyond sparkling like stars across the sky. A single lamp sat on top of the piano, casting a circle of soft white light onto Elliott's hands. It was the only light in the room.

He looked up as I approached, his notes trailing off midmelody as he rose and closed the distance between us. He swept me up into a hug, then kissed me gently, his hands lingering on my cheeks. "Man, I've missed you," he whispered. He held on to my hand but took a step back as if to get a better view. "You look beautiful."

"Thank you," I said. "I love the dress."

"I hoped you would. Lilly tried to veto the black, but I told her my vote counted twice."

I pressed my face against my hands, feeling like I was in a dream.

"You okay?" Elliott asked.

I nodded. "Just feeling a little overwhelmed."

He grinned. "In a good way, I hope?"

I almost laughed out loud. *Yeah, in a good way.* "You brought my family to Paris."

"I did. I thought you might want them here to celebrate."

My eyebrows went up. "Celebrate what?"

He didn't answer but tugged on my hand, pulling me gently toward the piano. "Come on. I want to play something for you." He motioned with his head. "Come sit beside me."

As soon as he began, I recognized the melody from the pages I still clutched in my hand. It had a simple, peaceful center and bright undertones that created a joyful, hopeful countermelody. Somehow the entire work felt like the promise of every good thing life had to offer. I generally liked to watch Elliott's hands while he played, but this time I was riveted by his face, by the sincerity and love in his expression.

When he finished, I sniffed and wiped my eyes. "How do you *do* that?"

"Do what?" he asked softly.

"How do you write all that emotion into your music? It's like . . . poetry without words."

"All I had to think about for this one was you." He leaned forward, whisking a tear off my cheek with the pad of his thumb, then kissed me softly. "I love that music makes you cry."

I huffed. "Most of the time it's hugely inconvenient."

He chuckled, then reached for the sheet music, sliding it out of my hands. He lifted a pen off the piano's music stand and tapped the blank line at the top of the title page. "Do you want to know what it's called?" His eyes were bright and hopeful.

Oh. My. Word. "Yes, please," I whispered.

He clicked the pen open, then, bracing against the top of the piano, wrote the words *Veux-tu m'epouser?*

Elliott put down the pen and took my hands. "Emma, *veux-tu m'epouser?*" The French rolled off his tongue with such ease it sent shivers clear through me.

Somewhere over my shoulder, a voice whisper-yelled out of the darkness, startling me mostly because I hadn't realized there was anyone else in the room. "It means 'will you marry me?'" the voice said.

"Travis, shut up," Lilly whispered. "She knows what it means."

"Sorry," Trav said. "Just trying to help."

"You two are really spoiling the moment," Gram said.

"Shhh!" Ava's voice quieted them all. "She can't say yes if you all don't *shut up.*"

Elliott's shoulders shook in silent laughter. "Are you still glad I brought your family to Paris?" He reached into his shirt pocket and pulled out a ring, holding it up for me to see. "Marry me, Emma. Please say yes so the hooligans over there can just cheer already."

I held up my hand, and Elliott slid the ring onto my finger, the diamond sparkling brightly under the piano lamp's pale glow.

I leaned in and kissed him soundly, then said loudly enough for everyone in the room to hear, "*Oui, monsieur*. Of course I'll marry you."

My family erupted into cheers while we kissed again. They gathered around the piano, hugging us and patting us on our backs, Dad and Trav reaching forward to shake Elliott's hand. Through all the commotion, my eyes stayed on his, hoping he recognized in my gaze just how much I loved him.

Trav clapped Elliott on the back, then draped his arms around our shoulders. "Okay, think about this: a joint reception for the four of us. You guys bring the music; we bring the beer."

Lilly appeared beside Trav. "Seriously? Are you completely out of your mind?"

"What?" Trav grumbled as he dropped his arms. "It's a good idea."

I wrapped my arms around Elliott's neck and leaned in close. "Thank you," I whispered. "For the music, for my family . . . for everything."

"Even Trav?" Elliott asked. He raised an eyebrow.

I laughed. "Even Trav."

"You have my heart, Emma. Forever. There's no undoing it now."

I leaned in and kissed him softly. "I wouldn't have it any other way."

THE END

About the Author

JENNY PROCTOR WAS BORN IN the mountains of Western North Carolina, a place she still resides and considers the loveliest on earth. She and her husband stay busy keeping up with six children and a growing assortment of pets. She loves to hike with her family, read whatever book she can get her hands on, and eat delicious food she doesn't have to fix herself.

Jenny hopes Love Notes, a reflection of her love and appreciation for good romance and classical music, inspires you to listen to Mozart and kiss your significant other as frequently as possible. Love Notes is her third novel.

To learn more about Jenny and her books, visit her website at www.jennyproctor.com.